NO USE CRYING NOW

Christine Eyres

To the girl who waited for the birth of her baby in
King Edward Memorial Hospital, on 12th December 1977,
and cried.

A Fallen Woman

IN 1965, Doog became pregnant, *fell* pregnant, they said. And then came the string of labels she was made to wear like a leaden necklace of ugly signs so the world would know she was a *fallen* woman. Except she wasn't a woman. She was still a girl. And she was exiled before the world had time to know anything.

The doctor, nurses, church officials, a social worker, even her own parents, called her unfit for motherhood, selfish, precocious, incapable of caring for a child, the ruination of a young man's life, immoral, immature, neurotic. They said it was in the baby's best interest to be placed with a *normal family* with a *real* mother and father. *Forget him*, they said. *Forget that any of it ever happened.*

And then they put a syringe in her arm.

She woke up screaming for him, but her baby was gone. They sent her home to resume the life from which she'd been banished. A life of secrets and silence.

*****

Doog can't forget. The grief returns over and over again. It is with her now as she sits in the ute outside the Sandy Bay Post Office twenty-five years later. Seagulls on the pavement in front of the car thrust out indignant necks and screech as they fight over chips dropped by a child. They claw her mind away from the memories and back to the present. The rusty corrugations of the roof of the small post office blur in a mirage of heat. Her eyes fuse onto the mustard-coloured paint blistering on weatherboard walls. Every fortnight, Doog drives to Sandy Bay to pick up supplies for Bedarra station where she's employed as a governess. She enjoys the break from the station but the small town still retains the memory of a night all those years ago

When she first came to work at Bedarra, driving on her own through this empty land had terrified Doog. Not now. Now she drives across the endless station country towards where the great bowl of the sky upends onto the flat line of the horizon, windows down, singing at the top of her voice like a mad woman. No one to hear, no one to judge. Being out in the middle of nowhere feels safe, peaceful. But as soon as she turns off the main road towards the coast, the same tightness clamps around her chest. And when she arrives in the tiny town with its row of small shops and sees the jetty reaching out over the Indian Ocean, the yearning returns.

Being in Sandy Bay brings back grief. Guilt and shame – she refuses to accept any longer. She's found stories of other women. She's not the only one. For years she thought she was the only one to have been so wicked. Now she knows there is a whole history of wickedness that was inflicted on young girls like herself and the shame has lifted. But grief has its own agenda. She is powerless against it.

And the anger, she refuses to let that go. She has a right to keep hold of anger. The cruelty of what happened to her, the unremitting blame, the agony of the hours of labour without any medication and, after the birth, the assault of the syringe filled with mind-numbing drugs and something to dry up her milk, her powerlessness to stop them … to stop herself lapsing into unconsciousness. And then the emptiness of indescribable loss. Most of all … the loss. Her baby stolen.

Yes, she will hold that anger. It makes her determined to find him despite the odds.

*****

Mail for Bedarra station lies on the passenger seat along with the newspapers. Paul Keating's grey face stares up from the front page of the *West Australian*. Doog picks up the bundle of mail and sorts the bulk of it into a pile for Matt, the manager of Bedarra. There's one for Mrs C, the station cook and one from her daughter, Annie, from Sydney. She'll read that later. She needs to pick up a prescription for Mrs C. Metal screeches on metal as she pushes the ute door. It partly opens. Doog twists her body to extract herself from the vehicle through the small gap. *Bloody Matt, should have fixed that by now. It's weeks ago he hit that roo.* No wonder none of the other staff want to drive the ute. She's the only one skinny enough to get out of the door. The seagulls scatter with angry cries as she pulls herself together on the pavement.

Out of the ute, under the northwest sun, Doog feels exposed. Down the street, a dog lifts its leg against one of the verandah posts of the general store. A couple of old men sit on the bench of the pub's shady verandah, the same ones every fortnight when she comes to town for the stores. Her eyes scan the few cars parked outside the chemist-come-newsagent, knowing she has nothing to fear in this small town. But shame leaves scars. Again, her eyes are drawn to the end of the main street where the jetty stretches out into the ocean. Again, she wonders if she's come back to the right place. It's the jetty that she remembers that awful night when Dad stopped for petrol and a pie.

*****

Through the years, friends, colleagues, relatives had not known about Doog's loss, they never guessed the pain she hid from view. No one would have seen that she didn't go a day without mourning for that part that had been ripped from her, at the same time cosseting the love that was embroidered on her heart during the brief moment she had held her baby in her arms. The world would have only seen the girl who tackled her high school studies

without veering. The young woman who went on to teachers'
college and put all her energy and focus into being a top student.
They wouldn't have known the girl who felt unentitled to grieve
because she was not worthy.

When she gave birth to Annie, Doog experienced a new terror,
almost unable to believe she was allowed to keep her baby girl. As
Annie grew into a joyful toddler, she vowed for her daughter's
sake to change. For Annie, she unearthed joy and playfulness and
she buried the sadness. The years passed, the baby transformed
into a beautiful young woman and grew ready to spread her wings.
The yearning that had lain semi-dormant repossessed Doog. A
search for any record of her son's birth had proved fruitless years
before. It was common practice for the adoptive parents to be the
only ones named on the birth certificate. But she was sure the
church had been involved and figured out that there must have
been a reason for her father to have taken her so far away from
her home in Fremantle when she became pregnant. She learned
that childless couples often paid a good deal of money to the
church for arranging an adoption. If she had been sent all that way
up north to give birth, it surely must have been where the adoptive
parents lived.

At the end of 1990 she surprised everyone who knew her by
resigning from her teaching job, and when Annie left home to
study at the National Institute of Dramatic Art in Sydney at the
beginning of 1991, Doog tidied up her life while she waited for
the wet season to pass. By the end of March, she was on her way
north. Right up until the day she left, her mother avoided talking
about her planned trip. Not that Doog had spelled out where she
was going. She hardly knew what she was doing herself and the
subject had not been broached in all those years. But Claris, her
mother, was the sharpest woman she knew. Claris must surely
have guessed something.

*****

After visiting the pharmacy, Doog wriggles back onto the torn seat of the ute and starts to head out of town on her drive to Bedarra station. *Bugger. The stock agents.* She slams the brake pedal to the floor and yanks the vehicle into a dusty U-turn in the empty street. Tyres skid on gravel as she pulls up to the open roller-doors of the stock agent's shed. She dashes in and signs for the supplies for Bedarra.

Gary tucks a carton under each of his bulky arms, asking how the preparations for the camp draft are going. Gary would yack all day if you let him. Doog gives him a tight smile, tells him Matt has everything sorted and heads back to the ute. He pokes his grin and his bad breath through the window and tells her to tell Matt, *Them salt licks haven't come in yet. Should be 'ere next week.* She nods, then revs the engine more than she means to.

Two kilometres north she takes a turn inland off the main road, spraying another coat of dust over the scrub lining the dirt track.

The ute lurches. *Concentrate,* she reminds herself. A vehicle can be halfway swallowed by a rabbit warren out here. There's no way she's giving Matt the satisfaction of rescuing her. Negotiating the track through the wide land loosens the knot in her gut and she lets out the breath she's been holding. The desert always does that to her.

She's glad Mary isn't with her today. Mary, from the Aboriginal community, often comes to help on the run to town, and she's good company. The young girl gives Doog an insight into what's going on with the Aboriginal kids. But right now, she's grateful to be on her own. She hadn't expected to like Bedarra but Matt's kids — she didn't anticipate. They need her. They've burrowed their way into the crack in her heart. Reminded her she needs to be needed. It's the last thing she'd expected to find in this outback place, a job she loves. Once the red country gets into your skin, they say, you belong to it. When Annie left home, this place had pulled her back. The need to look for the child stolen from her all those years ago couldn't be ignored any longer. But now there's more. Even if she doesn't find what she's looking for. And what are the chances? Helping these kids, that's given her something else, something she hasn't felt for years. She winces as she thinks of her daughter. Poor Annie. Doog hopes she's been a good mother even with a chunk missing from her heart.

*****

When she drove north up the Western Australian coast a couple of months ago and reached Sandy Bay, she thought she recognised the place where Dad had stopped that dark night. The little shops, the jetty at the end of the street, even the name sounded familiar. But most coastal towns up this way are similar. She couldn't be sure. A job she found as a barmaid at the pub came with basic accommodation. During the next weeks she scrutinised every young man around the age of twenty-five. Many were just passing through but, on the weekends, young blokes from stations around the area came in *to sink a few tinnies*. Surprised at how many stations there were, she found a map in the library. It was old and yellowing but the librarian said things didn't change much out here. She tried talking to the young blokes – deleting them if she found they were too young or too old. One was the right age and colouring. Her heart had leapt when she found out his birthday was June but the following week, she saw him in town with his family. He had an identical twin.

She'd asked herself over and over again what she thought she was doing. She had nothing to go on except the fact that she was sure he would be dark and perhaps look like Alex, his father. She had no names. There had been no records to be found in the Department of Child Protection. What was the likelihood that her son would have stayed in the district? Even if he grew up around here, he would most likely have taken off like most young people when they were old enough.

After a month, working and living in the pub wore thin. She told herself she should go home and forget about it. Then anger would resurface and she couldn't let go. There was a small town further up the coast, Lonsdale, the name somehow seemed familiar. She should go there. But before she could work out why, she saw an ad for a governess on the biggest station in the district, Bedarra. It was just over an hour inland, surrounded by other smaller stations. She could base herself there and explore the area when she had time off. What did she have to lose?

Matt answered the phone at Bedarra, briefly acknowledged her greeting and asked a series of questions.

'Yes, I have my qualifications and records of employment with me,' she assured him. 'I can fax them to you.' And then she added that she had all her Red Cross certificates up to date.

A warmer note crept into the manager's voice as he asked her about the Red Cross certificates. 'My wife Tanya died almost a year ago,' he said. 'She was the one who steered the kids through Distance Ed, but she was an ex-nurse, so she also took charge of the flying doctor's kit.'

'I'm sorry,' mumbled Doog. 'How awful, for the kids, and you, of course.'

'Yeah, well, we're managing but, Ms Wilson, can I ask you a favour? You need to understand that on a place like Bedarra we have our own jobs, but on top we all muck in to keep the station running. Everyone has a stint on kitchen duty, for example.'

'Sure,' said Doog. 'I think I'd enjoy that.'

'The thing is, Ms Wilson,' said Matt. 'It would be a great help if you could take over responsibility for the flying doctor's stuff.'

'Not sure I ...'

'No,' interrupted Matt. 'Nothing to it. But I'd need you to call into the local hospital and do a quick training session on what's in the kit and how to use it. Then you can register as Bedarra's first aid responder. That would really help us out.'

'The name's Doog. OK, I can try but it's a bit of an unknown for me.'

'You'll be right,' said Matt and the phone clicked.

*****

The track meanders through pink sand and grey-green spinifex. Her mind wanders back to her first weeks at Bedarra. The people were as craggy as the country. Mrs Cameron, the station cook, had thrown a tea towel to Doog before she'd even asked her name.

'Look like you could do with a bit of time in a feedlot. There are stick insects with more meat on their bones,' she said. 'How ya gonna help knead the dough with them arms?'

It was like being back at school with big Doris bullying her. 'I'll manage', she said, mustering her coolest voice, although, by the time she'd done the obligatory ten minutes of kneading while on kitchen duty, her city arms felt fit to drop off. If Frankie could see her arms now, she'd be impressed. Frankie, Francesca, had been her best friend since they were eight. They went through high school and ended up in teachers' college together. They joked about not letting their arms get wings like their mothers. She's fitter and stronger than when she first arrived at the station, and it feels good. She misses Frankie. They told each other everything … well, not everything. When she disappeared that time everyone, including Frankie, thought she'd gone over east to help Gran for a while. The secret is still a hole in their friendship.

A dry creek bed in a deep gully is just ahead. Doog slows and pushes the gearstick into low range. She grips the steering wheel firmly but lets the car pick its own way slowly over the rocks. She's done it many times, knows it's easy to lose control of the wheel and end up sitting on a boulder. She's confident now and has to admit to a pride at being able to handle this farm vehicle. *You're off the chain, Mum,* she can hear Annie saying.

When Doog had answered the ad to tutor the children through the distance education program, it hadn't taken much to figure that in this remote place her business would be fair game for everyone to stick their noses into. She'd put out signals that she just wanted to do her job and be left alone. She'd made up her mind not to care if they thought she was standoffish. But it's not that simple at Bedarra. People like Mary, well, all of them really, have an uncanny talent for chipping away at any wall you try to put up.

The last thing she wants, though, is for anyone to know why she's up here. She's not even sure she's come back to the right place. All that time ago when she came up here with Dad, they'd been driving most of the day before they had stopped at what she's almost sure was Sandy Bay. But after, they had driven at least another hour inland before they had reached their destination.

Fremantle

DOOG couldn't remember a time when her parents, Claris and George Wilson, hadn't struggled. Struggled to pay the mortgage to the bank, struggled to put food on the table and buy clothes for the small family. George struggled stoically but Claris seemed to brew her anxieties, making them heard through her silent moods and the banging of pots and pans. In South Fremantle where Doog was born, it seemed, as she grew, that everyone in the area clung to the same life raft.

Her father had returned from the war after serving in New Guinea and found a job in the council administration with the help from the church. Claris had worked in the office of a fish-canning factory but when the men returned, like the rest of the women, she was forced back into the home *where she belonged.* She tried not to resent it. She made her home and the church her life, but she missed the challenge of the work and the companionship of the other women.

Doog's life revolved around school and her friends. She didn't think of her family as poor. Everyone was the same and life was good. The beach, the river and the port of Fremantle were all within walking distance and never dull. They swam and climbed around the boat harbour and watched the fishing boats come back with their catch. Sometimes she and her brother, Charlie, managed to score a free fish or octopus from the men on the boats, which would earn them rare praise from their mother. Meals were usually three-course and basic.

'Eat up those broad beans,' Claris would snap as Doog tried to sneak them into her hanky on her lap. 'Your father works hard to grow those.' Meals of stews and mince with home-grown veggies were eked out with soups and puddings. There was a fuss at the beginning of every school year. Pencils and exercise books to buy, new school shoes for fast-growing feet.

'The government goes on about free education in this country and then the schools give you a list of things to buy. What's free about that?' said Claris every January.

Growing up, Doog tried not to resent the amount of freedom given to her brother while her mother seemed to monitor her every move. Vanity, Claris declared, was a sin. She should give no credence to how she looked. It was shallow. Character, ethics, goodness of her heart were far more important. However, Doog noticed her mother would comment warmly about the lovely blonde curls of other children. Doog had straggly red hair. Claris would admire the blue or brown eyes of other children. Doog's eyes were green. Charlie, her brother had blond curly hair and blue eyes. Charlie could do no wrong. But you couldn't help loving Charlie. He was always happy and never got nasty like some of her friend's brothers.

Sex education was non-existent except for snippets she gleaned from her friends. Her mother and father rarely broached anything approaching the personal, let alone sex. After she turned thirteen, her mother came to her bedroom door and thrust a book at her.

'Here, it's time you read this. You are growing up now.' She said before almost running back to the kitchen.

Doog quickly read the small booklet, which explained how cats had kittens, and sheep had lambs. It had a picture of something called a uterus where a baby lay curled. When her first menstruation arrived, she had her friends to thank for not being completely in the dark. However, they couldn't help with the awkward confrontation with Claris, and the embarrassment of her mother, thin-lipped, producing a sling-like structure to put around her waist to hold a pad between her legs.

Their unorthodox headmistress, Miss Florence Beckett managed to blunt the embarrassment. Flo, they called her affectionately, and when Doog first started high school, she remembers dismissing Flo as too old and staid to know anything useful. But one day the lower-school girls were told to assemble in the quadrangle. Tall, willowy Miss Beckett stood on a box, wafting in the wind and looking down upon them.

'Gels,' she said after the preamble about their bodies changing. 'You should always remember boys have a saying: *Candy is dandy, but liquor is quicker.*'

Doog had to consult one of her Italian friends to translate that. Then Miss Beckett had produced a paper bag, like the ones hanging in the toilets, pleading with the girls to use them. From a pocket she produced a menstrual pad and a tampon on a string, waving them in the air with abandon and insisting they were part of growing up.

'Please remember gels, they are nothing to be ashamed of but when they are soiled, pop them in the bag and into the bin. It would not be a good look to go dangling them through the school or the town,' she said with a smile that made Doog want to hug her, like she'd never wanted to hug her mother.

That day, for the first time, it felt OK to be a girl.

*****

Alex was the brother of one of her Italian friends, Lucy. Lucia, her mother called her, and Alex was Alessandro. Both children scowled when their real names were used, especially in front of their friends. Now Doog thinks how beautiful these names are.

Alex and Doog became friends from the start. She could play cricket as well, or better, than most of the boys. She could kick a football and bait a fishing line. The pair would often meet at the beach or the river. Sometimes Alex would bring a bottle of home-made lemon cordial and she would sneak some of Claris's Anzac biscuits out of the tin. She couldn't believe that Alex, with his beautiful brown skin and eyes with long curling lashes, had chosen her instead of one of the other girls.

They found a cave in the cliffs along the most inaccessible part of the river and it became a favourite place for their little picnics, especially in winter when they could look out at the rain bouncing off the water and watch the black swans fishing and the dolphins playing. Alex started to stroke her arms and hold her hand. He told her she was beautiful but she laughed. How could she be beautiful with her pale freckled skin and her red hair that wasn't curly enough? Then one day he leaned over and kissed her. She didn't mean to scare him off, but she wasn't expecting it and reared back, hitting her head on the rock wall and he didn't try it again. But she'd wanted him to.

It was a spring day in the school holidays when they arranged to have a picnic one afternoon. Claris wouldn't be back from the church women's guild until evening Doog made cheese sandwiches while she listened to the radio. People were protesting about the Vietnam War. Alex turned up with an old blanket to sit on and a bottle of Italian wine. Grappa, he called it. Said his grandfather made it and wouldn't miss a bottle.

'We can have a swig and hide in the sand at the back of the cave,' he said.

They had more than a swig of the sweet wine and almost immediately Doog felt warm and fuzzy. She heard Miss Beckett. *Candy is dandy but liquor is quicker*, but she didn't resist when Alex started to cuddle and kiss her. She kissed him back, hard and long. They fell back onto the blanket. He started to caress between her legs. She held her breath and pressed back against his hand. She didn't want him to stop but she knew she had to stop him. 'I have to get home. It will be dark soon,' she said. He nibbled her ear and reached under her jumper, squeezed her breast, played with her nipples. An exquisite feeling took possession of her. No part of her wanted him to stop. Not her mind, not her body. Between her legs she felt him pushing inside her. She was wet and slippery but suddenly she felt like she was being ripped apart. She gasped, he slowed down and kissed her. She found she was crying but she held him tight and pushed against him until she felt she was filled with him, joined to him. She wanted to cling to him forever. Then with a strangled cry he lifted his head and she felt wetness running between her legs. He rolled off her and lay with his arms still around her, laughing. They were both laughing but she thought of her parents and her laughter stopped.

After that, he became like an obsession. She couldn't wait to see him again. Every few weeks they gave their friends the slip and climbed around the rocks to the cave. Each time she told herself she would not let him *go all the way* but each time, as soon as they kissed, her good intentions melted. When her second period failed to show she started to worry. She vowed she would not be alone with Alex but she longed to be with him. She thought of him constantly. It was normal for periods to be all over the place in the first few years, she had heard. But was it normal to miss three? When the fourth month still brought no bleeding, she knew she had to tell her mother. Claris would be furious with her but she would know what to do.

Maroney

A WALL of heat hits Daniel Maroney as he stands on the metal steps that descend from the plane. The tarmac throbs. He fumbles in his bag for sunglasses. The rest of the passengers, mainly hulking big blokes in shorts and steel-capped boots, tramp towards a depressing collection of huts. He follows with flies feeding on the sweat on his face. This is it? Sandy Bay? His hopes for air-conditioned comfort take a dive.

He's on the bus. A cloud of red dust obliterates the road behind, infiltrating the vehicle that careers over the corrugations, coating his nostrils. Sheep daub the red landscape with grey, but apart from that, no trees, no pasture. Nothing but the flat, straight road, sporadic rings of spiky grass and a few rocky outcrops. He has landed on another planet. He looks down at the date on the copy of *The Sandy Bay Courier* that he picked up at the airport desk half expecting to be in another time but no, it's still the fourteenth of May 1991.

Two days ago, he had stood in the editor's office.

'Where?'

The editor had lumbered over to a map on the wall.

'About here.' He pointed. 'You catch the plane to Sandy Bay. Then you hire a four-wheel drive. I want human-interest pieces on the families that live out that way. You might look at the historical angle from a land-care point of view. Sounds like a lot of that country has been farmed almost to death and the smaller landholders are struggling. We could be looking at the end of the family-run stations, the demise of an Aussie icon.'

Maroney stared. His next job would be in the back of beyond? And who the fuck wants to know about land-care in the never-never? He was about to protest but the boss told him how he liked Maroney's reporting on the forest fires down south. He said he was the best man for the job. The old toad has a way of sweet-talking you into to his way of thinking. Always manages to manipulate the staff into jobs they never would have chosen. Toady went on with enthusiasm about the growing interest in the north.

'Tourism is growing in leaps and bounds with grey nomads getting more adventurous each year, turning up in all sorts of obscure places.' He sticks his chin forward, his bulging eyes above his large nose boring into Maroney's. 'Crikey, mate, you should be thanking me instead of looking as sour as green grapes We're coming into winter down here and you're off to the sunny north.'

Maroney had scowled his way out of the office. Back at his desk, he complained to his friend and work colleague, Maria. 'I'm being exiled to the most isolated place in the whole fucking continent — the planet — for what?' To collect stories about cow-farming in the desert?' She laughed at him. She and Rod, her husband, had sometimes suggested camping trips and watched him squirm at the thought of it.

'You swearing, Maroney? My, my, he has upset you, possum, but just think, maybe a dose of the great outdoors is what you need.'

'Yeah, well, thanks for the sympathy, mia amica. You're gonna feel terrible when you see the headlines: *Journalist Lost in Western Desert.*'

Not for the first time, he thinks he's had enough of working for the paper. He wants more autonomy. But what else would he do? Freelance work is tempting. However, that would mean more travelling and he'd done enough in his twenties to last a lifetime. Now he just wanted ... he's not sure what. But he likes Fremantle. His new apartment, bought with a lot of help from the bank, overlooks the river. It's not far from the city centre, with a gym and a pool in the building. He likes the routine of going home each day, working out for an hour before taking a glass of wine and a book onto his daybed on the balcony, to the peacefulness of his river view. There is an almost obsessive need within him for routine. He recognises that. It makes him feel safe. But most evenings he eats by himself in a city café. There's nothing lonelier than that.

He'd walked home, his mood blacker than the river. He'd headed straight for the pool on the ground floor, the knot in the base of his belly, worse than usual. Like the boss said, maybe he should be happy with this assignment, but the thought of going north puts a vice around his gut.

He dived into the pool, swimming underwater for half a length, the blue silence calming. As he broke the surface a child screamed. He spun around, but then realised it wasn't a scream. The child squealed with delight as her father threw her into the air, letting her go and pulling her up when she began to sink. Maroney went back to slicing through the water. The sound filled his head each time he came up for a breath. He tried to concentrate on his strokes but gave up and heaved his body out of the pool before the memories had time to surface.

*****

The bus drops him off at the town's only motel — a row of single-storey semi-attached boxes. He knocks on the side of the screened door with the sign OFFICE rusting above. A disinterested-looking bloke with several days of stubble on his chin emerges from the gloom, scratching his crotch with one hand and pushing the register over the counter with the other. A TV flickers in the room behind.

He takes the key and walks across the treeless car park to his room, glad to be away from the air in the tiny office — a fetid concoction of beer, hamburgers and smoke. That and the thought of the journey ahead of him, sour in his stomach.

Bedarra

IN the rear-view mirror, a frown corrugates the space between Doog's eyebrows. The sun is savage out here and the expensive cream she pushes into her face every night doesn't seem to be doing much, not that she really believes the promise of younger-looking skin from its anti-ageing ingredients. *And ask me if I care.* Age has its compensations. She tenses as she thinks of living through the confusion of adolescence again.

The station hands at Bedarra are a rough-hewn bunch but their old-fashioned manners still surprise Doog. When she had first arrived, she would see them out fencing in the paddock, stripped naked to the waist, covered in dirt. They'd lift their hats. *Missus,* they'd say with a bob of the head. *Name's Doog,* she'd reply, at first with her eyes glued to the ground. A couple of them stand when she walks onto the verandah for dinner. It has taken a bit of getting used to, that and the nicknames, mostly to do with her red hair. Bruce, the head stockman, calls her Pindan. *That's what we call the earth around here,* he tells her with a proud note in his gravelly voice. She pretends the word is unfamiliar and just smiles. Names like the Red Queen and the Ice Maiden, they don't say to her face, but if the breeze is blowing in the right direction, she hears and sees more than she's supposed to as she leans on the tank-stand at the side of the homestead to have a quiet puff in the evenings.

When they sit and yarn after school, Mrs C loves telling Doog what the blokes say at the first breakfast shift. Says she keeps quiet and hears plenty, takes pride in what she calls being a fly on the wall.

'Matt reckons he's never seen that beautiful mouth of yours laugh,' she'd said the other day, cackling away while she peeled the potatoes. Apparently, Matt had said that Doog's mouth sometimes turns up at the edges when there's a joke at dinner, but that's it.

'Yeah, well, maybe they should think of better jokes,' she'd replied.

At first, she'd wondered if Mrs C was trying to stir her up. But the cook just likes to gossip. She's harmless. Mrs C's a real mimic and Matt would be surprised if he heard the laughter that often fills the kitchen. She once told Doog how the blokes all tried to guess her age. Col had said about thirty, but Matt had argued. He thought that Doog was pushing forty. He would, but of course he was right. According to Mrs C, he'd said it was the sun frocks that made her look younger. Said Doog looks like a hippy chick.

'A hippy chick!'

When Doog thought about it, she realised even Mary wore the station uniform of jeans and checked shirts. But that was not for her. The strappy dresses she liked to wear were practical in this heat.

That day Mrs C had mimicked all the men: Koop, who reckoned a bloke'd be wasting his time trying to chat Doog up. And then Col said if you asked him, that sheila had a poker up her arse and Matt, who got real cranky said, no one was asking him.

And then Mrs C had looked hard at Doog and said, 'I reckon that man's got a soft spot for you.'

'Who, Matt? That man hasn't got a soft spot in his body.'

*****

Those who live around the homestead are all white except for Mary. Her clan live down by the river. At first, Doog was too shy to go anywhere near the community. Matt was the one who taught her the protocol. He told her to go down and stand on the edge of the camp.

'Just wait there. You gotta be invited,' he said.

She did this, and felt like the girl at the party that no one talks to. Soon an old man looked up and waved her over. He said something she couldn't understand and pointed to the group of women sitting around a fire in a veil of smoke and the smell of eucalyptus. Some were sorting roots in a long wooden bowl, snapping off stems and throwing them into the fire. One stirred what looked like an enormous stew. She understood she should join them and sat down on the ground, crossed-legged, thankful for yoga lessons. She watched in silence while they continued as though she wasn't there. Several had small babies suckling. Toddlers wriggled in laps, all the time looking shyly from liquid black eyes. A few women smiled and she began to feel welcome. She would have liked to learn some of the language but struggled to hear what they said, let alone get her tongue around the strange words.

After that first day Doog has ventured down many times, taking her camera. She always asks permission to take photographs. No one seems to mind but she can't help feeling like an interloper. There's one old woman whose grooved face is a history that Doog would love to record but the bloodshot eyes don't respond to her smile and she doesn't risk asking.

*****

Unless mustering or something else takes them away, on most evenings the staff gather on the verandah for a sundowner before the meal. At first, Doog couldn't get used to fronting up every night but they're a jolly bunch and now she enjoys the communal ritual. The area is large enough for a long refectory table with room for a drinks trolley and a fridge as well as assorted armchairs at the far end. The blokes drink beer like water. Doog always found her mother's fear of becoming addicted to alcohol annoying, but out here the heat makes it tempting and she finds herself worrying about the same thing. The first night or two everyone had watched while she added a squeeze of lemon to a glass of soda water.

'There's scotch or gin on the trolley if you want to add a bit of zest to your life,' Matt had said when she first arrived.

'Thanks, but I'll just have a wine with dinner.' She'd winced as she heard her prudish voice and saw of one of Mary's black eyebrows dip like a sneer.

She usually excuses herself as soon as the meal is over to wander back across the dark, towards the donga. Just beyond the verandah, behind the kitchen, is the tank-stand where she stops for a cigarette. When she got the job, she told herself she would give up smoking but she hasn't managed it yet. The verandah is always well lit. From the shadows she has no trouble seeing and she remembers a night not long after she'd arrived, Mary sitting erect, patting her pouting lips, mimicking Doog with a napkin, saying: 'Well, anyone would think she was the flippin' queen'. They were all quick with their judgments that first night. Even Mrs C called Doog a cold fish, leering at Matt and saying all she needed was a good bloke to warm her up. Then came Col's voice teasing Mrs C about why she was so warm, said he'd bet she'd had more pricks than a second-hand dartboard. Doog had almost choked but they all just laughed including Mrs C. Then came the clattering of dishes and they drifted off to an early night, leaving silence.

Most nights now she stands behind the tank smoking her cigarette and breathing in the stars. They always seemed so very near in this part of the country. They had loitered in her memories like a half-forgotten dream. The last time she was up this way they'd somehow given her hope. It'd been a cruel place, except for

the stars. After she takes her last draw and stubs out the cigarette,
she continues to her donga to shut her door on the world.

23

The Motel

MARONEY walks across the blistering tarmac to the concrete verandah outside his door where a small wrought-iron table and two chairs stand rigid and uninviting. On the table, a stainless-steel dog bowl half-full of bottle tops and cigarette butts. *Classy!* Inside, water the colour of gravy fills the toilet bowl although the candlewick bedspread, an orange remnant of the fifties, makes him smile. The mirror has acne but the air-conditioner hums, and right now that's all he cares about. He catches sight of himself in the spotty mirror. Rivulets of sweat run through the dust on his face. He looks over to the window and tries to resist the compulsion to make sure it will open. He opens it.

The shower is surprisingly decent. With the dust sluiced down the drain, and having changed into a fresh T-shirt, shorts and sandals, Maroney's mood lifts. Time to locate the car. It will take him only a few minutes to realize nothing is far away in this town. A short walk around the corner from the motel he finds the car yard. A few cars gleam. He passes a young boy with a polishing cloth in his hand. Everything else is stained with the same red, including the outside of the office, which once must have been painted white. He's shown the car. It's huge.

'There's just me. Have you got something smaller?'

'Where you goin', mate?'

'I'd like to explore the station country inland from here.' He explains that he's a journalist, wants to do some stories about the region.

'This is what you'll want, mate. Anything smaller out that way, you'll bust an axle.'

Great, just what he needs to hear. Still, he can't bring himself to confess that he knows bugger-all about off-road driving. Aside from the embarrassment, the bloke might refuse to hire out the vehicle, so Maroney swallows that thought and asks for the direction to the post office instead.

'Just around the corner in the main street, mate. Can't miss it — red box out the front.'

Maroney sits for a while in the car, trying to befriend the gears and the indicators. It wouldn't be a good look if he were to rev out of the car yard in low-range or switch on wipers and lights instead of the indicator. In the glove box is a manual. He'll need that. The only four-wheel driving he's done was years ago. Trouble is, he wrote on his job application — experienced off-road driver. *Lies, they always get you in the end.* His little second-hand Alfetta 2000 in Fremantle only leaves the underground car park for an occasional trip to the theatre in Perth or a Sunday outing to the hills with friends. At home, he walks everywhere. He focuses once more on the Land Cruiser and drives out of the yard. Carefully.

Just around the corner is the building recognizable as the post office by the logo peeling on the iron roof and the postbox, which looks like a dusty red dalek from *Dr Who* standing out the front. Maroney enters the tiny building and arranges to rent a postbox to have his mail sent to. The general store is across the road. Some snacks will help to keep him awake on the drive and he should stock up on a few offerings. They might be handy to make him more welcome wherever he lands up. He'll head east but he hasn't decided yet whether to drive slightly south to a station called Pardee or more north to one called Bedarra. He'll see if he can

work out the best road from the survey maps that he dug out of
the basement of the newspaper. Inside the general store, yellow
cauliflowers, broccoli and beans bound and wilting in plastic lie
on shelves. Fresh food seems out of the question so he settles for
an assortment of nuts and chocolates and then heads for the pub.
A bit of alcohol won't go astray.

He finds out later that by the time he arrives at the motel after
his last purchase, there are people in the small town who have
worked out what the city bloke with the pasty face is about.

The Guvvy

A DEMOUNTABLE serves as the schoolroom at the back of the Bedarra homestead. Inside, an extravaganza of charts and art colours every surface. Dinosaurs, monsters and the solar system dangle from the ceiling. Students spill on to the porch for art and craft, and the concrete floor is a chalky history of hopscotch and other activities. Jess, the elder of Mat's two daughters, is out there, working on a collage for her Year Five art project. Her shoulders slump while she mechanically glues paper on paper. Doog watches through the open door, at the same time listening to the youngest of the Aboriginal children, Molly, stumble through the words of her first reader. The girl on the porch looks lost and Doog's forehead corrugates with concern. The rest of the children work on the phonics sheets she's prepared. Independent little Cassie, Matt's younger daughter, works in a world of her own but Jake, the eldest of the Aboriginal children, is gazing out the window to where she knows he'd rather be. She'll need to coax him through the lesson, unlike Sam, his cousin, who finishes his task quickly and dives into the activity corner.

A rush of warmth for her little bunch fills her. *Her little bunch.* She's feeling a possessiveness she knows she's not entitled to. When Matt's away, Mary usually looks after the children, but if Mary is tied up Doog is happy to tuck Jess and Cassie into bed and read them bedtime stories. And the other three children claim just as much a part of her. A part she never knew was there to give.

The kitchen is around the other side of the homestead. The children take turns, mid-morning and lunchtime, to collect trays of sandwiches and fruit from the cook. Doog guides the children through the curriculum from 8.30am until 2.30pm. The School of the Air provides the highlight of most days. Jess and Jake are in the older group, while Sam, Cassie and Molly join in with younger children from the stations in the district. They all delight in connecting with their little friends, whom they see only a few times a year at school camps. Although she has only five pupils, Doog is flat out trying to fit everything in and wonders how she ever coped with thirty-five.

When school finishes in the afternoon, she likes to prepare the lessons for the next day. After that it has become her habit to stop off at the kitchen for a cuppa with Mrs C before continuing on to the donga to spend some time on her own.

'You never did say how you ended up out here, love.' Mrs C doesn't let up with the questions, but somehow, she manages to get away with it. Doog has been tempted several times to confide. That would be a mistake. The cook swirls flour over the table and pummels a great ball of pastry dough for an apple pie. From her seat at the table, Doog watches, her hands wrapped around a mug of tea while she yields to the nostalgic smells of the kitchen.

'Can't say I miss teaching in the city,' she says. 'Used to love it but things have changed. No autonomy anymore, and the testing and analysing … we hardly have time to teach. And it's different now. If a child gets hurt, you'd be sued if you put your arm around any of them to comfort them. Instead, they get icepacks.' She lets out a mirthless laugh. 'Bloody icepacks! They nearly drove me mad.

'Anyway, with that and other things, in the end, I told the department to stick their job.'

Doog stops to drink her tea, annoyed that she's still annoyed. 'I told myself if I got away from the city, I would save some money, maybe enough for an overseas trip.'

'You must have been earning good money as a school teacher.'

'Yes, I couldn't complain about the pay,' she says. 'But I spent it all, every penny … not sure why.'

But even as she speaks, Doog knows why. Her mother drove her nuts with her penny-pinching, *remember the depression*, ways. Maybe it was her sad way of challenging this woman who always seemed to be able to invade and manipulate her headspace. She had to get away, and when Annie won a scholarship for NIDA in Sydney, and her brother offered to pay Annie's accommodation, Doog was free. She swallows, remembers trying to share Annie's excitement, remembers trying not to miss her even before she'd gone. And afterwards, the visceral pull of this northwest region.

Doog glances up at Mrs C, knowing the cook's waiting to hear more but she also knows anything she says will be common knowledge on the station within days. You can't help liking Mrs C with her good humour and energy. She would put younger women to shame. Breasts and hips bulge from her thin cotton dress and her hair is a frizzy catastrophe. She jokes about her sturdy arms — bossy, she calls them. They're tanned, and firm from the daily bread-making and from carrying great steaming casseroles or giant pans of roasted vegetables from oven to table. Legs like bread dough, and ankles to match, disappear into flat black lace-up shoes. No one could be less like Doog's mother.

'Tell me about your mother, Doogie.'

'I wouldn't know where to start, Mrs C. I love her, of course I do, but sometimes she makes it bloody hard. She can't let go of how tough things used to be after the war. It got worse when my father died.'

She doesn't add: *The church rules her life, and she would love it to rule mine as well.*

'Yeah, I've met the type. You feel like you want to shake them and say, for heaven's sake relax and enjoy life while you can.'

Doog nods and gazes out the window. The ever-present clank-clank of an old windmill is soothing as she watches the boys strengthen the fence around the home paddock. A young Brahman has been separated from its mother and brought into the house yard. *Give him a cuddle whenever you cross the yard,* Matt had said. Said he wanted to get the calf used to people, that when he grew into a two-tonne stud it would make him easier to handle. Doog had no intention of cuddling it, but the cries of the orphaned animal got to her and now she's thankful it grazes contentedly and comes to be rubbed and patted.

She turns back to Mrs C. 'We should have been good friends, Mum and me … done things together, but we can't even shop for a loaf of bread without an argument.'

'Ah, mothers and daughters — often a difficult relationship. Yet they say we all turn into our mothers.'

I'll never turn into my mother. Doog feels her resentment rising.

'Talking of mothers, I wish we could do more to help Jess. She's still hurting bad after the death of her mother. But Brenda is a treasure. If anyone can get a smile out of Jess, she can.

Not long after Doog arrived at Bedarra, she met Brenda, the mother of Jake, the oldest of the three Aboriginal children and auntie of the other two. She felt an instant connection. There's a warm gentleness about Brenda, also strength reflected in the bones of her handsome face. Brenda used to help Matt's wife with the school's curriculum. When she first approached Doog, with eyes cast shyly on the dusty ground, to ask if she could help with the kids, Doog was so grateful she could have hugged her, and during that first meeting they talked for a good two hours about the needs of each of the children. Brenda told Doog that she didn't think Jake would last long at school.

'Wantin' to be a man and be doin' man things since the moment he could walk, that one,' she'd said. 'But Sam, he smart, that one. And Molly, she pretty smart too. They need to learn things, go to high school in town.'

Doog had nodded, pleased. It makes her job easier when parents value education. Now, on the weekends, Brenda is the one she seeks out when she visits the community. Brenda has told her the names of the other women. Some of them she knows from previous visits. Only a few ever speak to her in English, and once again she attempts to get her tongue around the language. It takes a while to work out which woman is the mother of Sam and Molly. These kids have lots of aunties. She's gradually learning about some of the traditions of their culture and tries to understand the etiquette. Watching Brenda, she learns there are certain conventions to follow, certain times to speak, times to wait to be spoken to. She also learns there are places that women can't go, not even the Aboriginal women. This had surprised her at first, but she remembers being told off when she crossed a line over which, *women must not step* at a yacht club in Perth, and it's still almost taboo for a woman to go into the front bar of a pub in *white* Australia. She winces as she thinks of Annie's father leaving her in the car outside the pub after football matches. She and the other women would be brought lemon squashes while the boys whooped it up inside with their mates.

Brenda seems to have a story attached to most things on the station country. There's a story to explain how the waterhole was formed and one about why the wagtail flits around near the ground instead of soaring into the air. She wants Brenda to tell these stories in the classroom. Doog is eager to carry them into art and other lessons. Sure, Jake, Sam and Mollie may have heard them but good stories should be told over and over.

Dark Enough For Stars

'G'DAY. Mr Maroney?'

A shadow falls across the map Maroney has draped over the wrought-iron table. He squints in the direction of the soft voice. A black form with an outstretched hand blurs against the glare.

'Name's Neville, Nev. Hear you're going out to Bedarra, bro.'

Maroney's only slightly surprised. He'd already guessed that he'd been under scrutiny when the girl at the local café had asked him where he was going. It's her friend who works in the post office and no doubt the café girl had told another friend until, like a Chinese whisper, the news had reached Neville, who Maroney will learn, works at the service station. He stands and shakes the hand before pointing to the other seat, out of the sun.

'Hello, Daniel Maroney, most people call me Maroney. Why do you ask?'

'That's my mob's country,' says Nev with a smile.

'You know the road out there, then?'

Nev's eyes dance. 'Yeah, bro. Bin away for a while but go out there when I can.'

'Well, I haven't actually made up my mind about which station to visit first.'

'Mad if ya don't go to Bedarra, bro. Biggest and best around here. And the campdraft's comin' up.'

Maroney resists asking what a campdraft is. Sounds like he'll have plenty of time on the journey to ask about the station. 'So, you're after a lift?' he asks.

The large smile grows even larger, Nev's white teeth in startling contrast to his dark face. Black curls bounce when he nods, giving him a boyish look.

Maroney feels relief flow through his body. He'd been trying not to think about the lone journey into unknown country, trying to tough it out and not admit to himself that the prospect filled him with dread.

'OK, maybe that's made up my mind. I hear the track's a bit rough. It'd be good to reach the station before it gets too hot. How long d'ya reckon it'll take?'

Nev strokes his chin, takes a deep breath and rolls his eyes. 'Depends,' he says finally.

'On what?'

'Track's changin' all the time. Rabbits, wind, cyclones in the wet season. Sometimes the dunes gobble it up and you have to drive around to find it again.'

'What about the track to Pardee?'

Nev shakes his head. 'Same, Bro. Better off going to Bedarra.'

Maroney's skin starts to prickle and it's not just the heat. He takes in a lungful of air. Nev will never know how grateful he is to have company on this journey. They arrange to meet out front at sun-up.

The next morning, in the hush of the dawn, when Maroney drags his bags from the motel unit, Nev is standing by the car with a small backpack and a carton of food — gifts for his family. In Fremantle right now, the roads will be bumper-to-bumper, cars and trucks spewing fumes up to his apartment. Here, the only smell comes from the dewy wattles lining the verges, their golden blossoms sparkling in the early morning sun. The wide streets of the small town are quiet except for the distant chug of a generator.

They pass the empty showground and the silent football field along with a few small, weatherboard houses on large lots. They stop at the 24-hour servo on the main road, where Nev works. Maroney fills the car's large fuel tank, and they buy bacon-and-egg toasted-sandwiches for breakfast along with cups of hot chocolate. He doesn't want to admit how good it all tastes. White bread hasn't passed his lips in years. His usual breakfast — muesli with yoghurt — is followed by a cup of green tea when he gets to work.

During the first hour, Nev talks non-stop. He answers questions about Sandy Bay and the countryside and the station. Maroney stores the information, grateful for the distraction from the endless track. They could be the only two people in the world. Out in front, and on both sides of the track, the flat land reaches as far as he can see. The same spikey grass and a few gnarled bushes are the only interruptions to the tedium.

Maroney reluctantly curtails the speed to a crawl to negotiate rocky outcrops that threaten to disembowel the vehicle. Nev points up ahead. 'Better stop a minute, bro. Bunny booby-trap.'

Maroney can't see the rabbit warren in front of the car, but when Nev gives it a kick, the track subsides. They could have been bogged in that for days. Kilometre after kilometre of spinifex, termite mounds and occasionally stunted trees with bleached trunks, break the monotony of the red dunes and swales, grey with rabbit poo. Kites whistle overhead, casting sinister shadows, hunting rabbits. He tries not to think of the rabbits. At the boys home, one of his chores was to trap the creatures. A little crushed paw would be hanging, bloody and limp. They never made a sound, just looked at him with eyes that still haunt. He was taught to kill the maimed animals after he extracted them from the steel teeth. To hold them by the ears and chop the back of their vulnerable necks using the side of his hand. Then, he had to skin and disembowel them. The soupy smell of fermented grass and warm blood mixed with that of shit and urine … even now, the thought makes his gut churn.

About midday, when Maroney is sure they must be nearing the station, they reach a clump of white gums that, according to Neville, marks halfway.

'Are you sure? We've been driving all morning.'

The midday sun bleaches the landscape and sucks at Maroney's resolve. He grabs his hat from the back of the car. He needs a pee and heads towards the gums on the side of a dry creek.

'If you're off to shake the snake, mate, just watch out for others.' says Nev.

Maroney stops and looks back. 'You mean …?'

Neville nods. 'Yep, mean buggers. King Browns, and a few queens too, I reckon.'

OK, right here will do. Maroney turns his back. The next minute Nev's standing beside him waving his baton around like they're about to perform a duet. Maroney looks at the sky. He didn't bank on this being a communal activity. Curiosity, though, gets the better of him. He lowers his eyes to see if Nev's is bigger than his. *Big kid, you haven't done that since …* He pushes away memories, but he can't help grinning as he shakes his head. *You're losing it, Maroney,* he tells himself.

They boil a billy in the shade of the largest gum. The midday heat presses down, heavy with silence. After they've eaten a sandwich, they set off again. Maroney forgets to keep the speed down and slams into a sharp rock. The vehicle starts to swerve and he slowly brings it to a standstill.

'Flat tyre,' comes Nev's soft voice.

'Shit!' Maroney's head drops onto his tired hands clutching the top of the steering wheel. He has never changed a tyre. He has helped a few times but it's not the same.

'It's OK, bro,' Nev seems to know what he's thinking. 'I can do it.'

Nev unloads their luggage from the back of the vehicle and lifts up the mat. The spare tyre, the jack and the tyre lever—all there.

Maroney can't ever remember feeling so hot. He tries to help and by the time they get the wheel nuts off he feels ready to expire. When they finally heave the spare tyre into place, he tries not to let Nev see that he almost weeps with relief.

A few kilometres on, the sandy track forks and Nev points the way without hesitation. But at the next fork, he points left, and then looks back, frowning. It dawns on Maroney that Nev probably scores his lifts from shearers and contractors who know their way. Now, with each fork in the track, he can see the confidence disappearing from the no-longer smiling face. He stops to look at the map but out here it's meaningless to someone who hasn't done an orienteering course. Like the one Maria's husband, Rod had wanted him to go on last year. Nev's not smiling or laughing anymore. He looks embarrassed and worried. And he's not the only one worrying.

The sun still beats through the back windscreen on its feverish journey to the west. A layer of fine dust covers the inside of the car. Maroney has to remember to stop licking his lips. The only result is a gritty tongue. Groups of kangaroos, some with small heads peeping out of pouches, begin to rouse. They seem to wait, disguised as bushes, before deciding to casually hop across the track in front of the vehicle. Unpredictable emus revel in an erratic crisscrossing of the country as if their job is to keep him alert. In among that lot, are rabbits and the odd brush turkey that slows their journey even more. The light continues to lengthen the shadows. The track peters out.

Maroney shuts his eyes and claws down the rising panic. He doesn't look at Nev. *How can you get lost? You're an Aborigine, for Chrissakes!* He's heard all the tales of travellers lost in this sort of country. It's sinking in fast that, even if the two of them survive, he's going to look like an idiot, setting out with no preparation for getting lost or breaking down. The list of things he should have brought is suddenly obvious. At the very least, he should have put in a couple of extra jerry cans of fuel.

The country stretches on all sides. They're in the centre of this emptiness. He feels small.

'Jeez, Nev. I don't fancy being stuck out here all night.'

'No,' says Nev softly, a look of misery transforming his face.

Maroney feels like a jerk. Kneading his forehead, he forces himself to think.

'OK, I've got water and a lighter. I suppose it could be worse,' he says, but he's not sure how.

One thing is clear. They can't continue in the failing light. Scouting around they find firewood and after the long drive, Maroney is glad to let go of the steering wheel, feeling the tension ease in his shoulders. It also feels good to walk across the flat earth towards the sun. He stops to pick up sticks, tapping away the dirt and, hopefully, any insects. This is the first time he has been back to the bush since the boys home. Swore he'd never return. Now, holding a bundle of dry twisted sticks, he stands motionless, becoming aware of the intensity of the changing colours in the limitless sky. He takes a long, deep breath, and although it seems fanciful, he feels the peacefulness of this place entering his mind and body. The alarm he felt when he first knew they were lost is subsiding. He should at least be nervous, but all he feels is a deepening calm in the middle of this … this space. An idea for an article germinates in his mind.

Becoming aware of the pleasant aroma of smoke-tinged eucalyptus, Maroney starts back towards where Nev has made a fire. Invisible birds perform a boisterous finale to the day, and then as if bidden by an unseen conductor, create a deep absence by sudden silence. The crackling of the fire is the only sound in the hush that follows. The western rim of the sky glows, pregnant with the ripened sun. Maroney slowly turns, the full 360 degrees. Dark scrub fringes the circle of the land with a vivid orange halo. In the east, violet and magenta tinge the sky, coalescing to grey. He's centred in this great ring and lifts his face to the ever-darker blue infinity above. Continuing to the fire, he squats on the sand and he and Nev open some warm beers. They eat potato chips that Nev has bought for his family. Maroney's eyes fix on the flickering fire. His mind absent, while he feeds small sticks to the flames.

'No, man!' Nev stays his hand. 'Ya don't want a fuckin' great whitefella's fire; ya can't see nothin'.'

And sure enough, when the flames die down into glowing embers, although there's no moon, Maroney feels he can almost touch the stars. Again, he feels small, but there's no fear. He lies back, almost floats, sedated by the dignity of the great dome above. *Centred.* That could be the title of the article. Then the toad would really think he's lost the plot.

There's a rustling noise and when he sits up, he feels the hairs on his neck prickle. A dark face has joined them at the fire.

'Jesus!' He jumps to his feet.

'It's all right, bro, it's me uncle,' whoops Neville, jumping up to pump the older man's hand, slapping his shoulder.

'How you goin', Unc?'

Nev introduces an older, smaller, more bent version of himself. The same infectious grin, the whites in large eyes shining in the light of the fire.

'Silly buggers, whatcha doin' out 'ere? Enjoying the great outdoors are ya?' Unc doubles over, cackling with laughter as he slaps his thigh.

'Got a bit lost.' Nev mumbles to the ground.

'Well, Bedarra's just two Ks over there, but if ya wanna stay here the night …' More laughter.

Maroney is already pushing sand on the fire with his boot.

The Homestead

THEY pull up to the steps at the bottom of the homestead verandah. A man in lanky blue jeans and a checked shirt uncurls from a chair and descends the steps to meet them. *An arrogant-looking sort* is Maroney's first impression. Unc rolls out of the vehicle.

'Look what I found over by the two-mile trough,' he says. 'Lost as a couple of ants in a termite nest.' The old man bubbles with mirth.

'Been away from home too long, Nev?' The man smiles for the first time while he shakes Nev's hand. But the smile doesn't linger as he turns to Maroney.

'Matt's the name. I'm the manager of the station.' he says. 'Welcome to Bedarra.'

Nev and Unc take their leave and walk off. Their chatter and laughter float back through the warm air as they meld into the black night.

'Can I interest you in a coldie?' says Matt, pointing to the verandah steps. Maroney's perplexed. He's being offered a beer by someone who can't crack a smile. Matt sprawls into an old cane chair on the verandah and indicates another to Maroney. He wasn't behind the door when they handed out good locks, Maroney thinks. Must be over forty but the single women in Fremantle would be lit up by his olive skin, his full head of thick dark hair and his tall, powerful-looking frame.

He tells Matt about being a journalist with the *News Weekly*, based in Fremantle. How he hopes to tour around to a few of the stations and get an idea about the life in the region.

'OK by me, so long as you don't mind bunking down in the shearers' quarters. We're a bit full at the moment. We have the Distance Ed mob here sorting out the radio for the kids. The station owner, Mrs Le Carre — '

'Jean Le Carre?' Maroney feels his antennae go up. Jean Le Carre owns one of the biggest pastoral companies in Australia.

'Yep, that's her — she got us hooked up to the latest and greatest so we can get the kids' school without relying on the flying doctor service. While they're here you can never get a word in edgeways between them and the guvvy so we leave them to it.

'The guvvy?'

'The schoolteacher, or governess if you like. You'll meet them all tomorrow.' Matt points the way back down the verandah steps.

'Whose kids?' asks Maroney as they walk past sheds towards the shearers' quarters.

'Mine, and some of the Aboriginal kids on the station.'

'So, you're married?'

'Was. The wife died a year back. Breast cancer.'

'That's rough.'

'Too right it's rough. A seven and ten-year-old shouldn't lose their mother at such a young age but it can't be helped and the staff all try to fill the gap.

They reach the row of wooden rooms skirted by a narrow verandah. Matt opens a cupboard full of bedding, stowed in plastic bags, and shows him the small bathroom.

'No hot water until the chip heater gets lit in the morning, I'm afraid.'

Matt slouches off into the night, leaving Maroney gazing through the glassless window. He wonders whether to be terrified of what might crawl in during the night or simply be pleased he can get out.

The next morning, still half asleep, he looks around. A breeze drifts through the window, crisp and unpolluted except for the faint smell of horses. He stretches, aware there's no tension in his shoulders for the first time since … when? The sight of a large beetle on the bed dislodges the last vestige of sleep. Maroney flicks the sheet and the creature is on the floor lumbering towards the door. Several geckos fix their over-sized eyes on him from the wall beyond the bed. *That's close enough, you lot.*

Outside, an orchestra — dogs barking, men yelling, and horses' hooves drumming on baked earth. He struggles into jeans and T-shirt. On the verandah bench he pulls on his boots and wipes off the fine coat of ash. Black cockatoos lazily chew on the nuts of the casuarinas casting meagre shade over the shearers' quarters. On his way to the homestead, he passes a mountain of mallee roots, great rolls of fencing wire and rusting machinery between ramshackle sheds. Contented chooks scratch oblivious to the axe cleaving the blood-soaked tree stump.

The smell of bacon lures him to an out building beside the homestead. He tries the screen door.

'Boots off, round the back,' comes a sharp command.

'Pardon?'

'No work boots allowed in my kitchen, and I don't want them scattered all over the front. Kitchen rule number one. Unless your name is Jean Le Carre or Queen Elizabeth you come through the back door.'

Through the screen, he sees a dumpy woman pointing a wooden spoon around the side of the building. He has the urge to declare that his boots are new, RM Williams, almost a fashion statement in Fremantle. However, he walks around the building, parks his boots neatly at the back door and enters the kitchen, feeling as sheepish as his woollen socks.

'Any chance of a coffee?' He tries to look friendlier than he feels. Instinct warns him not to cross this woman.

'Kettle's on the stove, cups are on the shelf above, coffee and sugar below.' The woman points with her chin, which is not exactly made for pointing. One arm is wrapped around a large bowl perched on her hip while she wallops the contents with the wooden spoon.

'You're a bit late for breakfast. Seven o'clock is the last shift.'

'That's OK, I'm never too interested in breakfast anyway.'

'You won't last two minutes out this way if you don't eat.' The woman waves the spoon, coated with cake mixture at him.

'Make yourself some toast, and there's left-over bacon under that cloth.'

That's an order rather than a suggestion, he decides. 'Cheers, I'm Maroney by the way, Daniel Maroney,' he says, aware of the scrutiny of the small black eyes.

'A bit of Irish in you by the sounds of it, Catholic no doubt. I'm station cook. Gwen Cameron's the name. Most people call me Mrs C.'

Maroney finds a stool and settles down with his bacon sandwich, glad of his decision not to turn vegetarian. And instant coffee never tasted so good.

'How many people work at the station, Mrs C?'

'They come and go. At the moment, there's Matt the manager —'

'Yes, I met him last night.'

'And Bruce, the head stockman. Darcy and Mandamarra, Manny we call him. They're the main stockmen. From the community.'

'The community?' Maroney imagines two stockmen coming all the way from Sandy Bay. But that can't be right.

'The Aboriginal community,' Mrs C says without missing a beat. 'Then there's two roustabouts, Koop and Col. And young

Mary. She helps me and sometimes works in the yards if she's needed. And Doogie looks after the kids and occasionally helps Matt in the office. Oh, and there's a young un, just started. Snow — poor kid — green as a tree snake and twice as scared. Apparently, he's a magician when it comes to fixing machinery.'

'Is Doogie the person they call the guvvy?'

'Yep, that her. After Matt's wife died, he advertised for help with the kids' schooling. The first year was a bit of a disaster. A couple of young things turned up but they only lasted weeks so Matt made sure the next ad specified someone mature with experience.'

Mrs C cracks egg after egg into the bowl, beating the mixture between each one. She shakes a small cellophane packet and the smell of cinnamon for one disorientating moment transports Maroney to another hand beating cake mixture. He returns his focus to the cook. The mixture, poured and scraped into a tin, disappears into the enormous oven.

'Matt was getting desperate. Young Jess, his eldest was becoming a bit of a handful.'

Maroney finds himself wanting to lick the bowl and spoon before Mrs C pushes them under the running tap and wipes flour with the heel of her hand into a scrap bucket. She pushes it towards him.

'You can throw that to the chooks on your way back to the shearers' quarters. Leave the bucket on the stump, someone'll bring it back when they're coming this way. I can't be gasbagging to you all day.'

He's herded out of the kitchen after gulping down his last mouthful of coffee just in time to see a Land Rover, trailing a cloud of red dust, kids hanging out of the windows, driven by a red-headed woman.

Leaves and Lizards

THE children dive out of the Land Rover in a tangle of legs and arms and small cloth bags They're down at the waterhole before Doog has time to get out of the vehicle.

'Doogie!'

Cassie is pointing to Sam. Her urgent voice sends a jolt of alarm through Doog. She reaches the bank, and Sam, his hands firmly clamped on the neck of a large bungarra, deft feet dancing to avoid the thick tail lashing patterns in the earth near his feet.

'Put it down, Sam, we're not here to collect goannas.'

'But Miss, he's got a hook in his mouth.'

She looks more closely. A hook complete with bait and a piece of fishing line pierces the hard lip of the scaley mouth.

'That was careless of someone,' she mutters. 'OK, wait, I'll get the pliers.'

Back at the car, a rummage in a rusty toolbox uncovers some pointy-nosed pliers and she returns to the ring of children surrounding the skinny brown boy.

'He's not going to like this. Would you like to help hold him, Jess?'

The silent girl turns her head to the side without a hint of interest.

'I'll hold him,' yells Molly.

'All right Molly, but we'll lower him to the ground first. Hold tight to that tail or he'll whip you, and watch out for those claws. You got him, Sam?'

The boy nods, his face set in a determined grimace as the lizard hisses. It takes all Doog's strength to cut through the shank of the hook and manipulate the pieces out of the hard mouth.

'You're a hero, Sam.' She ruffles his hair. 'You can let him go now.'

For a moment, the lizard stands, head raised, frozen like some prehistoric exhibit in a museum case, before rocketing into the reeds.

'Now you lot, remember what we're here for.' Doog points to her wristwatch. 'You have half-an-hour to each collect at least thirty different leaves — think about size, shape, colour. Have you all got your water bottles?' The four heads nod. 'Bum bags?'

'Sam hasn't got his, Missus,' Pipes up Molly.

Doog turns to Sam and raises her eyebrows. He grins before running back to the vehicle, grabbing the small bag and buckling it around his waist. The bags contain a mini-survival kit: two bandages for snakebite, a couple of Band-Aids and a box of matches to light a signal fire. In this flat landscape getting lost is more than a possibility. Rocks, bushes and tracks all look the same, although probably not to a kid like Sam. Doog's sure that both he and Jake could teach her a thing or two about survival.

'Make sure you can see me, or the car, or the billabong at all times. Now off you go.' They bolt away. 'Keep with your partner,' she yells after them.

A large rock protrudes into the billabong, worn smooth and shiny by the constant stream of water and generations of sliding bottoms. A ghost gum genuflects to the pool, bestowing speckled shade. The sun dances on the tree trunks like stage lights and makes Doog wonder how Annie is getting along at her drama school. And then her thoughts drift to her brother, Charlie. His offer to help with Annie's expenses came out of the blue. They were close once, before her pregnancy and then an unspoken-of rift rose between them. Charlie had been clever at school and she'd heard their parents arguing about how *this business* could ruin his chances. Afterwards, when she returned home, he was still a schoolboy and she ... she was different. In those days the education of a boy was paramount but not so important for a girl, who was expected to marry and become a mother. *Certainly not the other way around.*

Red dragonflies flirt with each other in the limelight. Upstream a waterfall splashes and flashes, sunlit over rocks. The only other sound is the ever-present choir of cicadas. The leaves the children gather will be used for a variety of lessons she has planned. There's satisfaction in stretching the scant resources of the station. She enjoys the autonomy and loves that she's trusted to fill the curriculum requirements of Distance Ed. In the city, she felt hemmed in by rules and regulations. *But then following rules never was my forte. If I'd followed rules, I wouldn't have ...*

Voices pull her back to the present. The children are downstream from the waterhole. Sam is with Cassie, the younger of Matt's girls. They're pointing and laughing at something. It's the older one, Jess, that Doog's eyes search out. The girl dawdles, her dark head down and shoulders slumped, oblivious to Molly, who darts around like a wagtail, picking up leaves. Frustration fills her. She doesn't feel qualified to help the girl with her grief.

She glances at her watch. 'Cooeeeee!' she yells with a beckoning wave to the children before heading back to the Land Rover.

'Do you think Jake will be home soon?' she asks in the car on the way back. 'Where's he gone anyway?' Brenda's boy, Jake, is Sam and Molly's cousin, and often skips school, much to Brenda's frustration. If the men go mustering or droving Jake finds a way to join them. Even if they don't give him permission, even if they say he should be at school, he waits and follows. Bruce has told Doog that they can be on the other side of the station rounding up a mob of cattle and suddenly Jake is working right alongside them. Underneath Bruce's gruff exterior, she senses a soft spot for Jake. Bruce treats him like his young apprentice.

'Important business, Miss. Gonna be big corroboree when he comes back.'

Doog's not sure what this is about. She'll ask Brenda.

'Well, he's going to miss out on the special broadcast tomorrow.'

'Tell us, Doogie?' begs Cassie.

'You'll have to wait and see but I'll give you a clue,' she says, winking at Sam beside her. She tries to catch Jess's eye in the rear-view mirror, but the girl stares out of the window, her huddled form cocooned in loss.

'There's going to be a special guest all the way from America and he's green and grouchy.'

'I know,' pipes up Sam. Doog shakes her head and puts a finger to her lips.

'Let's wait till tomorrow,' she says as they pull up at the homestead. 'Put your bags in the schoolroom and I'll see you in the morning at eight-thirty sharp. That means you too, Molly.' Doog bends down and peers into the irresistible black eyes and presses the flat nose on the cheeky brown face. 'No sleeping in.'

'Righty-o, Missus. Can I come over your place, Missus?'

'No way! I've had enough of you lot for one day. Skedaddle all of you. And Molly … please… call me Doogie.'

The children would love to visit her quarters. It has become like forbidden fruit. Right from the start, Doog had claimed privacy when she's not working, and Matt has helped by making the staff quarters off limits.

After an hour of preparation for the following day's lessons, she tidies the schoolroom and heads to the kitchen to grab her afternoon mug of tea and a slice of fruitcake.

Mrs C eyeballs her as soon as she walks in. 'Got a reporter from the city staying a while, a nice young fellow. Comes from Fremantle — same as you. You could have a lot in common, you two.'

Doog wills her face not to betray her. 'I doubt it,' she says, feeling the muscles of her shoulders stiffen while she pretends to look out the window. She knows she's being illogical but she doesn't want to share this place with anyone from Fremantle. She wants it all to herself. She changes the subject.

'I'm worried about Jess, Mrs C. I can't get her interested in anything.'

'Poor little thing. She's not letting go. Perhaps talk to Matt about a holiday or something to divert her.'

Doog gulps down her tea and heads for the door. 'Yes, I'll give it some thought. I'd love to find something to put a bit of sunshine into the little soul.'

'You need to slow down, girlie. We all seen you up with the magpies goin' at it seven days a week. *Flat out like a lizard drinking,* Koop says.'

Koop is a walking lexicon of Australian clichés, Doog smiles. She knows her need to keep busy is bordering on obsessive, but it's how she copes. The few hours when she loses herself in jogging, writing her diary or her photography — that's enough.

She drives the ute to the shed, walks away, leaving it unlocked with the key in the ignition. She'll never get used to that. The staff quarters are a collection of dongas that Matt scored cheaply from a mining company. According to Mrs C, the company fossicked around the area for almost a year, then left empty-handed. From the outside they are grim steel boxes with small windows, and Doog's heart had sunk when she first saw them. She had looked longingly at the old shearers' quarters. The row of wooden rooms and the railed verandah reminded her of old buildings in Fremantle.

'You don't want to live there, especially when the wet season comes,' said Matt. 'The rooms are not even screened, let alone air-conned. If the heat doesn't get to you, the bugs will. There are spiders and frogs and the occasional bungarra, and as soon as you put a light on at night, cockroaches as big as helicopters come calling.' The mention of cockroaches had sealed it. The donga it would be. Bugger character.

The two Moreton Bay fig trees that form a cathedral over the small structures with their enormous spreading roots and bloated branches, feel solid and protective. Her Moroccan cushions and rugs soften the austerity of her new home. There's a wardrobe, too big for her needs, and a dresser. A cloth with the embroidery of her grandmother drapes the top of the dresser standing against one wall. The cloth was the only thing she kept after Grandma died. On the dresser, a candle in a lotus-shaped holder sits between a framed photo of Annie and an empty frame. Each morning she lights the candle. It's a ritual left over from the fads she'd dabbled in when she was younger. OK, she *was* a hippy chick, but everyone was back then.

There are more dongas on the other side of the machinery shed where the rest of the staff is accommodated. And another donga sits next to hers. When she'd poked her nose in, there was no bed, just an old cupboard covered in dust and spider webs. It looked like it had never been used, although the light switch worked so she knew it was hooked to the generator. She let herself settle into station life for a few weeks before approaching Matt about the vacant donga. He looked surprised when she told him she would like to turn it into a darkroom. He agreed, saying he'd swap it for some of her masterpieces.

'Just a dabbler, Matt,' she said. The last thing she wanted was him snooping around. She hated to show her work until she was completely satisfied with it. Photography had become a passion since teachers college. She'd kept it up, making her apartment bathroom double as a darkroom but there never seemed enough time to indulge her passion. Out here, with fewer distractions, she was hoping to change that.

Now, there's time for a shower, and before dinner she wants to look at the map of the surrounding stations she found in Matt's office. In the flimsy cubicle at the end of the donga, the trickle of water is impossible to regulate. She has grown used to it, only occasionally cursing when she's not in the mood to be scalded. The plastic curtain dangling from a few remaining plastic rings always makes her smile. It is a far cry from the bathroom in her city apartment — moulded bench-top, generous tiled shower and the latest in stainless-steel fittings. But she doesn't miss any of the mod cons of the city.

There is only one thing still missing. It's out here, somewhere. But what hope of finding it? *Like finding a lost diamond in a wheat silo.* She tries to stay in the present. But the past zooms in on her. *Focus on now*, she repeats like a mantra.

At her desk in the donga, Doog's sarong clings to her damp body while she spreads out the map from the Lands and Surveys Department, which outlines the boundary of each station. She has written on it the names of some of the owners and the ages of any family they have. At dinner or other social gatherings, she keeps her ears open, trying to ask questions without drawing attention to her interest. This afternoon she looks for Pardee station and finds it's right next door. She has heard there's a young bloke living there who could be the right age. She pencils in a question mark and vows to find a way to check him out.

Folding up the map, she returns to her diary, jotting down sketches of the characters she has met in this far country. The station hands are entertaining with their tales, true and tall. The language is something she still hasn't got used to, nor the abuse that the station hands, black and white, male and female fling at each other. Yesterday Bruce yelled at Koop that he *Fuckin' couldn't knock the skin off a rice pudding.* It's not that it's new to her but sometimes it sounds like they want to kill each other. She cringes at, *stupid black bastards* or *useless white pricks,* and worse. Then, more often than not, they look up grinning and go on working side-by-side, sharing cigarettes and water bags, leaving her confused but relieved.

Doog catches herself staring at the wall. She can't concentrate on writing today. Jess's pinched little face keeps appearing in her mind. There must be something she can do. And the bloody reporter is here. The animosity she feels towards the reporter takes her by surprise. She wants this place to herself, a place where she can stay hidden for a while.

The Meeting

AT six-thirty Doog walks over to the homestead. Halfway across she stops and stands, eyes closed, her face absorbing the warmth of the sun. The orchestra of hidden birds before the deep hush at sunset always fills her with wonder. Three station dogs resigned to being chained up for the night look up with sad eyes as she passes. Their forty-four-gallon drum kennels, each with a worn hessian bag, is a far cry from the kennel of her friend Frankie's labradoodle with its upholstered thermal bed scattered with toys and cushions. A fourth dog, left free to take its turn on guard, bounces up to her to be patted. Doog turns away from the collection of long white emu and kangaroo bones strewn around each drum.

At the homestead, the purple of the wisteria blossom takes on a crimson tinge in the dying desert sunlight. Mary sets the table for the evening meal at one end of the wide deck. As Mrs C's apprentice, Mary has the sleep-out on the verandah of the kitchen house. Her duties start before dawn. It's plain to see Mrs C has a soft spot for the girl. She has told Doog she likes to keep an eye on Mary, although it's a fair bet that after working since daybreak, a cyclone wouldn't wake the cook once she has fallen asleep. Doog has seen the mooneyes and subtle signs that pass between Mary and Nev whenever he comes home.

At the end of the wet season most of Mary's community follows the route of their ancestors to the place of the wild geese and the crocodile. They always come back. This is their country. Not long after she had arrived, Doog tried to photograph the excitement of their exodus but what she ended up capturing was the emptiness of the silent space they left behind. Doog once asked Mary if she wanted to go with them. The girl told her she didn't want to miss out on her pay packet, said she was saving up. Doog wondered what she was saving for, but she didn't like to pry.

'What's for dinner, Mare?' Doog asks.

'Besides the computer geeks? There's a nice bloke from Fremantle.'

'Oh yeah?' Between the school excursion today and worrying about Jess, she had almost forgotten. 'What's a nice bloke from Freo doing up here?'

'Dunno, works for a newspaper, apparently.'

Doog moves to the side table and helps herself to a glass of red, wincing as she takes a sip. 'God, it's about time someone told Matt how dreadful this wine is.'

'Can't do that,' says Mary. She has a wicked grin, that woman. 'Maybe no one told you. His sister down south owns the vineyard.'

At the far end of the verandah Doog settles into one of the old armchairs. Today was a good day. Two of the men from the community took her and the kids to a place over in the breakaway country, where time has eroded and oxidised the ironstone into ochre. She still can't believe the colours. Red, even brighter than the pindan, and then yellow and green, and another colour that was almost magenta. That's why it's so great to have Brenda's help. She has already told the kids the story of Marlu, the ancestral kangaroo that was speared. How the different colours are the parts of his body, the red of his blood, the yellow bile and green gall — a creation story, Doog supposes. She can't wait to use that story in lessons. Great for art. No white ochre, though. That was a surprise. The mob use white on their bodies and faces whenever they have a gathering. But Brenda says it comes from another place, a secret place.

Doog's guessing one of the men who drove them out to the ochre couldn't have been more than eighteen. The other one was old and wrinkled with a wispy white beard. He was the one who showed the children how to grind the ochre using a smooth stone on a larger rock. Doog had taken empty tin cans provided by Mrs C. Her hands are still stained from brushing the different colours from the rocks into the cans and mixing them with water into a thick paint. It was fascinating to watch the men, using smaller rocks, bash the end of wattle sticks until the fibres were soft and pliable enough to use as a paintbrush. Her camera had clicked away as the children copied and made their own paintbrushes. They danced and pranced while painting each other's faces and bodies, and then printed their hands on the pieces of card that she had brought along. Even Jess showed some pleasure for a change. They all smiled their way home over the bumpy track, coated in the power of the ochre.

The long table gradually fills as the different staff members saunter up from their quarters, Doog stands as Matt calls her over to the top end of the table.

'Doog, this is Daniel Maroney, journalist up from Fremantle — wants to write about us. God knows why.'

Maroney reaches out a hand and smiles warmly. Doog tells him she hopes he enjoys Bedarra and tries not to be drawn by the disarming smile. She returns to the other end of the table and makes an effort to engage one of the visiting technicians in a conversation about computers.

Col and Koop are on kitchen duty tonight, carrying in large pots of stew with bowls of steamed vegetables and mashed potatoes.

'Smells all right, Mrs C,' says Koop. 'I could eat the crotch out of a low-flying duck tonight.'

Koop's expressions never fail to make Doog almost choke on her wine but only the journalist looks up in surprise as the pair set the meal down in the middle of the table. Everyone helps themselves and Doog concentrates on avoiding the journalist's eyes.

'Jesus, Bruce, d'you think you should taste it before you smother it with tomato sauce?' This comes out of her mouth before she can help herself. Her New Year's resolution, not to be opinionated, has failed. *You're turning into your mother, girl.* But Bruce, who reminds her of a bear with his great rounded shoulders and hairy arms, good-natured as ever, raises the sauce bottle to her with a grin.

'Cheers,' he says and reminds her of her brother. Charlie was the same — always good-natured, rarely challenging her. God knows, she'd baited him enough. What had she been trying to do? Make him mad? Make Charlie react in some way that her parents would notice? Show that she existed as much as he did?

At the other end of the table Maroney can't help noticing Doog. She appears to have given up on the technician and is now making an effort to engage Snow, the young blond bloke, in conversation. It looks like hard going. She prattles on about an ochre trip and then gives up. She never looks Maroney's way.

'Mr Maroney, what'd you say you came out here for?' Koop, the younger of the roustabouts, asks him.

'Call me Daniel, or just plain Maroney, if you prefer. That's what most people call me.'

'And?' says Koop.

'Well, I have to tell you it wasn't my idea but I must admit I'm warming to the assignment. My editor wants me to research life in this region, write a series of articles about how things are changing, especially on the smaller holdings.'

Doog concentrates on eating, but she finds herself interested in what this journalist hopes to uncover. Maroney turns to Matt and asks about stock numbers on the property and her ears tune into a conversation between Bruce and Koop. Koop has a friend who needs a dog and Bruce tells him that over at Pardee young Paul's red heeler has whelped.

'It's a good 'un, that dog of Paul's,' said Bruce.

Pardee. That's the station Doog found on the map and Paul must be the twenty-five-year-old.

After they've eaten the pudding, the men sit back patting full stomachs. She stacks some of the dishes and heads towards the kitchen still feeling Maroney's eyes on her. It's not her turn on kitchen duty, but if she leaves with dishes in hand no one will notice. *It's a woman's job, after all*, she thinks and again berates herself for being so grumpy. After dumping the dishes for Col and Koop to wash up, she escapes around the back to the tank stand. The air has cooled. *Halleluiah!* She lights a cigarette and gratefully inhales the peace.

'Not much for conversation, young Snow, is he?' A few minutes later the remark from the dark makes her jump and then let out a sigh.

'No.' She stubs the cigarette out on the wooden boards of the tank stand. 'And actually, Mr Maroney. I'm afraid I was just off to bed. Goodnight!'

She strides off towards her donga.

Maroney's left flabbergasted. He's always flattered himself that he could charm his way into any investigation without putting his quarry off-side

OK, mate, he thinks to himself. *You've either lost it, or she's a dragon. We'll give you the benefit of the doubt and call her a dragon for now.*

He leans against the tank stand and attempts to concentrate on the spectacular display of stars. He gave up smoking years ago and now he's sniffing the air, contemplating retrieving the almost whole cigarette that Doog just butted out. The lack of a lighter saves him from that lapse of dignity.

Sally Maroney

BACK in his room after the rebuff from Doog, Maroney diverts himself by spreading the station map out on the bed along with another. larger map of Western Australia that he brought from Perth. He has never had a talent for finding his way around a map and struggles to stop his eyes glazing over. Most of the placenames out this way are tongue twisters. The name of the boys home is indelibly printed on his mind. It was north of Geraldton, probably way south of here but still out in the middle of nowhere. Not quite desert, too much bush and not as red as this place. He hadn't thought about it for years but being up here has brought it back. The name doesn't appear on the map Was it a town or just a property? A property could have been taken over by native title and the name changed. It would have been so easy to have researched this back in Perth but, looking for the boys home was the last thing he expected to be doing and anyway, he can't see much point.

He remembered how, after they had landed in Fremantle they were herded into the bus and were driven for hours, falling asleep until they were jolted awake as the bus hit a rough dirt track with bushes swiping its sides, the scent of eucalyptus mixed with the smell of dust. At last, the bus slowed, and the boys all stared at the two-storey building made entirely of red-coloured rock rising in front of them. He remembers a large lemon tree laden with yellow fruit in front of the building. When they left the care-home in

England, they were told they would ride horses to school and eat fruit from the trees.

They never saw their cardboard suitcases again. Khaki shorts and singlets were handed out — no underwear, no shoes. He didn't wear shoes for the next nine years.

Maroney has not thought about his mother for years. They were taught to forget, told their parents were dead. They were orphans. Somehow, he knew his father was dead but he had no memory of how or when. There was some sort of accident, his mother sobbing, the neighbours hovering, whispered voices. He doesn't know that when his father had died, his mother, Sally Maroney, was at her wit's end by the time she sought help from the church. Almost a year had passed since the accident that killed her husband. He'd been down at the dock, west of Manchester, and his head had been smashed in by a huge iron hook swinging from the end of a crane. They said it was his fault. They said he was negligent but the bosses always seemed to get away with anything. Widows, such as her, received not a penny in compensation. Complaints were ignored. Hundreds of people scrambled for work with Manchester going through an economic downturn. Businesses were closing every day. Sally battled for a while, living on little else but porridge and turnips, but the rent went unpaid and the bailiff came knocking. She needed a job.

Being the barmaid in a pub was not what she would have chosen, not considered a respectable occupation for a woman but it was all she could find. In desperation she spoke to the priest. The shame of telling him about the mess she was in was almost too much for her. But he seemed kinder than usual and offered to help. He said he knew of a place through the church where her family would be cared for just until she could manage. The thought of being separated from her children was her worst nightmare. She had hoped there might be somewhere they could all be together until she got on her feet. But she tried to be grateful. She tried to make the children understand that she had to leave them for a while, that she would fetch them back as soon as she could. It broke her heart to walk away from that place with the baby howling. Kitty clung to her and her boy's eyes were wet while he nodded and tried to take Kitty's hand.

Dossing with a friend and working night and day for three months she visited the children once a week on a Sunday until she secured a small room and kitchen at the back of a shop. She had found a girl who would mind the baby while she kept working. The two eldest would be at school. Everything was in place for the return of her children. As she walked to the home to fetch them, she anticipated how happy they would be to be coming home with her. For the first time since the accident, fear loosened its grip.

But Patrick and Kitty had vanished. In vain, she tried to find them. There were rumours of children being taken to the colonies and she almost went out of her mind. Door after door she knocked on but always hit a stone wall. She never gave up the search for her children but she died just before the baby turned ten.

Rosie

THE following afternoon is Friday, the end of the Bedarra school week. Secretly chuffed at the way they want to hang around after the end of their lessons, Doog chases the children out of the schoolroom. Even Jess, who rarely speaks, reminds her that she said she would read another chapter of *Blinky Bill*.

'Sorry, we ran out of time today. Monday, Jess, I promise. If I look like forgetting, you remind me. By the way, I might need you to come with me tomorrow. Could have a special pick-up to do.'

Jess says nothing, but at least there's a look of curiosity in the dark eyes that lock onto Doog's.

'Tell you in the morning, kiddo. Secret girls' business — just you and me.' Doog puts a hopeful hand on Jess's thin shoulder and smiles but there's no response. She's had an idea but she needs to get an OK from Matt first. She'll catch him at dinner tonight.

When Jess leaves, she starts off in the direction of the kitchen for afternoon smoko but veers when she sees Matt stride into the machinery shed. *No time like the present,* she thinks. By the time she catches up he's peering under the bonnet of an old Chamberlain tractor with the young bloke, Snow. Doog watches while he walks over to the side of the shed and picks up a wrench from a clutter of tools on the bench. He throws it to Snow, along with a string of directions, and then turns back the way he came.

'Can I to talk to you for a moment, Matt.'

'Can't it wait till later, Doog?'

'I just wanted to get you alone to ask you something.'

Silently cursing him for being so difficult she stands her ground. She's learned that Matt likes to intimidate people with his dark good looks and his bark. She's also learned to ignore the display of blokieness that she knows he hides behind. With an exaggerated sigh, he plunges his hands into his pockets and slouches back towards her, his black eyebrows, as usual, guarding his eyes.

'OK, what is it that won't wait?'

'It's Jess, Matt.'

He looks blank.

'Jess? Your daughter?' Matt sweeps an arc on the dusty earth with his boot. Doog can see his jawbone working. 'Yeah, yeah, what about her?'

'She's hurting. She's still taking losing her mother real bad. I've been trying to think of a way to distract her, only thought of this last night.'

He says nothing.

'Look, sorry I'm springing this on you but I missed you before school this morning. I think it could work.'

'Go on,' His voice is hoarse.

'I want to take Jess over to Pardee Station tomorrow. Paul's red healer whelped a few weeks ago. I want to get the kids a pup.'

Matt's head shakes from side to side. 'You get some bright ideas, Doogie but this ain't one of them,' he says. 'We don't need anymore dogs, and certainly not from that young smartarse.'

'Matt, the station dogs are working dogs. All I'm saying is it would do those kids good to have a pet.'

Hands still dug deeply into the pockets of his jeans, Matt turns his back and stares out across the paddock. She waits.

'OK, do what you have to, but it stays out of the homestead, right?' He starts to walk away.

'No!' She calls after him. 'No, Matt, like I said, it'll be a pet. It won't be like the other dogs. Needs to be part of the family.'

'Jesus, Doogie.' He turns with a twisted smile. He shakes his head again, and she knows she's won.

The next morning, she gently nudges Jess awake. 'Come on, kiddo.'

'What?' Jess rubs her eyes.

'Like I told you yesterday — secret business. A surprise for everyone. Shush, don't wake the others.' Doog wonders if she should feel guilty for finding a pretext for checking out Paul from Pardee. No, she's confident that the idea of getting the kids a pet is a good one.

When she has bundled Jess into the car, she puts a bowl of cereal on her lap.

'There's fruit and muesli bars in the back if you want something else.'

Jess asks where they're going. When Doog tells her, she fixes Doog with a look of disdain before turning her gaze to the side window. They travel the track between the stations in silence apart from the low chug of the diesel engine. Acacia bushes lace the air with a faint scent that sweeps across Doog's face through the open window. The tranquility of the early morning, with the sun slung low in the sky behind, fills her with a serenity she never knew in the city. Mobs of kangaroos and emus slow their journey. She waits for them to move off the track wishing Jess would, just once, turn and share her delight at seeing these creatures. Her camera sits on the back seat but she resists taking anymore shots of the animals. Three times they stop while Jess schleps out to open and close gates.

Doog has phoned Paul, to make sure the pup is available. He'd seemed happy enough for her to come over and check out the litter. Matt doesn't seem too struck on him. Smartarse, he called him and Doog wonders why. However, when they pull up to the Pardee homestead, Paul's nowhere in sight.

'Come on Jess, he's probably out working in the paddocks. We'll go find Connor. He's bound to be in the shed or the stables.'

Doog sees Jess's eyes brighten. She likes old Connor, the Irishman who turned up at the station about twenty years ago, with his beat-up Holden and his caravan. He visits Bedarra about once a month to have a drink with the boys. He's a favourite of the children, with his magic tricks and his stories. He's the reason she brought her camera. She'd like to capture some of his story in a portrait of his careworn face.

The shed is a corrugated-iron structure, with extra bits constructed from any available material tacked on over the years. It holds a jumble of machinery, tools, tyres, cans of paint and chemicals. There are old fridges, drums of stock food and supplements. In the midst of all this sit two motorbikes and a T-Model Ford. At one end is a stack of hay bales and Connor's van. They find him around the back of the shed, grooming one of the horses.

'Well, I'm blessed,' he cries, a smile splitting his face. 'Here's me feeling a bit lonely, thinking I could do with some company and two lovely ladies turn up. If that's not the luck of the Irish, I ask you.'

'How are you, Connor?'

'Never better, never better.' Connor still has a head of thick hair, a large lock of which always falls over his forehead. Behind round, steel-rimmed glasses, his eyes are brown pools. 'Here now, let me be putting this lady in her boudoir.' The smell of fresh hay sweetens the air as he leads the horse into the stables then reemerges with a wide grin. 'Come to my van and we'll have a nice cup of tea.'

'Did Paul mention we were coming?' she asks.

Connor turns and winks and pats the side of his nose with his forefinger. At the caravan he stops.

'Here, young Jess, I have something to show you.'

They follow him around the van where a temporary enclosure has been set up among the hay bales. A tired-looking red heeler lies on her side exposing a row of flabby teats, while all around pups pounce and tug and torment her.

Jess's face lights up. 'Oh look! They're so cute.'

Connor pushes the wire aside so they can enter the enclosure.

'Aye, they're cute all right, but they're getting too big to stay with Ruby. She's worn out, poor old girl. Three are spoken for and Paul's keeping one but that still leaves two. Don't know what's going to happen to them, do we Ruby?'

Jess is already holding the smallest of the pups, a female, stroking it, and kissing the top of its head. Doog sees delight transform the cross little face. Her eyes meet Connor's and she nods happily.

'What do you reckon, Jess? Do you think we could give a puppy a home?'

Jess looks up at Connor and then at Doog. 'What will Dad say?' she whispers.

'I've already asked. He doesn't mind,' Doog says. 'Which one's it to be?'

Jess's arms fold possessively around the pup.

'I think that's decided then.' Doog laughs and gives her thin shoulders a squeeze. 'Now what were you saying about tea, Connor?'

Connor likes to talk. Doog watches as he sets out morning tea, including fruitcake. Tucked into the bench-seat on the opposite side of the table she listens carefully as he chatters away.

'Where's Paul now?' Doog asks when she can get a word in.

'He's gone over east.'

Doog tries to hide her disappointment. She had been hoping to check out the young station owner today. Paul has no brothers or sisters and her heart gives a leap when Connor confirms he's twenty-five.

'Why has he gone over east?' Asks Doog.

'Gone to the horse sales in Tamworth. Hoping to pick up a quarter horse.'

'What! For the campdraft? Matt's not going to like that.' At the dinner table Doog has repeatedly heard references to the debate about introducing the American quarter horse to campdrafts.

'Ah well, there's some that want to hang on to the Australian tradition of using stock horses, but there's those that says we need new blood brought in.'

'And what do you say, Connor?'

'A bit of new blood doesn't hurt. Keeps the breeding strong.' She'd heard the old man has doted on Paul since he was a boy.

Jess sits cross-legged on the floor, the sleeping puppy coiled in her lap, a look of bliss on both their faces. The gentle light from the open side of the shed reaches through the window of the caravan and illuminates the small scene. Connor is still chatting and Doog lifts the camera, managing to shoot half a roll of film before Jess looks up and scowls.

'Well, give my regards to Paul and tell him the children will thank him for the pup at the campdraft. What do you think we should feed the puppy, Connor?'

'Ah, yes.' He looks at Jess and tells them the pup is only part weaned so she needs to learn to drink milk from a saucer. Connor puts down a dish of milk and shows Jess how to dip her fingers in and then let the puppy lick them. The delight that transforms Jess's face brings Doog close to tears. Connor tells them he's written down the mince recipe that he's been introducing to the litter. They should have calcium and a few vitamin drops, he says and takes them over to the house to collect the things they will need.'

The Pardee homestead is not quite the same design as Bedarra. They walk down the wide breezeway to the kitchen. As they pass the front room, she can't help noticing that, unlike Bedarra, it's lined with shelves of books.

'Paul's family were readers I see,' she says to Connor as he spoons white powder into a jar.

'Well,' says Connor from under his lock of hair. 'That boy's nose has never been out of a book since he was old enough to stand up upright. I don't think his parents were great readers, but him, he devours one book after another and his folks always kept him well supplied.'

Doog herds Jess and the puppy into the vehicle and once again they are rattling over the bumpy track between the two stations. Delight shines from Jess's eyes while she speaks softly to the tiny red pup.

'What are you going to call her?' Doog asks.

'It has to be something to do with red, maybe Ruby — no that's her mother's name. Something like roses. Rosebud or … Rosie. What about Rosie?' Jess smiles triumphantly.'

'Perfect!'

'I wish I could show you to Mum,' Jess whispers into a furry ear, making Doog's heart ache.

The Watcher

MARONEY is aware that he has become the watcher. He watches the station hands in their uniforms of jeans, checked shirts, elastic-sided boots and Akubra hats. He watches how they fling themselves off and on horses, how they herd cattle in and out of pens, through chutes and on to trucks brandishing their hats and yelling obscenities. He watches Matt barking orders and walking off, head down, avoiding eye contact. He enjoys watching how Mrs C growls and grumbles at everyone but how she makes sure nobody forgets anything, especially lunch. And Doog, he's no closer to her than when he first arrived. He watches her crossing the yard from her donga to the homestead in her sun frock and her Blundstone boots. A battered straw hat usually hides her face. She's always busy with the kids or sealed in her donga. At dinner she manages to sit as far from him as possible. Her mane of red hair falls to her shoulders in the cool of the evening and her freckled face always has a freshly scrubbed look. She avoids talking to him but her green eyes sometimes wander his way. He can feel her watching him watching her.

Tonight Maroney has maneuvered himself into a place beside Doog at the dinner table. They hardly have time to say hello before Matt announces that Mrs Le Carre's personal assistant is coming to visit the station.

'Willie Albers will be reviewing the lucerne trials,' he says. 'And he wants to put the station records on the computer now that our system has been updated. Can't say I'm looking forward to that, but just try to be half-civilised while he's around. Like, watch your fuckin' language for a start.'

Everyone laughs. A joke from Matt is a rare thing.

Afterwards Maroney steels himself and follows Doog out to the tank stand. He makes his footsteps heavy enough so as not to startle her again. She looks up unsmiling. They both start to talk at once. Him, sounding lame, saying he wanted to catch her away from the others, her apologising for her rudeness last night. They both apologise, talking over the top of each other.

Maroney hesitates. He doesn't want to scare her off again. Doog is obviously also struggling.

'Look, I drank too much last night. I know that doesn't excuse me.'

'No, I rather barged in on you. Sorry about that but I hear you come from Fremantle and I'm curious about what brought you up here.'

'Look, I don't want to be rude, Mr Maroney, but neither do I need a stranger poking his nose into my business, and this is sort of my special place. I come out here to be alone.'

'Fair enough.' Maroney holds his hand up in a gesture of surrender. 'I promise I have no intention of prying into your private life. It's just that I never heard the word *guvvy* before I came here and I think your role as a teacher in this unique situation would be of interest to our readers.'

He watches her struggle to light a cigarette. The leafy molasses aroma drifts to his nostrils. Craving sears his nerve endings and he thrusts his hands deep into his pockets. Doog's arms wrap stiffly across her chest while she drags on her cigarette, rocking slightly, staring at the ground. He's feeling a bit out of his depth. The people he's used to writing about mostly clamour to be interviewed. 'Anyway, no pressure,' he says. 'I'm sure I can find lots to be going on with but I would like to get to know you a bit better, story or no story.'

She turns to him, no smile, just pins him down with a suspicious look in her eyes, her sharp chin raised in challenge as she lights another cigarette.

He finds it hard to concentrate. The smell of the tobacco gnaws at him. 'You like a smoke?' He said feebly.

'And what of it?' She snaps.

He holds up his hands. 'Yes, absolutely none of my business. It's just that my antenna sticks up if there's the slightest opportunity for an OP.'

'OP?'

'Other people's,' he explains. 'I'm an ex-smoker, but I can't resist bumming one now and again, especially after a good meal and a glass of red wine, a rather demeaning and embarrassing habit, I grant you.'

'Help yourself.' She pushes the packet of tobacco towards him. 'Papers and lighter are inside. I only smoke of an evening, and not usually this much.'

He draws the foul taste into his mouth, picks a stray piece of tobacco off his tongue and wonders again why he bothers.

'Doog,' he said. 'I've been doing this job for a long time, and something's not adding up. There's more to this than publicity shyness. Am I right?' As soon as the words are out, he curses himself. *Talk about the bloody bull in the china shop, Maroney. Pull your head in.*

She turns away, the moon catching the edges of her hair, a halo of light tracing the curve of her shoulders. There is a challenging strength about this woman but Maroney senses that if she feels cornered, she will run. He had to back off for now. He gazes at the stars and finishes the cigarette.

'Look, forget I said that. I'm not up here for long. I'll be out of your space soon but until then, it would be nice if we could be friends.'

She doesn't reply, but he catches the hint of a smile. There's something about her he can't put his finger on.

'All right, I'd better hit the sack if I want to survive this boot camp. Breakfast at six — right?'

They walk back through the casuarinas without speaking. She sees him to the shearers' quarters; her donga is just beyond. He hesitates on the verandah steps.

'Doog, Doogie, that's a strange name. Where did it come from?'

'You can tell you're a reporter,' she says. 'Nosy as hell … might get you into trouble out here. Nothing exotic. Just my young brother not being able to say Judy. It stuck.'

He tells her he likes it, and again, she flashes a half-smile, before she turns under the Moreton Bay figs towards her donga.

Too Big a Step

HE tells himself it's just his imagination. He has been at Bedarra for just four days but Maroney can feel this country softening him, opening something in him. His old surety has gone, but so has the sense of distrust he always keeps hidden, the sense that he needs to stay wary. Even after a night on the unyielding bed in the shearers' quarters, there's a peace that he hasn't known before. He feels like his fear is being eroded along with the rocks in this ancient land. He's not missing his old routine. How much does this feeling have to do with the balmy weather and the laid-back atmosphere of the place? He has to admit he has been a bit jaded by the job lately. Now, he's enjoying not having to front up to the office every day. Who wouldn't? But he suspects it's more. In the past when he listened to people rave about *being at one with nature* it had made his eyes roll, but now … this land, this space seems to be invading his very soul. How long can it last?

'There's something about this place,' he tells Maria on the phone. 'You're not going to believe this. I'm sleeping like a medieval monk in a bare room with a wooden bed and a prehistoric mattress. There isn't even glass in the windows. Mind you I'm going to have to rig up some curtains soon. The cockroaches are like Black Hawks. Doog said she'd help me. She's already found me a net canopy for over my bed.'

'Doog?' He can feel Maria's matchmaking antennae sprout from her head.

'Don't you worry about her, *Ficcanaso*. Worry about me.'

'How can I worry about you, Maroney? You're too much of a paradox. I've never seen you comfortable at a picnic, let alone out in the never-never.'

'Maybe I've had an epiphany,' he says, not sure he's joking. During the day, he's losing the confidence and reporter brashness that have taken him years to acquire and perfect. *Your crutches are no good out here, boyo.* The repartee that has become second nature to him and his city colleagues is met with perplexity by the station hands. Silence is accepted. Words are sporadic, and if no one speaks no one rushes to fill the gap.

Maroney's mind wanders back to the governess. He'll make an all-out effort to corner her whenever he gets a chance, get to know her. Story or no story she's too much of an enigma to resist. She's up before the birds, running down the track with that ruddy great camera slung around her neck. Even when she's not teaching, she's always flat-out helping Matt or Mrs C. The only time he sees her take a break is when she sits cross-legged on the ground talking to the woman called Brenda from the community. They laugh and draw pictures in the dirt and Brenda often has a wooden bowl with leaves and flowers and seeds. The two women pore over them and he hears Doog exclaim in delight.

This morning he had woken early. The poignant crowing of roosters stirred unwelcome memories of waking in the dormitory but he had breathed them away. He had listened instead to the carolling of magpies in the dreamy half-light of the dawn, content in bed until the sky shone blue into the room through the interlaced branches of the trees. Then he'd willed his body out of bed, instinctively seeking refuge in the kitchen, hoping that some of the surrogacy that Mrs C lavishes on the young station hands might extend to him. He wasn't disappointed.

'How's it going, luvvy?' Sweaty locks of hair plastered her forehead as she thrust a tray of baked beans into the warming oven at the bottom of the enormous slow-combustion stove.

'Cuppa?' She holds up the enamel teapot with both hands. It' is big enough to provide tea, along with the loaves and fishes, to the multitudes. 'I'm just about to make a brew — even if it's just for you and me.'

He gives her the thumbs-up. A cup of tea and the smell of bacon in the warm kitchen are almost enough for him. He doesn't need to eat but Mrs C takes that as a personal insult. He hopes to have a spoonful of baked beans on a slice of toast without drawing attention to his appetite, which is puny compared to the station hands.

'Wot'cha got on today, love?'

'Last night I heard Matt talking about bringing in some stock. I thought it would be good to tag along.'

The station hands file in on cue at six and collapse into chairs around the long table on one side of the large kitchen. They help themselves to bacon, eggs, baked beans, potato cakes and toast. He studies each one. There are bound to be some stories here.

Cholesterol's obviously not an issue out this way. He tries not to stare as they take three or four eggs and pile a mound of bacon onto their plates. Mugs of tea are poured from the oversized teapot, the broody, morning silence of the men only broken by the scraping of utensils and the slurping of tea. The skinny blond kid who he saw Doog trying to talk to doesn't eat much. Doesn't speak, either. Just consumes the scene and shifts those dark eyes to whoever else is speaking. As the teapot is topped up and passed around for the third time, Col asks Bruce about what's on that day. Bruce reaches for a toothpick from a Vegemite jar on the table and sits, hunched, head jutting forward, staring at no one in particular. His drooping brow and loose jowls remind Maroney of a bulldog.

Eventually, he breathes heavily through his nose and taps a toothpick on the table in Col's direction.

'You need to get over to the other side of the creek and look for those damned heifers,' he says. His voice sounds like pea-gravel forced through a drainpipe. 'And when you've found them, check that bloody fence. If they get in with the bulls, Matt'll have our knackers on a plate.' He starts to rise and hitches up his jeans. 'We need to tidy up all the jobs this week, 'cause next week we're flat out getting ready for the campdraft so I need the rest of you with me. We'll meet Darce and Manny at the home bore and bring the yearlings into the yards, and then we'll divvy up the jobs. Mary, you can help Koop with the ear-tags, inoculations and tick treatment. Snow, you'll be with me on branding. That's if you haven't fallen off your horse by then.'

Snow's eyes flicker and Maroney wonders if that's fear he sees. But the youth just nods and starts to rise. The mention of horses has put Maroney right off the idea of tagging along. The last time he was on a horse was at the home when he was twelve. He'd had no choice. He and another boy had been ordered to look for two missing milkers. He had almost shat himself. It was the other boy who saved the day. Left him holding the reins of his horse in the middle of the bush and went off to look for the cows. He found them all right and came back for Maroney. He remembers wondering what would be worse: the hiding they'd get if they didn't return with the cows or being left out in the bush all night. He was a good sort, that kid. Francis, they called him. He wonders where he is now. He straightens up and looks around hoping the blokes haven't noticed that his chest has caved into the past. The back of a horse is too big a step. Too big altogether.

'How long do you reckon it'll take to bring them into the yards?' he asks Bruce.

Maroney is planning to be there for the rest of the action but he knows the station is almost 2000 square kilometres. He'd expected the cattle to be rounded up by off-road vehicles, or even the helicopter that he's seen in the hangar at the end of the airstrip.

The head stockman picks at his teeth. 'Let me see now ... I reckon the whole mob should be just about up at the yards now, waiting for us,' he says with a hint of a grin.

How could that be? Maroney had expected it would take most of the day to round the cattle up from far and scattered locations. Bruce explains how, over the past week they had gradually shut down the windmills on the bores until all the animals have been forced to come in for water. Mrs Le Carre insists on horses when they're working with the stock. 'The cattle stay quieter and she doesn't want vehicles chopping up the landscape. And', says Bruce, 'I have no argument with that.'

When the boss had told Maroney he could collect stories from up this way, he'd been sceptical. Couldn't imagine finding anything interesting enough to write about but he's changing his mind. It's a different world and he's already planning a column called: 'Yarns from the Bush'. *Eat your heart out, Ragazza.*

Bruce's voice cuts in and he tells Maroney they will then cull out the yearlings and turn the rest around. The head stockman scowls as Mrs C chips in. She needs Mary back by 4 o'clock. And not to forget Mary goes to Sandy Bay with Doog for supplies tomorrow. Mrs C lays down the law, along with more food and nobody argues. She turns to Maroney.

'You'll need to pack a lunch. Don't think you can arrive at the kitchen any old time.'

Maroney flashes Mrs C what he hopes is his most disarming smile but she's no pushover and doesn't respond. He follows the lead of the others and picks up a small foam Esky. On the bench lie stacks of sandwiches made with enough leftover beef roast and mustard pickle to feed a city family for a month. Great slabs of fruitcake, more than he's ever seen at an office Christmas party, sit in open tins, along with Anzac biscuits. There's fruit laid out for the men to help themselves. And they do. Water bags are filled, and there's tea or coffee for the Thermoses. Maroney quickly wraps a sandwich and pokes an apple into his Esky. He fills a flask with coffee.

'So why don't I ever see Darcy and Manny at breakfast?' Maroney asks.

There's a silence. He feels the rest look at him as if he's as thick as mince, and then Mrs C says, 'They're free to join us but they like to eat with their own people.'

And he remembers being told that the two stockmen are from Nev's community down by the river. When everyone works together with the cattle and the horses there's not much difference to be seen but now, he wonders about the life of the others, how it all fits together. How some of the Aboriginal people seem to tread in both worlds. He makes a note to self to try and interview Darcy and Manny.

The final morning ritual is sitting on the back verandah pulling on boots. Bruce and Koop both have spurs and everyone has a large, black felt hat that Maroney soon sees is used for everything from brandishing at wayward cows to scooping water from a waterhole to pour over sweaty heads. As the others move off towards the stables, he notices Doog, and again smiles at the discord between her feminine sundress and those great work boots she wears. Matt's kids walk towards the kitchen with her, the little one chattering all the way.

Second sitting, he thinks and heads off to the lavatory.

There are two lavatories, wooden boxes, not much bigger than telephone booths. *Dunnies.* He remembers how strange he thought that word was when he first arrived at the boys home. Thankfully they're parked in the shade of the casuarinas. No matter how hot it gets he has no intention of sitting with the door wide open like some of the men. Blocks of camphor in various stages of disintegration hang from bent wire attached by nails to the wooden walls. The smell of camphor is not strong enough to mask the odour coming from the pit. After examining the seat for spiders and snakes he nervously shuts the door. He sits and wills himself to relax. *OK Boyo, it's dark. You're thirty-five. Say after me: You are not scared shitless.*

He holds his head in his hands. That quip would be funny if his gut wasn't beginning to lurch, if he wasn't having to hold back claustrophobic panic from the past.

Snake

DOOG watches Maroney as he heads to the lavatory. He's has been on the station for more than a week. More than once he has turned up at the tank stand after the evening meal. Always manages to cadge a cigarette. She has to admit she's enjoying the company of someone on her wavelength, who's familiar with her home town. He's a good conversationalist, she'll give him that. She's curious about a comment he made the other night about not having a family but it wouldn't be wise to ask about his personal life if she's to steer him away from her own story. When he starts with the questions, it's easy enough to maneuver him back to talking about art, books and movies.

Maroney turns, before entering the dunny, salutes with a beamish smile and does a funny little bow to her and the girls. She grants him a nod, then herds Jess and Cassie into breakfast. She's keeping her eye on him. For the first time in a long time, she feels herself letting down her defenses. He's quite attractive. A bit of a clown but is that a touch of sadness she senses? A bit dorky, you could say. No, not really. The trouble is he won't fit into a box where she likes to put things and people, to be filed neatly. But no matter how nice he is, what sort of an idiot would she be to trust a journalist?

'I told you before, that mutt's not coming into my kitchen.' The blunt voice of Mrs C bags her attention.

'But …' Jess protests.

'No buts. It's not coming in. Good try, princess.'

'Rosie will be all right on the verandah,' Doog assures Jess, ignoring the rebellious scowl. The image of Matt. Doog rolls her eyes towards Mrs C and gives a small shake of her head. They both know that challenging the cook would be pointless.

'Don't you mind mean old Mrs C, Rosie,' says Jess to the pup.' Then she follows the others into breakfast, martyrdom written all over her sharp little features. She plonks herself down with an exaggerated sigh and Doog turns away to hide her amusement. The display of pique is a relief after the almost impenetrable wall surrounding Jess since Doog's arrival at the station.

Rosie has won everyone's hearts, even Matt's. The dog is intelligent and tolerant. Tolerates the children cuddling her, dressing her up and wheeling her around in a pram. She has become the centre of their world. Almost the centre of her teaching program. They research nutrition for puppies from the leaflets she's picked up from the Sandy Bay vet and write recipes for her food. The cook's even reluctantly given them time in the kitchen, but never with the puppy in tow. The children prepare the meat with vegetables and rice, weighing, measuring and calculating. While Doog mentally ticks the curriculum, Matt shakes his head.

'That mongrel gets treated better than most people around here,' he says as they meet outside the kitchen.

'Rosie's not a mongrel, Dad.' Jess glares at him and holds the pup close. 'And she doesn't like it when you growl.'

'Oh, excuse me, Miss Rosie.' Matt holds his hat to his chest and bows. 'I didn't mean to offend you. It's just that you are *sooo* ugly.' He meets Jess's eyes and grins.

'We know you don't mean that, Dad.'

'She's definitely better, Matt.' Doog says as they watch Jess walk away with her nose in the air. Maroney joins them.

'Wondering if you might spare some time to show me around the station?' Maroney says.

Matt glowers. 'I'm sure Doog has more than enough to do.'

'I didn't mean right now,' stammers Maroney, while Doog stares at Matt.

'Yeah well, there's routines in a place like this,' Matt snaps. 'Just don't go getting in the way.' He jams his hat on his head and strides to his horse, which is tied to the fence.

Maroney stares, his mouth open while Matt gallops away.

'Look, he's just a bit worried about Jess. But he's … he's right. There isn't much spare time around here.' She sees amusement in Maroney's blue eyes while he squints through his fair eyelashes in the harsh light. 'Sorry, I have to get back to the kids.'

'Come on,' he tries. 'Surely you can spare a couple of hours one afternoon to guide me to the waterhole the kids talk about.' There's an artlessness about his face that thaws her mistrust. She tries to ignore it.

'I was also rather hoping you'd introduce me to the people in the Aboriginal community. I've been trying to work out which language group they belong to but I haven't managed it yet. And so far none of you lot have been any help. It would be good to hear their stories and I've got a feeling it would make a difference if you were with me. I mean, I'm a complete stranger.'

Maroney seems to think she has, in some way, been admitted into the Aboriginal culture. But she hasn't, she's barely accepted. If it wasn't for the kids … She'll talk to him at dinner, she says. Right now, she needs to have a word with Mrs C before school starts, and heads back to the kitchen before he can argue.

'Almost forgot, Mrs C,' she says as she pokes her head around the kitchen door, 'did you manage to save me some sunshine milk tins?'

'You'll find six in a cardboard box just inside the storeroom. If you want anymore, let me know and I'll keep them for you.'

'No, six is perfect. Thanks, Gwen.'

Back outside, she's about to call the children to the schoolroom when a scream comes from behind the pile of mallee roots. Jess is running towards her, arms flailing, her face a mask of terror.

'Snake! Cassie's been bitten by a snake.'

Snake! Bitten! The words collide in Doog's brain.

'Get Matt … Dad … get your Dad,' Doog yells to Jess, and sprints towards the mallee roots.

Cassie lies on the ground her face contorted with fear. Rosie barks at the pile of roots. Doog scoops up Rosie and thrusts her towards Maroney, who's joined the small group of stricken children.

'Good girl,' she forces her voice to calm. 'You remembered to lie down. You'll be all right. Now please don't move, Cassie. Tell me where the snake got you.'

'My hand, Doog. It was trying to bite Rosie and I wouldn't let it, and then Rosie was trying to bite its tail and it ran away.'

'A King Brown?'

The girl nods.

'Don't even move your head, Cassie. I want you to breathe in deep like I taught you. Good girl, now let it out. Breathe in— breathe out — slowly, Cassie.' She hears Jess running back and turns around.

'Where's Matt?' She tries to push down the alarm she's feeling.

'No one's here, 'cept Snow. Think Dad's gone to check the four-mile windmill. Snow's gone after him.' Jess's voice trembles.

Doog closes her eyes for a moment and then looks up at the girl.

'Jess, you're in charge now, big girl. I need you to go to the homestead and ring the flying doctor. Tell them we think it's a king brown, and tell them how old Cassie is. Maroney needs to do something for me, and then he'll follow you. I want you both to bring back some water and the big umbrella from the breezeway.'

Jess runs off towards the homestead and Doog turns to Maroney. 'I need a piece of flat wood … shed.' She points with her chin while she opens the small pouch she always carries strapped around her waist.

'Cassie, I'm going to put the pressure bandages on now and then we're going to lie here together until the doctor comes.'

'It hurts, Doog.'

'I know, Possum, remember I told you it might, but you'll be all right. I just need you to keep real still.'

Maroney comes back with a couple of pieces of wood. His eyes meet hers and she gives him a grateful nod before he follows Jess to the homestead. Doog winds the bandages firmly from the bite all the way up to Cassie's armpit. With the scarf from her hat, she immobilizes the arm using a flat piece of pine. If Rosie disturbed the snake it might not have had time to inject venom.

By the time Maroney and Jess return with the umbrella, Doog lies on the ground telling Cassie a story. The children stand around open-mouthed and tearful and she asks Maroney to take them to the kitchen.

'Ask Mrs C to keep them busy until the doc comes,' she says.

Cassie's probably not listening but Doog continues with the story. The child is suddenly so small and frail … and young, but seems comforted by the sound of Doog's voice. Doog slowly lets the pressure off the bandage. Cassie is calm, too calm. She looks at her watch again. Time drags. Cassie's breathing seems normal, but how would she know? Her pulse is fine and she doesn't seem to have a temperature. There is redness and swelling around the bite but no rash forming. Hopefully it's a dry bite. Doog can't remember whether to let the patient have liquids. She looks at her watch again. Where the hell is Matt? He has no idea what's happening. He'll be beside himself if … she can't think like that. Despite his bristling and blustering, the girls are everything to

Matt. For his sake, for everyone, she needs to just concentrate on keeping Cassie calm and doing what she has learned to do.

At last, the roar of the King Air's turbo-prop engine passes over them. Maroney doesn't need to be told. He's on his way to the airstrip. A little crowd has gathered in a silent circle. Some of the people from the community have drifted up and Mrs C and the children stand with wide eyes and clenched jaws. Doog's camera is lying in the dust, not even a lens cover on it. She asks Maroney to take it back to her donga.

In what seems like an age later, someone points down the track to a cloud of dust and Maroney and the doctor race up in the Land Rover, with Matt and Snow following on horseback. Matt flings himself from the still-galloping horse. His face grey, he drops down beside Cass, his hands reaching, fingers upright, rigid knowing he can't touch her. The doctor takes his shoulders and moves him aside gently, his voice reassuring.

'She'll be all right,' he says softly.

Doog looks at the doctor. *Will she?*

He places a hand on Doog's arm. 'Well done,' he says. 'Did you loosen them every twenty minutes?' All Doog can do is nod as the doctor takes over and starts to remove the splint and bandages.

'The arm's a good colour,' he murmurs. 'Cassie, I'm just going to scrape your hand a little, to get a sample of the venom, so we can make sure what sort of snake it was.'

'A King Brown,' mumbles Cassie.

'OK, don't talk anymore,' says the doctor and turns to Doog. 'Has she been immobilised since the snakebite?'

'Yes,' Doog whispers, and as Cassie is lifted onto the stretcher, she suddenly feels teary. Handing over responsibility makes the weight of the past hours go to her legs. She feels Maroney's hand steady her as she tries to stand.

The doctor looks at Matt. 'You coming in the plane? I'm taking her to Lonsdale. It's better equipped for this situation.'

'Yeah,' he says, looking first to Bruce who is standing with the others. They'd all heard the unscheduled plane and guessed it meant trouble. Bruce nods, understanding he's in charge while Matt's away.

'Took the liberty of packin' a few things for you, boss.'

Matt yells to Doog from the Land Rover window. 'I'll ring you. Need you to do some stuff for the campdraft while I'm away,' he says and then slaps his forehead. 'Oh lord, Albers is due to arrive. I need you all to look after him. Doog, I'll ring you about that too.'

Doog nods, staring through him. The name Lonsdale is swimming around in her mind.

No Use Crying Now

THAT name — Lonsdale — she'd forgotten but it's where they were headed when the pains came, she's sure of it. The farmer's wife drove, with her stony face, not speaking, except to mutter: *You got yourself into this mess, girlie. No use crying now.* She's wiping the window of an old Dodge truck with a snotty hanky. Her mind squints through the miasma while she feels every bump in the corrugated track. The country all looks the same, the red dirt, the spinifex, small, tortured trees.

Doog pulls her mind into the present and goes to herd the children back to the schoolroom. Concentration will be out the window today. Drawing a picture and then writing a story about it will hopefully help them process the drama they just witnessed.

That evening Matt rings and there is relief and joy at the news Cassie is doing well. Matt asks Doog to find a file he has been compiling for the campdraft. It contains the names of the entries for the different events.

'I need you to go through last year's file, Doog. Tick off the ones who have entered this year and make a list of those who haven't. Can you get on the phone and ring them? Ask if they intend to enter. Some of the lazy bastards take no notice of the deadline and then whinge like hell when they find it's too late.'

'And what did you want to tell me about Mr Albers?'

'Just make him comfortable. Put him in the front room and show him the office and computer. Oh, and let him have the Land

Rover. I dunno, Doog. Just play hostess while I'm away. Sorry to lump this on you.'

Doog assures him it's no trouble.

'Just look after Cass, Matt. I hope you're both back soon.' Now that she's confident that Cassie will be OK, Doog can't wait to get into the office and look at the names and ages of the entries for the camp draft.

When they meet behind the tank stand after dinner in what has now become a nightly ritual, Maroney tells Doog he's planning to take off for a few days before the campdraft.

'I want to head north and visit a few of the smaller stations, maybe drive as far as Lonsdale and come back by the coast,' he tells her.

'I was planning to take a drive to Lonsdale soon.' It came out of Doog's mouth without her thinking. 'I've heard the coast up there is beautiful,' she adds.

'I don't suppose you could get away and come with me,' said Maroney.

'No way,' she said. With Matt's away and the campdraft coming. Too much on. I have school, remember.'

Maroney drives along a neglected track. After studying the map, he had found Newton station, the location of the boys home but it's too far south. He has no good reason or the desire to return to that place. His heart isn't in it. He's almost ready to admit that he needs to revisit his past but instinctively he knows that's not the way. However, he does need to satisfy the boss that he has investigated the small holdings around here. After that he will have no more excuses to remain in this country. It will be time to go home. He doesn't want to go home.

This is the fourth station since he left Bedarra. It has been a bruising encounter on his city-reporter psyche. There's not much evidence of the romantic outback on these smaller stations. He's wondering about his state of mind. He realizes he's missing Doog, so much it almost feels like grief. And this is the place for grief. Dejected cattle and flyblown sheep populate the desolate landscape. What do they find to eat? He wonders if some of the boys ended up working on places like this. It's further north but the land reminds him of the boys home. They were told they were being trained as farmhands, but the training wasn't up to much. They were just slave labour.

Kites circle over bones — white scars on bright earth.

The homesteads he has seen have been little more than hovels, with a collection of ramshackle sheds alongside. He used to hide in sheds like that. Miserable-looking dogs are tied to trees, the usual collection of kangaroo and emu legs scattered around. More bones.

On the first two stations, he'd been made welcome enough by careworn couples with frayed-looking kids of various ages. He was fed great plates of roast lamb and potatoes with frozen vegies. His contribution of cartons of beer was received with appreciation. A haggard man with leathery skin and enormous gnarled hands greeted him at the third station. As they sat at the wooden table eating mutton chops and drinking beer that night, Maroney learned that the man's wife had taken the kids and gone down to Perth to live with her mother. Bitterness flavoured the room lit only by a fifty-watt bulb. The scene reminded Maroney of an old sepia photo from the Depression. He wishes Doog could have been with him to take her black-and-white shots of these folk. She would have captured the mixture of strength and tragedy in their rugged faces.

He knows that he misses her and wants to share all this with her. He's tried to tell himself it was all a mistake, that he hasn't known Doog long enough, that he doesn't need to get involved with someone, but it doesn't feel like a mistake. Because everything feels right with her, everything is right, and he knows he's starting to want this woman so badly it hurts. But he can't pile his mess on to her right now. He needs to clean this up on his own.

He crosses a dry creek bed. Ahead, he sees the rundown homestead, and turns the Land Cruiser towards the house paddock. On either side of the track more bones bleach in the sun. They conjure up Father Timothy ranting Ezekiel from the pulpit:

The hand of the Lord was upon me and carried me out in the spirit of the Lord and set me down in the midst of the valley which was full of bones … and, behold, there were very many in the open valley; and, lo, they were very dry.

Ezekiel must have found himself in a place like this, thinks Maroney with a grim smile and finds himself singing softly:

Dem bones, dem bones gonna walk around.
Dem bones, dem bones gonna walk around.
Dem bones, dem bones gonna walk around.
Now hear the word of the Lord.

There must be artesian water. The track is lined with olive trees that he can see are watered by a homemade reticulation system. Green lawn surrounds the homestead and, as Maroney swats away the flies he is confronted by more bones, some with emu feathers or kangaroo fur still attached, but no dogs. The front door is open and he calls out. The place has a silent, deserted feel. Curious, he walks into the first room off the breezeway. The kitchen is like a scene from the Marie Celeste with plates of half-eaten food on the table, along with mugs and a teapot. No light comes on in the fridge when he opens it, hoping to find a cold drink. He's hit by warm, fetid air. Mouldy cheese and withered vegetables languish alongside other unrecognisable items. Every nerve in his body jangles when it sinks in that part of the silence is the lack of a generator. There's always a gennie chugging away in the background of these places. Just to make sure, he tries the light switch on the wall. No electricity. The hairs on the back of his neck are beginning to stand to attention. Maroney wishes he hadn't noticed the large freezer against the wall. He doesn't want to open it. When he does, he's confronted by a stinking mass of rotting meat. He slams down the lid and rushes back outside, heaving for fresh air. What can have happened? It's obvious no one has been here for over a week. After a search around the sheds, calling out to make sure that no one is around, perhaps lying hurt, or worse, he heads back to Bedarra as fast as the unforgiving track will allow, that song still in his head:

Ezekiel disconnected dem dry bones,
Ezekiel disconnected dem dry bones,
Ezekiel in the Valley of Dry Bones,
Now hear the word of the Lord.

.

Matt is still in Lonsdale with Cass. When Maroney tells Bruce what he has seen, he's irritated to see a wry grin creep over the stockman's face. Bruce shakes his head.

'I'll call the cops in Sandy Bay, but I think I can guess what's happened.' Maroney waits for an explanation. 'Dan has a helicopter. He hasn't been able to make a decent living out of the station since the recession-we-had-to-have, so he hires himself out for mustering to other stations. Sometimes he's away up north for weeks. He had a couple of backpackers from England looking after the place. Bet they couldn't hack it and high-tailed it out of there They probably let the gennie run out of fuel and then couldn't get it started. Dan couldn't organise a piss-up in a brewery. Bet he left them with bugger-all training.'

'I hope you're right,' says Maroney. 'I'd hate to think of a couple of English kids taking off on foot — I've heard of kids like that dying of dehydration in this sort of country. And what would have happened to the dogs?'

Bruce pushes his hat back and scratches his head. 'Reckon they would have found their way over to the station next door. They know the missus there — Bonny. She feeds them if Dan goes AWOL, and most likely the police'll find Dan's ute abandoned at the airport. Anyway, I'll give them a ring.'

The episode had given Maroney a fright but has also given him a story he thinks could be a winner. Fremantle has a few backpacker hostels. This story could be a reality check for starry-eyed kids.

'I was right,' said Bruce in his gravelly voice. 'Dan's car was found at the airport a week ago. The police contacted Dan. He's up in the Kimberley mustering. Yep, and Bonny's got the dogs, I phoned her.'

'I'd hate to have to come back and clean up that mess,' says Maroney.

'I can guarantee it won't be Dan doing it,' says Bruce. 'He'll pay Bonny or one of the other station wives. They're always glad of a bit of casual money.'

That night, Maroney wonders what the boss will make of this story. He stands behind the tank staring at the sky. After dinner, Doog went straight to the office — to sort out stuff for the campdraft, she said. She seems to be relishing the job Matt gave her. *Cruel woman — why have you abandoned me?* He sighs and walks to his quarters. He'll fill the night writing. He needs to dissect and interpret what he has seen. What makes people addicted to this hopeless, terrifying, seductive land? He wants to make sense of the feeling that this country is somehow embracing him.

He had sworn never to live away from the city again after he'd left the boys home. He'd loved the part-time job as a paperboy in Perth, chatting to people on the streets. After the years in the bush, he felt alive, excited, had a sense of belonging. He smiles as he remembers the cheek of the young boy who hounded the people at the *Daily News* for an in-house job. He'd started as a gopher, eventually the cadetship and uni. Now what's happening? Maybe it wasn't so much the countryside around the home that he hated … was afraid of. It was the people. He'd been so focused on avoiding any trouble, hardly noticed the environment, except the few times he went out to check the boundary fences. Him and another boy. Took them two days to walk all around and fix any holes. They'd camp out. Scared the shit out of him. But not as much as the dorms in the dead of night.

Paul

'SORRY, Mr Gorski, but we don't have any spare blankets.'

Paul gives the flight attendant a sideways look. Bloody airline! They must think everyone's used to living in the Arctic. They're ten thousand metres above the Nullarbor on a five-hour flight across the continent from east to west. The plane is freezing. It'll be good to get back up to the warmth of Pardee. He hates flying but the new horse he bought in Tamworth is worth it. She's a beauty. He can't wait to show her to Connor. He closes his eyes and steers his mind north along the rough track around the lake. In the late afternoon light he sees the vibrant red of the earth deepen, and the shadows turn purple. He hears the Major Mitchells screech from the white gums. Wading egrets, painted gold in the sunset, ripple the mirrored surface of the lake. In the stillness, spindly legs and reeds pierce reflected sky and clouds. Land in this region can be as boring as batshit, but not Pardee.

A wave of grief hits him as he thinks of his parents, who got themselves killed driving back from Sandy Bay one night. Hit a roo on the track and rolled into a deep gully. Both died instantly the police told him. Anna and Tony Gorski, born in Poland, immigrated to Australia after the war and made their way to the outback as if to get as far away from society as they could. He owes them so much but right now he can't forgive them for dying … and for not telling him what he had a right to know. He doesn't want to think about it again. In his mind he journeys back to the station.

On the west side of the track, the red earth has pushed up a line of rocky outcrops, gouged by deep gullies and lined with low trees and scrub. He loves the breakaway country, especially the mesa. No one gets to go there, except him. That's his place. Well, not his. He has no right to call it that, although the Aboriginal people, the original owners, don't seem to want it. But who knows? Maybe, they want it just to be left alone. There are tales of it becoming taboo after a massacre years ago.

The trolley comes down the aisle and the flight attendant hands him pretzels. He buys a beer. The seat becomes more uncomfortable with every minute. A child screams two seats behind him, and the fat man in front keeps farting. Again, he escapes to Pardee. The monthly tourist run is going well. Some of the townies are great but others frustrate the hell out of him. They just don't see how amazing the place is. Makes him cringe when they talk about bush-bashing, and he tries not to see red if they mention roo shooting. What they don't get is the interconnectedness of nature. Most of it already wrecked — farmed to hell. *We have to look after what's left. The fuckin' writing's on the wall.* They see beauty in the lake and the waterholes with their fringe of amazing ghost gums, but they need to be told about the fragile creatures whose homes are the stony plains. They need to be told just how ancient the spinifex rings are, and how the mallee scrub may look dry and gnarled, but it's a whole ecosystem. They're all astounded by the rock, of course. Past the breakaway country, it's as if the belly of the red earth flattens out except where she's given birth to one huge rock, which stands like an orphan on the plain. It's their own Uluru.

On the full moon he drives anyone who wants to go to the base of the rock. He gives them the full-on explanation. Some of their eyes glaze over but he doesn't give a shit. They're his captive audience so they can damn well listen. As they climb, following the trail of painted white rocks, he tells them about the plants and animals — how they all have a purpose. Flowers, medicine, bush tucker. Each one is special. Grief hits him again as he thinks of his parent but that's one thing he'll always thank the old man … Tony, for. He and Anna, even though they originally came from Europe, had a feeling for this land. Life was tough back when the folks first came to this country and they had to work hard, but they'd taken the time to learn its history. They taught him to respect the land and every living thing in it.

Surprise stirs Paul to find the anger he had been stewing in since his parent's accident has cooled. He shuts his eyes tight, can't cry here. He must have been only about five years old when Tony showed him the dark secret hole at the base of the rock. He'd pointed out how the roughness of the rock was worn shiny and smooth by bodies penetrating back and forth — since the Dreamtime, he'd said — to reach the permanent supply of fresh water.

But the old man waited a few years before he told Paul the rest of the story: how the white explorers captured blackfellas, fed them on salted beef, and then denied them water until, half-crazed with thirst, they led their tormentors to the precious holes. That's what the tourists don't get, how this land was the mother to her people before she was taken by strangers to be used and abused. Even though it all happened generations ago, the blacks remember. They steer clear of the place now. Just as well, he thinks. This way they don't have to deal with Connor. Paul loves Connor but he can be a frustratingly bigoted old bugger.

Dad … Tony … started the full-moon tradition. Whenever Paul was home from boarding school he'd go along for the ride — never got sick of it. In the dry season, Tony would lead the tourists up the path to the top of the monolith, real rock-wallaby country, and then he'd open the Esky. In his Polish accent, he'd command the tourists to be silent, and they'd shut up, every one of them. The sun setting fire to the land had them all agog. But a couple of times a year they could sit, champagne in hand and watch the earth and the eastern sky light up in a celebration of the full moon rising. And then, they'd all turn to watch the sun sink in the west. It still gives Paul goosebumps to think about it.

The plane is flying over the salt country. He must have dozed off. Thank God, they'll land in Perth soon. He wouldn't have missed the horse sale for the world but he's been going crazy not knowing what's happening at Pardee. Connor will have managed while he's been away but he hates not being in control. He'll be stuck in Perth for the best part of a week while he organises the transport of the mare to Pardee. He should relax and enjoy it, could even look up an old girlfriend. He wonders what Tennille is doing now. Toenail, him and his mates called her when they were at uni. She was a bit of all right, Toenail. But she's sure to be hooked up with someone else by now.

How pissed off Matt will be when he sees what a prize he has scored. He outbid them all for that horse. The bloodline of the American quarter-horse, Ballinger — they don't come much better than that. Most station folk don't like the idea of using anything but Australian stock horses for campdrafting. Why do they have to be so bloody set in their ways?

He had complained to Connor about the district being in a time warp. He thought Connor agreed with him but he always has a bob each-way, does Connor. *You'll be up against a strong tradition, lad,* he can hear him saying. He always calls him lad … and he's right … tradition is getting stronger, especially with all the talk of foreign ownership. Folk are fierce-proud of the history of the stock horse and you can't really blame them.

Paul remembers spouting off about the need for new blood and he can hear Connor saying: *You could be right, m'boy.* But Connor didn't look at him. He had turned back to the saddle he was mending and then he said *But I t'ink you'll be on your own.* Connor's accent always gets stronger when he feels uncomfortable.

It was just after Tony and Anna had died and he'd found the biscuit tin. Paul regrets it now, Connor's been like a father to him, but as he walked away, he'd said: 'I've always been on my own.'

An Introduced Species

THE next evening, as the station staff gather for dinner, Col pulls the ute up in a cloud of dust beneath the homestead verandah.

'What are ya?' yells Mary, and then stops and stares with the rest of them.

From the car door, first one long leg and then another emerges, followed by the elegant body of a young woman. She's dressed in what could be called station clothes, jeans, checked shirt, an Akubra hat and sunglasses but she looks like she has just stepped out of the pages of *Australian Vogue*.

'Everyone, let me introduce Willie, Willie Albers.' Col grins and rolls his eyes at everyone as he follows her up the steps.

The young woman takes off her Akubra and flicks the mass of dark curls that tumble around her face. She offers a small, manicured hand and, after quick introductions, Doog ushers her inside to freshen up. Fifteen minutes later she re-emerges in a linen shift; crisp and white against her dark hair and smooth brown skin.

Doog watches bemused while those gathered, including Maroney, stand open-mouthed, and then scramble to sit beside Willie. She would look right at home on the catwalk of the Miss Universe competition. Maroney is quick to grab the seat next to the newcomer and talk excitedly with her all night. The first chance she gets, Doog quietly leaves, sure that no one has noticed.

She returns to her donga, forgoing her nightly puff at the tank stand.

By the time she reaches the kitchen for breakfast the next morning, Maroney has already gone.

'Grabbed a cup of coffee and a bacon sanger, and was off to meet the tree hugger,' chortles Mrs C. 'Bruce gave them the Land Rover. She came to breakfast at the early shift. I thought the blokes' tongues were going to fall into their baked beans, but I've got a feeling that one knows how to handle herself.'

Doog knows she has no right to feel resentful, but she does.

Maroney is at the shearing quarters collecting his notebook when Willie turns up in the ute.

'Don't forget your lunch, Dan,' she calls. 'Not sure how long we'll be.'

Strapped into the passenger seat he notices that Willie is at home in the off-road vehicle. She's dressed the same as a man, in shirt, shorts and the requisite Akubra hat. He takes note of the rainbow scarf knotted at her neck. Her legs disappear into the steel-capped boots that many of the men wear when not riding, but no man ever had legs like that.

'We'll drive over to the eastern border first,' she says. 'I want to show you what our destocking program has done. Just in the last three years we've brought back five species of native grasses and many species of other flora as well as fauna.'

When Maroney asks about which species Willie reels off the names and promises to give him a list when they are back at the homestead. She becomes animated. It's plain to see she loves her job, goes on about how vital it is to understand the connection of all living things from the smallest organisms the largest species of plants and animals. 'And it's not just for the flora and fauna,' she says. 'We need to convince station owners of the economic advantages of destocking in some areas.'

'What economic advantages?' Maroney needs hard facts if he's to write about this. Zeal is not enough.

Willie tries to explain the importance of maintaining a diverse environment and tells him about the native bee and the dire consequences of its decline. She'll give him some reading on the subject, she says.

All creatures great and small. Maroney has a quiet chuckle and Willie looks at him with a frown. He assures her the only thing he's laughing at is himself. A couple of weeks ago he wouldn't have believed he'd be out here contemplating writing a story about the native bee.

They drive on and to Maroney the first two paddocks look the same as much of the land up here: baked earth, sparsely covered with clumps of dusty grass and spindly bushes. He notices small, gnarled trees still standing but the remains of many more lie, white and ossified, disintegrating into the soil with the help of termites. The land looks tired, worn out, as papery as old skin. He wonders if this is natural. Australia is always referred to as an old continent. She sure looks old around here.

When they pass through the third gate, the transformation is obvious. In this paddock everything looks alive. There are trees with an understory of bushes and grasses. The sounds of birds and insects thrill the air. Out of the car, it actually feels cooler and he breathes in the difference.

'I'd like to bring Doog back here in the late afternoon light to get some pictures.' He tells Willie about Doog's photography.

'I'll show you where the water trough is,' Willie says. 'That's where she'll get great shots of the wildlife.'

When the track widens out, Willie pulls down hard on the steering wheel and turns the vehicle around. 'Now I want to show you what we're doing with the tag.'

'Tag?'

'Tagasaste, tree-lucerne. It's a great fodder, but it's an introduced species so it has to be managed.'

'What's so great about it?' He writes the name in his notebook.

Willie waits for him to get out and open and close a gate before going on. She's flushed with enthusiasm. She explains that like all legumes it gathers nitrogen from the air and puts it back in to the soil. 'The latest research shows that it might sequester carbon as well.'

'This is great, Willie. My boss's one redeeming feature is that he's interested in the environment. If I can knock up a good piece on this, I just might keep the old toad happy enough to let me stay a bit longer.'

'Sounds like I have a better boss than you,' she says with a happy grin.

They turn down a track along the fence line and eventually come to another gate. When he jumps out to open it, Maroney sees the land slope away into a wide valley. Through the middle is a thick winding belt of bush, which he guesses must be a creek line. On either side are long lines of shrubs that look like low hedges. In between the shrubs are tracts of land about four or five metres wide where grass grows green and lush. On one side of the creek, cattle are grazing. Now the land feels alive, thriving, prosperous.

Willie points to the shrubs and explains that the tagasaste can grow into a decent-sized tree but the cattle keep it grazed into low bushes, which prevents it from flowering and seeding.

'This soil is hungry,' she says. 'And the roots of tagasaste reach down deep. It stops the salt rising to the surface.'

Maroney thinks of the saltpans that he saw from the plane. He'd wonders if the damage to the environment is irreparable. He comments on the greenness of the grass between the rows of tagasaste. Willie tells him the green is a result of the nitrogen deposited by the tag.

'It feeds the grass,' she says.

'So is the aim to get this stuff growing all over the station?'

'Far from it.' Willie says and again tries to explain the long-term advantages of diversity.

Maroney can see an angle for his story. He'd read once about a tree, logged almost to the point of extinction in America, before it was found to contain a cure for a type of cancer. Surprise strikes him again at his newfound interest this subject. Since he started working for the paper, he's always preferred writing about the arts and the cultural scene. He had no desire to revisit the bush, let alone write about it. Being at the boys home probably did that to him. He hadn't thought much about it. Now he's telling Willie his ideas for some articles.

Willie smiles. 'Sounds good, Dan. All the same, I'd run anything you write past Jean or me before you publish. She's pretty jumpy when it comes to the press and Bedarra. Might be safer if you want to keep on her good side. We've both had experience of journalists making it up as they go along.'

Maroney assures her he'd be happy to write the stories and pass them over for the facts to be checked. This subject is all new to him.

On the way back, Maroney asks if this is the only station in the district practicing these methods.

'There's a young fellow over at Pardee who's right into it,' says Willie. 'He's passionate about the environment, destocked massively lately. I think his parents died and he's got free rein, but otherwise, no. Most of the station owners think we're off with the fairies.'

He makes himself a promise to visit Pardee as soon as he can.

The Gathering

DOOG has been going through the entries for the campdraft and the rodeo. She puts aside the junior and ladies for now and goes through the open entries. There's lots of information on the forms but more about the horses than the riders. To her frustration, it is not a requirement that the riders state their birth date.

'For heaven's sake do we need to know when the bloody horse was born but not the rider?' she says to Bruce.

'Makes perfect sense to me,' says Bruce.

For the next couple of afternoons and evenings she sits on the phone carrying out the task Matt gave her. She tries to engage the mostly young men in conversation and jots down notes trying to get a picture of them.

'You don't sound very old,' she tries with one young man. 'Old enough,' comes the terse reply.

This exercise makes her realise how big the event is. Some people are travelling hundreds of kilometers to participate.

Mrs C looks up when Doog walks through the screen door of the cookhouse and sits at the table. The cook pushes the teapot towards her.

'Where's Mare?' Doog asks, when she can get a word in.

'Probably down by the river. Families are coming in from further along the creek. Jake came back last night and they're here for the campdraft as well. There'll be a shindig tonight for sure. Maroney will want to be in on some of that, I would imagine.'

Jake has been missing from school. Brenda had been evasive when Doog asked about him but she had established that he wasn't sick and had assumed that he'd gone fencing with the men.

'So, where's Jake been?' she asks.

'Initiation, I hear.'

'Christ! Really? Seem's a bit young.'

'That one's tough. You don't have to worry about him. He'll be as proud as a young bull. Being a man — one of the clan — that'll be worth a bit of pain to Jake,' says Mrs C.

'What does it entail?' Doog asks, not sure she wants to know.

'I don't think this first bit is too bad,' says Mrs C. 'The boys eventually reappear with a scar around their upper arms More could happen when they're a bit older but it's all pretty secret.'

On the way to the shearers' quarters, Doog thinks about Jake, and what Mrs C had said about him being made part of the clan — belonging. From her visits, and from Brenda, she's been trying to learn about the ways of the community. They're friendly enough, always laughing and joking, but there's an undercurrent of distrust.

'Can't blame them,' Mrs C had said. 'They were virtually slaves on these stations a few years back. Got paid in a few groceries and tobacco. And then their kids got stolen and taken away from their country.' Doog had heard these stories years ago but up here the appalling reality sends a chill through her. Some of these people would have suffered grief and anger and the feeling of powerlessness that she knows all too well.

Doog doesn't know much about the small mob down by the river but it always seems like one big family to her. She has seen the way they look after each other. They fight and squabble among themselves but once when she was down there talking to Brenda, a policeman came to ask some questions about a brawl in Sandy

Bay. The wall that went up was like concrete as they responded to the questions in evasive monosyllables. She knows from the dinner-table conversation they do the same if Bruce is pissed off about something and wants to know who's responsible. He says he's got Buckley's of finding out. She's seen him express frustration but she also senses his admiration for the way they unite.

Mary and Maroney wait in the shade of the Moreton Bay Figs, where Doog joins them. Mary, in T-shirt and jeans, carries a bag. They near the camp and suddenly she's not beside them anymore. Later, she's sitting with the other women, bare-breasted and wearing a lap-lap. She's shed the station and sits in another skin pounding seeds and remembering language.

Doog and Maroney walk along a track beside the mostly dusty creek bed, to the billabong where the people come together in the dry season. Doog tries to explain to Maroney what she has learned about these gatherings.

'I think tonight is like a family reunion. We'll be welcome because it's the just the lead-up but after that there are other ceremonies. Some for men only, and other times only women. I'm sure this first day is our only chance to be here.'

Near the billabong the worn track weaves between a clump of white gums and acacia. The white-trunked trees are always a striking contrast in this country and Doog's eyes rove, automatically on the lookout for anything that will make a good photograph. She squints as she spots the almost camouflaged figure of Snow squatting in a low fork of a tree, overlooking the riverbed. She glances at Maroney but he hasn't noticed. And, not for the first time, she wonders about the shy young man in the tree.

Before talking to anyone else, Doog seeks out Watarra, who seems to be the most important elder of the clan. She nods to him and explains to Maroney that they need to stand and wait. Eventually, the old man beckons them forward and she gives Watarra a greeting from Matt and all at the station and shows him a box of biscuits from Mrs C for the mother of the initiate. The old man rattles off a short string of strange words.

'I think he's asking who you are in language,' Doog says, and introduces Maroney.

'This one comes from Fremantle. He would like to understand the ways of the station, the ways of the people, *all* of the people.'

Watarra beckons to a second man, who says that they are welcome and leads them to the circle.

'Watarra understands English, then?' asks Maroney.

Doog repeats what Brenda has told her. How the community are trying to hold on to their language that was outlawed not that long ago. They try to speak language whenever they're able but it's in danger of dying with the old people. She pulls out her camera and indicates she'd like to take photos.

'Yeah, yeah,' says the man, seemingly unconcerned, and he flops down beside them.

'I didn't tell you,' says Maroney. 'My editor was so impressed with the story about the snakebite he wants to send a photographer up to the station.'

Doog stares at him, not trying to hide the fact that the idea of another journo poking his nose into things appalls her.

'I hope you checked with Matt,' she says testily.

'Nah, I told the editor, no need to send a photographer. Save your money, I said to him. We have a great photographer right here on the station. She knows the place and gets stunning results. Trust me, I said.'

She stares at him aware that her mouth is open. 'What are you on about, Maroney?'

'You, I'm talking about, you. When I took your camera back to your room after the snake bite, I saw your photos on the wall.

They're amazing. Simplicity combined with powerful drama. Doog, they're great shots. And how many people still persevere with black-and-white? I love what you do in the darkroom. It's brilliant.'

'But I'm an amateur; I can't take photos for a newspaper,' she says.

Maroney explains that a lot of what the paper buys these days is freelance. Anyone can submit a photo of a topical event and hope their photo will be chosen. He insists she's good. Says she's better than most, as good as most of the pros he has known. Along with being astonished she's aware that she's elated by Maroney's approval of her efforts, her art, he calls it.

'But hey!' He puts his hands up in a gesture of acceptance. 'It's up to you. I'm only trying to save you from having another stickybeak around.' What Maroney doesn't say is that he's feeling territorial about the station. There is a lot of mileage to be gained out here and he doesn't want to share it. He will tell her that later.

For an hour, they sit, fascinated by all the activity. Doog spies Darcy and Manny. The two stockmen look different without their checked shirts and jeans, sitting on the other side of the fire with the younger men, clowning around while they paint each other with stripes and dots, applying the white ochre with the chewed ends of sticks or their fingers. Occasionally a new group arrives to be greeted by shouts and slaps. They carry gifts — a kangaroo, a bungarra, or perhaps a brush turkey. The newcomers deposit their offerings by the fire and melt into the various groups. Doog shoots off two spools of film.

'What's happening?' asks Maroney.

'Your guess is as good as mine. Like I said, a big reunion, while everyone is arriving. How about we go see the waterhole and come back later?'

Maroney nods and she speaks to Watarra and looks around for Brenda to tell her they'll be back. Brenda sits talking and laughing with a group of women Doog has never seen before. She's introduced to several aunties and cousins.

'They don't mind?' asks Maroney.

'Nobody seems to mind much what you do around here, as long as you follow protocol — the laws of respect. Good manners, if you like.'

On the drive to the waterhole, the scene of Brenda with all her aunties and cousins sitting around yarning and laughing stays with Doog and she feels a twinge of envy. Her family seems so scattered, distant, absent.

Silence fills the vehicle. She's not the only one with things on her mind. Maroney seems deep in thought, as well.

'How long do you think you'll stay up here?' she asks eventually.

'Well, it depends on the editor.' I've told him I've had no luck interviewing the *guvvy*.' He looks hard at her, shrugging his shoulders and holding up his hands in a helpless gesture. She pokes her tongue out and turns back to the road. 'Actually, I am hoping to stay a while. Almost offered to use some of my holidays but the boss pricked up his ears when he heard about Willie and the innovations in land care that Mrs Le Carre is interested in. I've managed to keep him happy with the stories I sent about the smaller stations, how they're struggling to hang on since the price of wool dropped. And the snake bite helped. He's keen for more at the moment.'

'And so, Maroney? You want to stay?'

'Yeah, besides anything else the campdraft's coming up. I'd love to stay for that, but there could be a problem.'

She'd noticed his reaction when he was talking to Willie last night. He'd looked a bit shocked, but she couldn't hear. She asks what that was about.

'Now who's snooping? If you must know, Willie has suggested I may have to find another station to stay at before the campdraft.'

She finds it hard to believe that Willie would ask Maroney to leave. It seems to be a tradition that any blow-in is welcomed at the station, especially at campdraft time but Willie has told Maroney the owner bans all media from the event. Doog remembers now. She did hear something about that when she first came to Bedarra.

'She said she'll put in a good word for me but apparently Mrs Le Carre is a bit jumpy when it comes to the press.'

Doog concentrates on changing gears as they drive over a patch of cap rock and then tells him she can't believe Mrs Le Carre would be that hard and fast with her rules. Surely, he can contact her and explain what he's doing. Life in the bush and all that. He needs to convince her he's doing a service and assure her he won't mention names. He needs to ask permission to stay and do a piece about the event — he could keep it generic. But this is the tenth anniversary. It should be celebrated, she tells him.

She stops talking. Maroney is turning to her with that look of surprise he often gets, and his lips twitch at the corners. Why is she encouraging him to stay, for heaven's sake? Less than two weeks ago she wanted him to drop off the edge of the earth.

He nods. 'Yes, I had already planned to give that a try.' He's silent for a moment and then says: 'Should I take heart from the fact that you're encouraging me to stay?'

Again, Doog concentrates on driving, aware that her face probably betrays her confusion. She pulls the Land Rover up at the end of a track leading to the waterhole. She could drive further to where it's possible to park almost at the waters' edge, but here the track leads to the most spectacular view into the gorge.

'It's just a short walk from here,' she says. 'After this long grass, there are rocks and logs, just watch out for snakes.'

'Since Cassie got bitten, all I see is grass, rocks and logs. I'm too paranoid to look up at the trees or the sky.'

'Just as well, Snoopy, you'd trip over a log and fall flat on your face if you went around this country gazing at the sky,' she quips, relieved that they're out of the vehicle, trying to hide what she's starting to feel near this man.

Maroney is ahead of Doog and she hears his sharp intake of breath and knows the feeling of the sudden ending of the track and the cliffs rising from the waterhole. She becomes aware that she needs him to like it, to be as enchanted as she is.

'It's magnificent.' He has his back arched and his arms outstretched as if to embrace the whole scene, and Doog finds herself wanting to hug him. The pool reflects the surrounding cliffs in fluid stillness, except to one side where the creek that feeds it cascades over rocks and continues downstream. White gums, startling against the black water, reach over the banks on both sides. The space echoes with cicadas competing with the solo drawn-out caw, caw of a crow.

'Sorry Snoopy, I told myself I wouldn't do this, but in this heat it's just too tempting. You're going to have to turn your back for a moment.'

She sheds her frock and boots in seconds. Eucalypt leaves have stained the water to the colour and clarity of black tea. She swims underwater until her lungs protest, then surfaces, shaking the wet hair from her face. Maroney is still standing on the shore with the look of a startled wallaby.

'Come on Snoopy, I won't peep.'

'Turn around then.'

'Are you in yet?' She looks over her shoulder. He's sitting on a rock, removing his shoes and socks.

'Keep your eyes on the cliff.'

She peeps. He's stripped off his singlet and shirt. His body is painfully white in this brown country.

'How're we going, Snoopy? How many clothes are you wearing?'

'No perving.'

She imagines him hobbling on tender feet over the stones to the edge of the water and turns. He's standing in his boxer shorts frowning at the water.

'Come on, you can't wear those great big knickers, they'll weigh you down and you'll drown.'

'That's it, I'm not coming in.'

'OK, but you don't know what you're missing.' She duck-dives into the blackness.

He strips and reaches her in the middle of the deep pool in a few strokes.

Again, confusion takes a hold as they face one another, treading water, his smile wrapping itself around her as she imagines an oyster wrapping around a pearl. She turns and strikes out for rocky cliff face on the far side of the pool.

'Time we were heading for home,' she says, when he catches up. The delicious freshness of the water, her nakedness, the whole damned mélange is conspiring. It would only take a small movement for the electricity she feels to be sparked. She swims to the shore, dresses quickly and heads for the vehicle to wait.

Back at the river bed the smell of roast meat and singed fur flavours the warm air. Flames and sparks fly skyward from the fire in the centre of the gathering. The light pulsates off dark bodies and shows the expectation on painted faces and the collective whites of eyes that turn to the gap in the circle. Doog hopes to capture some of the spirit of the occasion. But it's dark. Too much to expect of even her 800 ASA film ... perhaps with the tripod, if she pushes it in the darkroom. Who knows?

A loud nasal incantation cuts through the air, joined by the chanting of other voices, the clap-clap of sticks and the tap of boomerangs. The voices stop. And start again. Different groups joining in and fading out. She holds her breath as a tall man springs into the circle, brandishing a woomera in one hand and clutching a spear in the other. The night almost swallows his black form so that the white-painted markings seem to move, disembodied. She looks at Maroney. In the flickering light he leans forward, expectant. The tall man stops, looks around and then starts a graceful dance, occasionally pausing, twisting and stamping his feet. A smaller man with a kangaroo skin tied around his shoulders hops into the firelight with arms and hands bent in front of his chest. He too stops and looks up, sniffing the air before his watchful leaps continue.

Maroney's hand finds hers. She's not sure he realises. His face tells her he has been transported. Two more figures in demonic masks enter, and the kangaroo man bounds up and down making loud clicking noises with his tongue. The tall man leaps gracefully away from the threatening figures and out through the gap.

Doog leans over to Maroney and says she thinks that it was the story of Jake's totem, the kangaroo. How it saved his ancestor from the demons. Maroney grips her hand tighter.

'It's fantastic.' His eyes are alive with excitement as they meet hers. Again, she finds herself wanting to hug him. He connects to this magic.

She moves to the back of the circle where she's left her tripod set up. She won't intrude on the night by using of a flash but it's asking a lot of the film unless she can get the exposure just right. She sets up the camera and inserts a zoom lens, aware that it too, will compromise the light. She uses a whole reel of film. Most of it will be wasted but … if she gets one good shot.

With new film loaded she watches Maroney through the viewfinder, his pale skin and blond hair illuminated by the fire. She can see the shine in his eyes as a dancer comes closer with a beckoning motion. Maroney looks ready to offer himself.

The shutter clicks.

Somebody's Birthday

THE following night every male hovers around Willie. Doog tells herself she's not jealous, she's not so idiotic. She smiles her way through the meal. The conversation doesn't stray far from the campdraft

'I'm assuming you'll all be entering,' says Matt. 'What about you, Snow? Do you want a guernsey?'

The conversation stalls and all eyes turn to Snow. He reddens, but doesn't hesitate long before saying in his low, soft voice, 'Yeah, yeah, I'll give it a go.'

A few sceptical glances skip between the hands before they return to dissecting Paul's purchase of the new horse. When the old argument about bringing in new bloodlines starts, Maroney becomes embroiled in it. Doog leaves quietly. She walks past the tank stand and the machinery shed to the back of the donga before she pulls out her tobacco. The rational part of her needs space. There is too much to sort out already without added complications. And yet she knows if Maroney were to come looking for her, seeking her out with his artless grin, pretending to need a cigarette, rationality would be lost in the desert.

She rolls her shoulders; she's tense. She's starting to feel a bit out of her depth Matt is relying on her to help with the campdraft, but there's still the kids and … and tomorrow! She still has to get through tomorrow. The birthday of her first-born child always looms from the calendar to fill her with despair no matter how much she tries to prepare. Last year she'd planned to fill her day, to keep busy and had volunteered to run the winter sports carnival at the school. She'd battled to hold herself together. At the end of the day she presented the first trophy to a young boy with a golden smile and his chest sticking out in pride. As soon as he left, she lost it, unable to stop tears flowing. She stumbled away, saying she felt ill.

The next morning Doog stands at the dresser, in her running gear with a black bandana around her hair, wondering if she's being a complete idiot. Her little ritual of whispering affirmations as she lights the candle are not her anymore. But how, when do you stop? The glow of the candle reflects her pride as she puts her lips to Annie's image. And then she leans forward to the dark glass in the other frame and she sees … she sees … her own reflection. She shakes her head and stands quickly.

The sun weeps a golden fringe from the scalloped edges of violet clouds low in the eastern sky when Doog sets out on her morning jog. At times like this she thinks she should take photos in colour. She wants to celebrate the bush and everything in it. Mrs C asked if she wasn't scared wandering through the outback on her own but she's always feels embraced by it. She has never understood people, such as Annie's father, who are happy to live without nature in their lives. She remembers how he became anxious when she cultivated a jungle in their garden. She had worked to cover the fences and the sides of their home with vines and creepers and now wonders whether the tangle of jasmine that she encouraged over the front porch had strangled the marriage. On a camping vacation they came across an old Norwegian whaling station with great hulking vats that had been used to render the whale's blubber into oil, rusting into the sand dunes with vines climbing over them. He had bemoaned the fact that it hadn't been preserved while she could only celebrate the power of nature to obliterate it.

Her mind turns to the day ahead. Brenda will help in the schoolroom keeping Cassie and Molly busy with number games and other activities, which means Doog can concentrate on the three older children. She runs and runs. She runs through breathlessness and feels that she could keep on running, keep on and on and never stop, never look back.

In the schoolroom, the morning lasts forever. After lunch Doog tells the children to bring their bags of leaves and they all sit on the verandah floor. She keeps glancing at the clock through the window, wishing again that the time would go faster today.

In front of each child she has drawn three intersecting circles in red, yellow and green chalk.

'I want you all to sort the leaves into three sets,' she begins. 'The red circle is for the big leaves. The yellow circle you can put the yellow leaves into and in the green circle you can put all the green leaves.'

She watches while they work and waits, hoping for the right question. Sam doesn't disappoint.

'But what if they're big *and* green, Miss?'

'Ahh, I wonder if anyone can work out where to put them if they are big and green, or if they're yellow and green.

They will work through the maths syllabus classifying, sorting the leaves into sets and sub-sets according to colour, size and shape, as well as doing simple arithmetic. Brenda has promised to come and tell them more about some of the leaves. Bush medicine and bush tucker often come from these plants. Brenda's stories can be typed into the new station computer and printed. And when pasted into books along with the children's illustrations, the kids will end up with something that Doog hopes they'll be proud of.

For a science lesson, she plans to coax her students into thinking about such things as why the leaves of the spinifex are like needles, and why the leaves of gum trees change direction during the day.

'Try not to lose your leaves between now and Friday,' she tells them. 'We're going to use them to create some really cool art to decorate the shed for the campdraft. We can use the leaves as stencils, roll them with ink and lots of other things so if you get any bright ideas let me know. You're all responsible for shed decoration.'

'Can we use glitter, Doogie?' Shouts out Cassie.

'Yes, glitter! Bucketloads! And we'll raid the art cupboard and see what else we can find.' The children line up and she pins a homemade badge on each chest: a paper rosette with the words *Bedarra — Official Shed Decorator*. She's put on an Akubra from the dress-up box and imitates Matt's gruff voice as she shakes each small hand.

'Congratulations on your appointment to the shed-decorating committee.'

Only Jess rolls her eyes.

As soon as school finishes for the day, Doog escapes back to the donga. Her head feels ready to explode. After a shower she gulps down two Panadol. She lies on the bed and breathes deeply, trying to meditate, willing her mind to stop splintering. Maybe it's time to leave this place, time to move on. She never intended to stay, doesn't belong here. Maybe she doesn't belong anywhere.

Her mind drifts, drugged by the heat. She's feeling emotional despite the Panadol, or maybe because of it. She's made such a pig's breakfast of everything. That was one of Gran's expressions. Gran would have said. there's no use looking back, feeling sorry for yourself. The old lady used to maintain that everything that happened in life was for a purpose. She misses Gran and she misses Dad, the old Dad. The Dad before … again the scene of her mother and father arguing floats before her. Her mother is crying, but she hears her father again, *Struth Claris, you're too friggin' old and so am I. The little tart brought this on herself. The church has offered to help. There's no other way.*

She wakes with a start, feeling the sting of her father's words, but yes, he'd clearly said the church had offered to help. There is a soft insistent knocking at the door.

'Doog, Doog, it's me, Maroney. I don't want to disturb you, just checking if you're OK.'

Darkness fills the donga and she looks at the fluorescent hands of her watch. 'Oh lord, I've missed dinner.'

'Yeah, Mrs C has sent you a plate of chicken and salad. She said you weren't looking too good.'

'Just a minute, I'll be right out.' She tightens her sarong, slips her thongs on her feet and opens the door.

'Mmm,' says Maroney pulling a face. 'You look dreadful.'

'Thanks.' She takes the plate from him and places it on the chest of drawers. 'I had a headache, but it's all right now that I've had a sleep. You want a fag, I suppose.'

'That won't do *you* much good. You'd be better off eating … but if you're offering.'

Her defenses cave in to his dorky grin. She ducks back inside and grabs the tobacco pouch, a couple of glasses and a bottle of red wine from her stash. They walk over to the table and chairs on the shearing shed verandah and Maroney fills the glasses. She stands at the verandah rail and lifts her glass and her eyes towards the stars before taking a sip.

'What are you thinking about? Tell me, Doogie.' Maroney's voice comes from the shadows with a tone of concern she's unprepared for.

She takes a gulp of air. She can't stop her lips from quivering. Her first reaction is to flee back to the donga with some excuse but suddenly she wants to share this.

Her own voice comes in a hoarse whisper.

'I was just wishing someone a happy birthday.'

Maroney takes her glass, as she doubles over and great heaving sobs threaten to pull her down. His hands gently guide her into a chair.

'What is it, Doogie? Please, tell me.' He gives her a handkerchief, his eyes stricken. She shakes her head.

'Whose birthday?'

She nods sniffing and wipes her eyes, chest heaving. 'I should have seen that coming. Sorry you had to see it.'

'Good God, Doogie, don't apologise. You must know … you must know how much I … Please, tell me. Let me help.'

'Nobody can help. It's too late now. I just wish I could let go, could move on, but the truth is, you never move on.'

'Tell me,' he says again,

She looks at him, trying to decide whether to trust him. She needs someone to trust.

'I was a teenager when I had my first child. I don't think I knew real love,' she starts slowly. 'Not before … not before he was born. I held him. I wasn't supposed to. But one of the nurses took pity on me and laid him on my chest.'

'You were a relinquishing mother?'

'I relinquished nothing,' she says angrily. 'My baby was stolen.'

Maroney reaches forward to hold her hands, his face contorts with concern.

'Just for a moment. I held him close to my face and breathed him in, and in that moment, I knew such love. In that one moment, it entangled every cell in my body and it never let me go — not for one single day of my life. I have needed him … so badly, I'm … I was so ashamed.'

'Surely not ashamed,' says Maroney softly. 'Love is something to be celebrated. Why ashamed?'

'My mother, and my father, but especially my mother. I felt I'd let them down. And my brother, and later even my daughter. Her birth was so precious to me but there was always a shadow hovering, accusing. I found myself scared of loving her, scared of the pain if I lost her. And my son, if I ever found him, would he want to know why I kept Annie when I gave *him* away?'

'What about Annie's father?'

Doog thinks about the boy she'd met when they were both travelling in Italy. He'd grown into a lovely man but her unspoken past worked holes into the threadbare cloth of their relationship. They'd tried to mend it for Annie's sake but eventually it unraveled. Maroney is waiting for an answer.

'Michael?' He was … *is* a good man but I … I think I was too stuck in the past, and we ... He's happy now, with someone else, and I'm pleased for him.'

'And now,' says Maroney. 'What about now, Doog? I've seen you with the station kids. They worship you. Your connection to them is extraordinary.'

Doog looks at this man. He's showing such compassion and she needs that right now. Her voice cracks as she tries to thank him.

'I dare to hope I am learning to love again … yes, I believe I do love those kids, but I'll tell you something that may sound strange. It scares the shit out of me.'

'It doesn't sound strange,' says Maroney, and she sees a far-away look come into his eyes.

They sit in silence, savouring the shiraz. 'I like this place,' she says at last. 'This probably sounds crazy but sometimes it feels like bits of me are falling off. There's something about this space that puts me back together' She feels a warm breeze and listens as it ruffles the tassels of casuarinas. The stars seem closer than ever.

Maroney gives a soft chuckle. 'Coming to a place like this was not on my list of things to do in this life. My friends had a battle to get me to go the outskirts of the city for a picnic. And forget about camping. Yet out here, without all the material comforts that I thought I couldn't live without, I'm more content, more at peace than I've ever been.'

Doog finds herself smiling. She tells him she knows what he means. The thought of being a nun sometimes seems appealing — a simple life, routine, and no needless possessions; life of study and contemplation, and perhaps gardening. She laughs and Maroney laughs with her and says he sometimes has similar thoughts, although certainly not as part of a religious institution.

Doog points her finger at him. 'The thing about religious institutions is that they usually have a library and a vineyard, two of life's absolute necessities.'

'Yes, you may have a point there, but nothing would tempt me to ever go back to one of those places.'

She leans forward in the half dark.

'Go back?' she says.

Maroney picks up her tobacco pouch and rolls a cigarette. He doesn't speak, but she can see he's trying to find the words.

'Call me snoopy, Snoopy, but I'd say it's about time you told me about you. My secrets are out. What about yours?'

He sucks on the cigarette and breathes out. His eyes closed. There's an almost imperceptible shake of his head. 'I'm sorry, Doog. There are things I have tried to forget, things that have been sneaking up on me lately but I haven't processed them, even to myself. I'm not ready to share Doog. I'm sorry,' he says again.

'God, don't be sorry. I know all about not being ready to share. And I'm grateful that you let me dump my baggage on you tonight. I hope it doesn't spoil our friendship.'

Doog knows two things. She has a precious new friend and she's not the only one with an unhealed wound.

A Dark Room

AFTER school the next day, Doog is keen to see how the photographs of the corroborree have turned out. Her mind keeps returning to the phone call from Matt this morning.

'The doc needs to come back down that way tomorrow, Doog. He'll give me a lift but Cassie's not ready to come home for a few more days.' He wanted Doog to go to Lonsdale with the Doc and accompany Cassie home. 'I really need to be there, Doog. I've got a hundred details to tick off before the campdraft.'

Doog's mind worked furiously. 'OK, Matt,' she had started slowly. 'But what about if I drive to Lonsdale and pick Cass up, then bring her home? It's less than three hours away.' There was silence on the other end of the phone.' That could work,' said Matt. 'As long as you're careful. I must admit that would get me off the hook. The doc's starting to grumble that I'm using him like a taxi. I had to remind him of the size of the donation Mrs Le Carre gave his mob last year.'

When she hung up the phone she wondered if Maroney might like to tag along. When he went to investigate the smaller holdings, he didn't make it as far as Lonsdale after hightailing it away from the abandoned station. She'll talk to him tonight at dinner. She'll have to organise Brenda or Mary to keep an eye on the kids while she's away.

Floating below the solution in the developing tray, the image grows like an organism in vitro. Doog gently strokes the photographic paper until the timer stops ticking and rings. With plastic tongs she lifts the image by the corner and plunges it into the stop-bath and then into the tray of fixative. When she has rinsed it, she holds up the print. It's a good one. She can see this even in the dim redness of the safelight. An image in a strip of negatives hanging from the line above the makeshift sink is lit from behind by the red light. It catches her eye and gives her a start. The negative gives Snow dark hair and light skin. He's a bit of a mystery, Snow. He's usually tinkering with one of the farm vehicles when she parks the ute or the Land Rover up at the shed. She stops to try and chat to him but he's painfully shy so it's mostly a one-way conversation: her telling him what the kids have been doing that day. He shows interest but as soon as she asks a question about his life, his head bobs under the bonnet of the vehicle as quick a rabbit down a hole. He's the right age but she puts that thought out of her mind. Her baby had dark hair.

One more and she'll get ready for dinner. She turns back to the proofs. One stands out from the proof sheet. As small as it is, she can see it has the contrast and movement that she's after. She positions the negative and switches on the enlarger. One monkey, two monkey … she shifts the cardboard mask over the photographic paper until she's completed a test strip. When she's satisfied with the timing, she exposes the negative: One monkey, two monkey … after seven seconds she flicks the switch of the enlarger and transfers the paper to the developing solution

This time she holds her breath. Yes! This is what she was hoping for. This is good. The light, the depth of field, the focus, everything has come together to bring the image of the dancers to life. After processing the image, the excitement of success throbs through her. She thinks again, *just one more*. One negative image is dark, especially one side. Hair, face, body. In the reversed world of the dark room, it looks like an Aboriginal man but it's one she took of Maroney at the gathering. Is there enough light to show the need, the excitement in his face, in his body?

She turns back to the enlarger and repeats the routine. The image is not quite strong enough. She'll push it. It will be grainy but that could help get the mood she's after. The face in the image slowly emerges. With a feather, she caresses the hair and over the brow, following the river of light that runs down the side of his face, through his body and into the reaching arms.

While she rinses the developing tank and wipes the rest of the equipment her eyes keep wandering to the image that hangs up to dry. Maroney comes across as easygoing, but there's an enigma lurking behind that boyish demeanor. When she had invited him into the darkroom, she caught a look of pure terror in his eyes before he recovered, made a lame excuse and raced off. What could he be afraid of? Not the chemicals, surely. Some people do say they're bad for your health, but no, there was something else that scared him, something he couldn't name. She wonders if he's claustrophobic in small spaces.

On his bed, Maroney lies awake and shudders at the thought of being shut in the windowless donga. Regret drains from him in a frustrated moan. He would love to have seen Doog developing her photographs. The excitement in her voice when she had described the process had captivated him. Now, just thinking of being shut in that iron box in the dark, starts panic perspiring from his body. Before he can escape, memories pounce. The sound of a key, the image of a figure in black entering the tiny room at the back of the shed, where he's been locked up for hours, the hooded figure watching, a switch in his hand, while he strips. Calling him the son of a whore. Cold and cowering, he feels the cut of the switch and sits bolt upright dragging air into his lungs, forcing his mind to go blank. He can't go on like this.

The images are becoming harder to control, intruding when he least expects them, fragmenting him with disgust and fear. He must have sounded lame and he groans again as he wonders what Doog is thinking. And he cares so much about what she's thinking. What she thinks about him.

He'd screwed up every relationship by letting his past control him, not having the ability to trust. He tenses as he hears Gina, his ex, screaming with frustration about how he never let her in, telling him she needed a partner she could connect to, said he had as much emotion as a pet rock. He doesn't want the same thing to happen with Doog.

He's at a crossroads — time to work out which direction to take.

Lonsdale

LONSDALE is a ramshackle collection of small shops and houses. Doog drops Maroney off at the motel where she's booked them each a room, and arranges to meet him for dinner. On the north side of the dusty town, she turns off the road into a long driveway lined with date palms. Her heart pounds, hot in her chest: she knows that driveway. She knows the high-set building with its wide wooden verandah … these wooden steps that she forces her legs to walk up.

Cassie sits up in bed, basking in the attention of the nurses and doctor. Her face dimples when she smiles. Like a lot of station children, she has no qualms about chatting to adults. They all love her. Doog stays long enough to hear all Cassie's news and tell her what happening back home. She has brought cards made by each of the children, all of them with drawings of snakes. On the way out, Doog stops at reception and waits impatiently while the receptionist quietly argues with a woman who wants to take her dog into hospital to visit her husband. The large clock on the wall ticks loudly, incessantly. She wants to jam the hands, stop time ticking. What if she could wind it back twenty-five years? Would she have done anything differently? No use beating herself up all over again. The girl at reception looks up and gives a sympathetic smile. Doog smiles and keeps waiting. How will she explain to this young thing what she wants? She couldn't bear to see judgment in another person's eyes. *For crying out loud what does it matter what she thinks?* It has to be worth a try. When the woman leaves with her labrador on a lead and her nose in the air, Doog walks to the counter, her gut churning, and hears her own voice crack.

'Do … do you keep records, like from way back, like twenty-five years?'

'Depends,' says the receptionist. 'What sort of records?'

'Patients … patients who came to this hospital.'

'We have record books, but jeez, that was before I was born.' The girl meets her eyes with voice, gentle and empathetic. 'Dunno really. Ask Matron maybe. I can make an appointment for you to see her at one tomorrow afternoon, if that's any good.'

Doog walks out onto the verandah and rolls a cigarette. The haze of smoke obliterates the sight of the obscene date palms.

At the motel, Doog dumps her handbag and grabs a towel. It's a short walk to the beach. She breathes in the sight of the coast. She has missed it; she hadn't realised how much. In this part of the world, where the desert meets the sea, the water is crystal clear. For twenty minutes she walks south along the deserted beach, then strips and wades out through reef-dotted shallows, swims away from the shore until the old memories of Lonsdale Hospital dissolve in the warm water. Face down, her eyes open to the warm briny water. Floating. Without clothes, without the weight of life dragging her down. Her body in naked isolation, her mind melding with the sea. Floating. Fingers stretched, arms stroking gently. Bringing the underwater world into focus like a print in her dark room. She rolls, face to the sky, eyes closed. Time drifts. When she looks up. She's still the same distance from the shoreline. She swims slowly to the beach, tries not to look back.

Except for the circular patterns of tiny white balls made by crabs. the beach is pristine. Like Western Desert dot paintings, she thinks, but stripped of colour. Her footprints defile the patterns and there's a twinge of regret but tonight the tide will erase all traces of her intrusion and the paintings will be recreated. Sundrenched specks of ilmenite glitter in the ebbing tide. She sinks back into the warmth of the sand and stares towards the lazy horizon. When she and Charlie were little, they spent a lot of the summer at the beach at Fremantle. Their mother would sit in the shade of the old kerosene store and imagine dark shapes in the water.

The dark shape Doog now sees is her young self, conforming to the claustrophobic strictures of 1960s Perth. Could she have been braver, tried harder? No, she's been over that a thousand times. She had been powerless against her parents and the church. There had been no way they were going to let her keep her baby. Under the unwavering gaze of the sun, she swallows the ire. She's thankful for Annie, for the kids, for her life. She'll stop seeing dark shapes.

Back at the motel, the day washes down the drain of the shower. The stream of water is a treat after the dribble at Bedarra. Wrapped in a sarong she heads to the pool, thongs flip-flopping between her heels and the pavement. It always feels strange now, not to be wearing boots. She collapses into a chair beside one of the outdoor tables around the pool, notebook in one hand and a glass of wine in the other. Blessed be the motel that has a bar, although attracting someone to serve you is not easy. She rolls a cigarette but before she lights up, she closes her eyes breathing in the heady perfume of the white and yellow blossoms of a frangipani spreading overhead. She knows she should stay with the freshness of the frangipani. Give up smoking. But she won't. Not yet.

A shadow blocks out the sun. 'Mind if I join you?' She opens her eyes and feels herself grow lighter as she smiles back at Maroney's gawky grin.

The next day, Doog spends the morning in the hospital playroom with Cassie. The nurses say she's doing well and can go home tomorrow. They'll miss her, they say, and Doog believes them. Cassie's bubbly but contentedly placid nature makes her irresistible. Doog wonders if she's like her mother because, unlike Jess, she sure doesn't take after Matt.

Just before one o'clock Doog walks up the corridor towards the matron's office. She concentrates on putting one foot in front of the other, can't turn back now. Anyway, what's she afraid of? That she won't find out anything, or that she will? A smart looking woman in plain clothes welcomes her into the office. No starched white uniform these days.

Through the window behind the matron is a view of the palm-lined driveway. Doog looks at the matron's face smiling happily from a frame on the desk, together with a man and two grown children, a boy and a girl, the perfect happy family. The matron introduces herself. Jean, Jean Carmody, she says. Not Matron Carmody. With an elegant wave of a smooth white hand, she indicates the seat on the opposite side of the desk. Her warm smile lifts Doog's hopes. When she starts to explain what she wants, her mind shuts down and the words get jumbled.

'I was here … before … as a patient.' Her voice falters. She picks up a pen and starts again.

'I want to know if …' Doog bites her lip only vaguely aware that her arms are out in front and both hands are around the matron's pen as if to snap it. She won't let herself break down. The woman will think she's mad.

The matron reaches across the desk and puts her own hand on Doog's. At last, Doog finds the words to tell the matron — Jean — what she wants, what she's hoping to find. Jean asks questions. *Does Doog have dates, names? Did she remember the doctor's name?* But Doog shakes her head. She'd never known the name of the doctor and can't remember any of the nurses' names.

She has written her name on a piece of paper, together with the date that is seared into her memory. She pushes it over the desk. Jean looks at it and chews her bottom lip. She looks thoughtful. Troubled.

'Excuse me a moment,' she says and heads into an adjoining room leaving Doog sitting in the empty office knowing there's a problem. Jean's body language had changed when she glimpsed the paper. Another dead end. What did she expect? But recognising the hospital felt like a good omen. Not that she believes in omens. But surely … this feels so close. Through the open door, Doog can see rows of metal shelves containing files and boxes.

When the matron returns, Doog can tell by the look on her face that there's no good news.

'I'm sorry,' she says. 'It's as I suspected. You see, my dear, there was a fire in the file room, some say deliberately lit, just a few years after you were here. It would appear that your records were among those destroyed.'

Doog tries not to cave in to disappointment.

'So, did they ever catch the person responsible?' she asks.

The matron shakes her head. 'I'm afraid not, my dear.' She stands, and Doog knows that she is dismissed. Empty-handed.

Lonsdale Library

BEFORE they pick Cassie up from the hospital at eleven the next morning Doog tells Maroney she wants to check something in the town's library. Maroney volunteers to pick up food and drinks for the drive back to Bedarra.

The Lonsdale Library is an old weatherboard house with a wide shady verandah in the middle of the small town. Despite the musty smell, the front room is as bright and cheerful as the young librarian who's tidying the children's corner when Doog arrives.

The breezeway up through the middle of the house is festooned with old black-and-white and sepia photographs in heavy black frames. Her eyes scan the faces in every frame while she follows the librarian. Through open doors on both sides of the breezeway, older books in drab covers retire on shelves. There's a photo of the hospital with the staff gathered on the front stairs dated 1946. Too old. They come to the back room devoted to local history.

Doog flicks through books and files. Most of them filled with the minutia of the small town, including mind-numbing accounts of council meetings and several books of recipes from grandmas or aunts. Another time she might have been interested to read the stories of early settlers and their encounters with the Indigenous people, but not now. She's about to give up when the librarian enters the room with a large book bound in maroon-coloured leather.

'I forgot,' she says, stroking the cover of the book. 'We left this in the meeting room after the historical society got together last night. It covers the period from after the war until about 1980. Tom Carter, our past president, put it together. It's quite detailed. I thought it might interest you.'

Doog hesitates before opening this last book. Her pulse quickens as she finds a chapter entitled: Lonsdale Hospital. The foxed pages reveal sepia and black-and-white images starting from the 1950s. One image seizes her attention — a group-photograph of the staff, taken sitting in front of the hospital in 1970. She forces herself to take a deep breath. She knows the faces of some of the nurses. She knows the face of the doctor at the centre, sitting on a chair in front of them. They are faces she has tried to forget. Small pale eyes behind rimless glasses take her back to the white iron bed. She stands and clutches the back of the wooden chair to steady herself. The faces, the smells, the clatter, the fear assail in the familiar rhythm of her nightmare. Her body arching up away from the operating table before the next avalanche of pain steals her last vestige of strength. Blinding lights, her arms strapped down, the invasive clinical hands, the utter humiliation of her legs hung in stirrups as if they were hell-bent on displaying that which was supposed to be so shameful. And then the sudden rush of warmth expelled between her legs … no more pain … drifting into the warm pink smell… a sound like a kitten mewing … immediately alert, reaching, loving, filled with a desire to hold.

Now panic threatens to consume her as again she feels the powerlessness of watching them take her baby away, strapping her wrists to the iron rails of the bed, the snake-eyed doctor looking down with a syringe. Anger rushes through her and she wants to open her mouth and howl, wants to tear the pages from the book and obliterate the names that swim beneath the photo. She forces herself to breathe as she walks over to the window and then returns to the table. With shoulders pulled back and teeth clenched, she picks up the book and takes it to the front desk.

'Can I get a photocopy of this?' She points to the picture and tries to keep her voice natural. 'Do you happen to know any of these people?'

'Yes, I do. That's my Aunty May.' The girl points and Doog's heart does a flip. 'But she died a couple of years ago.'

'Oh.' Doog can't hide her disappointment.

'Old Tom … Tom Carter, the one who put the book together, knows everything and everyone in this town. You could try talking to him.'

Drained and sweaty, Doog goes the library bathroom. There's still another couple of hours before she joins Maroney to pick up Cassie. She splashes water on her face and dries it with the hand towel that has crocheted edges probably done by a volunteer. She wonders if her mother still crochets for the Parish Women's Guild. She wonders if she ever thinks of her grandson.

Cassie talks non-stop as they start to drive back to Bedarra and then falls into a deep sleep on the back seat of the Land Rover.

'So, now that you can get a word in, tell me what you've been up to in Lonsdale.'

Maroney has been checking out the local newspaper, seeing how it's run these days. 'Computers are simplifying everything now which is a bit of a boon for these small country newspapers.' Doog keeps him talking on the subject, glad that he's not too curious about what she has been doing.

A couple more days in Lonsdale would have suited Doog. It would've been good to talk to Tom Carter. She called into Sunset Homes but he's visiting family in Geraldton. He's due home tomorrow when she'll be back at Bedarra. He must be a bit of a character. It was plain that the residents of the retirement village missed him. *Haven't had a decent laugh since he's been away*, one told her. *Calls us the Coffin Cheaters,* said another. *When did you say he was coming back, luvvy?*

Doog asked at all the local shops if they knew the doctor, but most of the people behind the counters were too young to remember, or care. Someone must know what happened to him but she's hit a brick wall and it will take time to dig under it. It would be interesting to know who else had their records destroyed in the fire? But any doubt about where her baby was born is now put to rest, so she has that to be grateful for.

Station routines are upset while preparations rev up for the campdraft. The kids are as noisy as a gumtree full of galahs. After steering them through the morning lessons of spelling, maths, reading and writing stories, Doog hopes to divert them with the activity she has been saving since before the snake bite. After lunch she ushers them into the schoolroom. On each of their little tables she has placed an empty sunshine milk tin scrounged from Mrs C. She has enlisted Col's help to cut a square hole in the side of each tin.

'Today we're going to make a camera,' she tells them.

Sam's arm shoots up and triumphantly punches the air, Cassie and Molly shout hooray. Jess and Jake stare at her.

The children gather around while Doog shows them her camera and they talk about how it works. Their eyes light up when she explains that today they'll be allowed to work in her darkroom, until now forbidden territory. Doog removes the lens from her camera and shows the children the hole and the shutter. She explains how the light bouncing off the image passes through the hole on to the film. It can do the same with the pinhole camera they are about to make.

'What do you think the shutter is for?' she asks. They look blank.

'It's like a little door,' she says. 'Like the one on my darkroom that I use to shut you lot out' She's rewarded by a giggle from Jake and wide eyes from the rest. 'What is shut out by the shutter?' she asks, and then gradually leads them to begin to understand how it works.

Holding up two black-and-white prints of kangaroos, Doog asks the children if they can see differences between the images.

'That one's fuzzy,' says Jess. The spark of interest from the girl gives Doog hope. It has been hard work trying to get her enthusiastic about anything, but Rosie seems to be making a difference. Jess is a capable student and does what's required but Doog aches to see her carefree and happy, as an eleven-year-old should be.

'Well spotted, Jess. Can anyone guess why it's fuzzy?'

Doog encourages the small group to think about movement. Movement of the camera or the subject.

'So, your first job is to choose what you're going to photograph with your pinhole camera,' she says. 'That's called your subject and it's good to start with something that doesn't move, so maybe not Rosie for your first shot.' They all start to look around and call out. 'No, don't tell me now. I'll give you ten minutes to walk around outside and decide, then come back and we'll make the camera.'

When the children straggle back inside, Doog shows them how to tape some foil over the hole in the tin.

'Now, you have to make another hole.' She demonstrates on a tin she's punctured beforehand. 'This time, a tiny one with this needle.'

After they make the hole, she herds them over to the darkroom. where they'll insert the photographic paper. The little group crowd into the donga unusually silent as she shows them the tanks where they will develop and wash their prints.

'Then we have to hang them up to dry,' she says pointing to the line stretched across the donga with pegs. They all giggle when she turns off the light and they look at each other in the red safe-light. She has decided to let them shoot and develop their first photo before they talk more about how it all works. That will be for another day.

The Day Before The Campdraft

ON the Friday before the campdraft Doog and the kids meet in the shearing shed to hang the artwork. It's a shearing shed in name only these days. Except for a few self-shedding sheep kept for meat, the station runs only cattle. On a platform at the back of the large shed a line of shearers once hung from slings. Now, the platform is the stage for social occasions. The baling equipment lies rusting out the back but the sorting tables have been kept for serving food.

The children's artwork animates the corrugated-iron walls. They've created life-sized portraits of themselves complete with collaged rodeo outfits. There's a lot of bling. Not just from the girls. Last week Doog had taped pieces of paper together so each child could lie down and draw outlines of their bodies. They had painted, glued and collaged fabric on to the figures to depict an outback fashion extravaganza. Next, each child was given another large paper on which to draw a station animal. Now five horses complete with glittering bridles and collaged saddles hang on the walls while patterns and mobiles of painted leaves hanging from the rafters and over the doorway wave in the breeze.

Once the artwork is hung, there is no more school for the day. The children are as skittish as a mob of emus while they wait for their friends to arrive. Doog's praying they'll keep out of trouble. She needs to finish the preparations but her job of organising the spectators and helping with the social side of things is not hard.

This is the most important event on the station calendar, and as a new chum she's enjoying being trusted to be a crucial part of it.

The arena at the mustering yards, about 200 metres from the homestead, has old post-and-rail fences still standing from the start of the century, obviously strong and very high. Matt had told her the northwest cattle of the past were even bigger than the huge animals on the station today.

The folk out in this country, black and white, are more comfortable on the back of a horse than anywhere else. Horses, steers and bulls, many of them from the surrounding stations, fill the yards behind the arena. The children are squealing as their friends from Distance Ed arrive. Doog has to stop herself from crying out when she spies them prancing around far too close to horses, cows and enormous bulls.

Over to the other side, bright blue capsules, portaloos, hired from Sandy Bay, stand like a row of aliens in the sunburnt paddock. She heads towards them to make sure they are all well stocked with loo-paper and towels. A few guests have already set up their marquees with the requisite Eskies on top of picnic tables and she pauses to chat as she passes the roped-off area.

Many are camping in the home paddock beyond the loos. The people in from the other stations come with portable fencing for their horses. Some are metal rails but some string up electric fencing to make small enclosures. Most of the horses wear blankets of checkered misery — it's too hot but it keeps them clean. There are caravans and tents, but many of the station folk have horse floats akin to road trains with accommodation up front. Doog's glad they're well away from the staff quarters. The word is that some of the young ones party well into the night and things end up messy. Dust billows from the long strip of land roped off down the far side of the mustering yards where the riders practise for the events.

On the way to the shearing shed she sees Maroney shifting bales of hay for seating during the Saturday night shindig. He's handling them with ease. *He's fit for a journalist,* she thinks, and immediately rebukes herself with a smile. *What would you know about how fit journalists are?* He's gazing towards her but she pretends not to see him. Needs to get on, still got things to tick off her to-do list.

Bruce grabs her arm as she passes and ignores her protests while he steers her towards the stage.

'Need someone to test the mike with me, Doog. Wanna stand by your man?'

'I told you before, you're not my man, Bruce,' she says screwing up her face.

'I'm crushed,' he says with a brawny hand on his heart as he pushes her up the steps.

She and Bruce had made a fool of themselves singing one night when everyone got a bit merry at the evening meal — Koop's birthday, she remembers. He hasn't forgotten. He's ready with a blanket and Cassie's teddy bear in his arm. The others gather round and there's no way she's getting out of it.

The microphone crackles and makes ear-splitting whistles. Doog sees Maroney sit down on a hay bale he's maneuvered into place. He leans towards the stage, his elbows on his knees, face propped in his hands. Watching. The microphone settles and Bruce sprawls against a crate, legs out in front, pretending to upend a King-Brown beer bottle. She bends over him and starts to sing 'Stand by your Man', trying not to convulse into giggles as he slides to the floor. She covers him and gives him the teddy while she sings about giving him two arms to cling to and belts out the final lines.

Before anyone can make a fuss, Bruce grabs the microphone. He waves one of the King-Browns around and starts imitating Slim Dusty, singing 'I'd Love to have a Beer with Col' in his deep voice. He's changed all the words, and as the verses go on everyone gets a mention, even Snow who turns red all the way to the top of his ears as people turn to look at him.

Doog laughs as she watches the communal clowning of the staff. It's good to laugh ... and forget other things for a while.

Maroney walks over to her as Bruce finishes. Everyone claps and cheers and Koop yells that Bruce should be the lead act tomorrow night. Bruce is protesting and saying *No bloody way*, but you can tell he's pleased.

Maroney leans over and whispers, 'Tammy Wynette, eat your heart out.'

She rolls her eyes. 'So, what are you doing on Saturday night?

'What do you mean?'

'Everyone on the station is expected to perform. Can't come to a party and not contribute.'

She holds up her clipboard with the list of names. 'Look. Koop's on guitar, Mrs C's singing a song with the girls. Think about it.

'Snow,' she calls. 'Got a moment?'

Snow's permanent look of fear turns to terror when she asks him the same question.

'Come on, Snow, you must be able to play something. What did you do at school? We've got a clarinet here somewhere.'

Snow shakes his head. 'No,' he says. 'But ...'

'But?' She's no letting go. 'But?'

Snow's looking terrified and she's starting to feel sorry for him. 'I ... I can play the didge.'

Now it's her turn to be surprised. 'Right,' she says and writes *didgeridoo* next to his name. 'Lookin' forward to it, Snow.'

At the front of the shed the barbeques and the spit are all ready to be fired up first thing tomorrow. Connor's taking care of that.

He did a great job last year and people kept him topped up with his favourite tipple so he's more than happy to take it on again.

Doog ticks things off her list: microphone, spare leads, coloured lights. There's a freezer full of ice in the big shed and another up in a shed near the grandstand. People bring their own picnics but there'll be a pig and two lambs on spits and plenty of steak, sausages and chops for the barbecue. Mrs C. is bound to have a table in the shearing shed close to collapsing under the weight of cakes and other goodies. Nobody will go hungry.

A thin moon smiles cream against the violet sky. It's dinner and an early night for her. As she walks back towards her donga the low hills beyond poke their breasts towards the sunset. Maroney catches up with her and wants to know what Matt will be doing while the rest of the staff is buzzing around like blowflies in a dunny. Station lingo is rubbing off onto him.

'Matt's up to his expressive eyebrows sorting out the events. It's all very serious.' She leans closer. 'Matt has to sort out the buckles and ribbons for the winners and runners-up.'

Maroney scowls as she defends Matt and she smiles. They pause for a moment to watch some of the station hands practising over in the long paddock, weaving in and out of forty-four-gallon drums and sending the horses careering around sticks.

'Bloody Norah!' Maroney exclaims. Col's upside-down reaching from his horse, almost to the ground, to pluck small flags from the earth while he gallops flat out. Doog realises it's making her heart race as well.

'I've got no idea what to expect tomorrow,' he says as they walk back to the staff quarters. 'I'm counting on you for some great photos. You'll be well paid for any the paper accepts.'
She pulls a face at him. 'Hmm, I could do without that pressure, you know, Snoopy.' But she can't help smiling.

Campdraft

ON the day of the campdraft, the station hands on the first shift slouch in to the kitchen. It's not yet 6am but Mrs C is ready with the tea brewing in the pot.

'Where's Matt?' says Bruce. 'I thought he'd be first here this morning,' he grumbles as he pours himself some tea.

'He and his sister are having breakfast with the aristocracy up at the marquee,' says Mrs C with a sniff of her out-of-joint nose. 'They brought their own chef.'

'Hope his sister doesn't talk Mrs Le Carre into buying her wine. That'll be the end of Matt's job,' says Koop with a grin.

'I'll just have toast,' says Snow. 'Not that hungry this morning.'

'Here, get that into you, you'll be needing it, trust me.' Mrs C pushes a plate of fluffy scrambled eggs over the table.

Mrs C has been doing this job for a long time. She knows the *boys* won't be in the mood for the usual belly-extending feast. She has made a light breakfast with stacks of buttery toast to tempt nervous stomachs. Except for the scrapes of knives and forks on plates and the slurping of tea, there is silence. After the usual three strong cups, the staff straggle out to the back verandah.

Now they have been fed, the men might be awake enough to talk. Maroney tries to ask questions about the campdraft. They pull on their boots and give inaudible mutterings and grunts.

'Weather's good for the campdraft,' he says cheerily to Bruce, who raises his head with a blank look on his face, nods and keeps attaching his spurs. The men pick up their hats and head for the stockyards.

'For a festive occasion I don't sense much festivity. That lot look like they're off to a funeral.'

'Nothin', love, just nerves,' says Mrs C, who's come out to fetch an armful of wood from the box on the verandah. 'They might appear to be cocky as galahs most days, but you think about it. How would you feel if you were about to go out and perform in front of Matt and the boss lady, and you thought the honour of the station was depending on how you rode?'

'So, it's all pretty competitive?'

Mrs C throws back her head and lets out a guffaw. 'Competitive? That's the understatement of the year. You obviously don't know how much effort and money goes into these events. These horses', she adds, 'aren't just any old hacks for the station hands to check the fences with. They're the best Australian stock horses money can buy.'

'I hear it's horses only at round-up?'

'Yep, Mrs Le Carre won't have any motorbikes or other vehicles on the property. Reckons it damages the place, them crisscrossing and leaving tracks. Insists they use horses only for working the cattle so the hands get lots of practice.'

When Mrs C disappears back into the kitchen, Maroney sits on the small verandah at the back pulling on his boots. No need to hurry, he decides. He pulls out his notebook to catch up on his notes before he walks up to investigate all the activity at the stockyards.

Up in front of the arena, a row of marquees has sprung up next to the large one erected for Mrs Le Carre and her entourage. There's no sign of the owner yet, but a chef tends a stainless-steel barbeque and sitting at a table draped with a white cloth are Matt and his sister.

141

Maroney walks past, waving good morning and is close enough to see they're attacking what looks like eggs benedict on ciabatta with smoked salmon complete with garnish. At the end of the thoroughfare, he turns, looks around and watches for a moment. He's trying to get a handle on this gathering. It's obviously a big deal. But who knows whom, and how many blow-ins are there? He passes two men leaning on a fence, talking in loud voices. 'Be buggered,' one says to the other.

Before coming to Bedarra, he'd never heard of a campdraft and wonders whether this well-kept secret that seems to be a quintessential part of station life has any part in the tourist industry, or is it strictly local? If he's not careful, he thinks, he could find himself on the travel pages writing articles for the growing grey-nomad market.

A crowd begins to settle into the other marquees with huge Eskies, chairs and picnic tables. People have come from stations and small towns, some over two hundred kilometres away. The small grandstand on the other side of the arena with an Australian flag flying on top, also fills up. The festive hum in the air drowns the ringing of cicadas. Over to one side, riders warm up, thundering up and down the paddock, weaving between posts sticking up from the baked earth. Dry leaves and twigs snap and crackle beneath his feet as he walks over the mat of oatmeal-coloured couch grass. Dung-laced dust clouds the air and coats his nostrils. Lucky for him he doesn't mind the grassy smell of horse dung. Another story is seeding itself in his mind.

Koop passes and kicks a clod of earth with his boot. 'Dry as a dead dingo's donger,' he remarks with his crooked smile.

Everything looks in place. Doog knows she's done all she can but she walks around rechecking. Her camera hangs around her neck, and she's starting to relax enough to think about taking a few shots. This place is a menagerie of young good-looking men.

They are different shapes and colouring but they all have a tanned, athletic look. She gazes into each face not sure what's she's hoping to see.

Matt's at the bar near the end of the grandstand, looking hassled. He sees her and calls her over.

'Doog, the bloody lead from the freezer to the generator out the back is a mess. Don't want anyone tripping over it, pulling it out. Warm beer would be a fucking disaster.'

No please or thank you, not even a smile. She wants to snap her heels to attention and say, *Yes boss, anything you say boss. Three fucking bags full, boss.* She knows the tension's getting to him so she lets it go.

A group of men is standing around the bar, even though it's not open. She takes a mental photo and gets a satisfaction out of entitling it *Natural Habitat of the Male of the Species.* After she has attended to the lead, she pauses, leaning for moment on the rail of the long paddock. A striking young rider on an equally striking horse practises galloping at top speed, zigzagging in and out of a row of forty-four-gallon drums.

Doog continues towards the events ring and stops by a post to reattach a sign pointing to the loos. After that she strides up the thoroughfare when the young rider from the long paddock passes leading his magnificent horse.

'Oi!' She yells. He turns. 'You're supposed to lead horses round the back of the ring. We don't have time to be picking up dung from the pedestrian area. You must know that.'

He tips his hat and gives her a contemptuous smirk. 'Aye, Aye, Missus Boss-Lady, I'll remember next time,' and he keeps walking in the same direction.

'Young man,' she hisses loudly to his back so that he turns again. 'You can call me Doog or Ms Wilson, but if you ever call me Missus Boss-Lady again, I'll take to your balls with an elastrator.'

She sees the smirk replaced by a bemused look on his face before she flounces off.

Her confrontation with the cheeky young rider has thrown her. She knows she came on too strong but his arrogance had aggravated her. Back to the shearing shed to check on the catering. Then her job is finished until the evening

She glances at her watch. Almost time for the events to begin. She has the list of names of the male riders. She'll cross off those that look too young or too old. She's not sure about colouring. Surely someone born with dark hair can't turn into a redhead like herself but she's heard that it's not uncommon for dark-haired babies to turn blond.

Blundstones and Akubras

THE spectators interest Maroney more than what's happening in the ring. The older men in their jeans, elastic-sided boots and Akubra hats, often leaning against a post with a beer in hand, are the Australian cliché. The younger men and the women in similar attire are more likely to be occupied rubbing down the horses, helping the kids with their animals, carting water. Outside the shearing shed he has a long yarn to Connor. He's an interesting old cove. Maroney doesn't want to risk intruding but he has to wonder why a man leaves his country and everything he knows to ends up in the middle of nowhere. 'I've heard Paul is into some pretty radical farming practices,' he says.

'You'll need to come over and see for yourself,' says Connor. 'That lad understands this country. The results speak for themselves.' The old man's voice sings with enthusiasm as he tells Maroney what Paul has done. Maroney wonders about Paul, a young bloke like him living such a secluded life. Apparently, he has been through environmental studies at uni. Maroney wants to meet him, perhaps interview him.

He leaves Connor and continues up towards the grandstand, his eyes automatically scanning for Doog. He spots her under a tree at the far end of the row of portaloos. Even from here he can see from the way her thin body caves in on itself that something is on her mind. She's greedily sucking on a cigarette, but she straightens up when he approaches and greets him with a tepid smile.

'Are you OK?'

'Yeah, just had a run-in with a young bloke and then found out it was Paul from Pardee. I probably should have kept my mouth shut but his arrogance got right up my nose.'

'Then he'll be the type to have forgotten about it, so you should too.'

'I was just coming over,' she says. 'It must be almost time for the open to start.'

'Yeah,' he says. 'I watched a bit of the juniors and the novices, but I can't really see what the point is.'

'I think you'll find the open more exciting. Keep your eye on the horse after the rider cuts the steer out of the yard. The aim is to maneouvre the steer around those two pegs in a figure of eight.' Doog points to the open ground beyond the ring. 'And then the steer needs to go through those two pegs over there — that's the gate. They only have forty seconds.'

They prop themselves against the fence as a group of steers is let into the yard. The first rider, hesitating only a few seconds, indicates a small white steer and cuts it away from the rest. At one stage the rider has it on its own before it bolts and returns to its mates. Once again, man and horse work as one until they separate the steer and follow it out of the yard. Maroney finds himself silently urging the man to succeed. The steer charges away again and the horse springs into action, twisting and turning, nudging the steer on the course around the two pegs. The man, the horse and the steer seemed locked in a battle of wills until the steer, eyes rolling with panic, races through the gate and is left in peace.

'That horse's backbone must be made of rubber,' he yells to Doog. 'The way it bends and twists at that speed is unbelievable.'

'That's an Australian stock horse, been bred for cattle drafting since settlement. They're strong but agile. Just about all the horses you see here are stock horses, except Paul's of course. Trust him not to conform.'

'That could be a trait to be admired,' he says, and smiles as she screws up her nose.

'Well, I bet that young smartarse doesn't do anything much in the campdraft. He might do all right tomorrow in the rodeo events, that's what the quarter horse is more suited to.' Doog recognises her animosity towards Paul is unreasonable. She needs to lighten up. 'It's the campdraft that counts around here,' she continues. 'A lot of the old diehards reckon the rodeo is just a bit of fun while everyone gets over their hangovers. Too American for their taste. Mind you, I've heard it's catching on around the tracks.'

They stop talking to watch Bruce go through his event. The head stockman shows he's worthy of the job, guiding the steer around the course without fault. Maroney thinks about the origins of the campdraft, a competition to let the stockmen prove their skill. He's glad to see Doog's clicking away with her camera as she weaves around the other spectators to get the best angles.

'I think that could be our winner,' she says.

Next comes Paul, and to Maroney's eyes, he matches Bruce's performance.

'No, not as smooth,' declares Doog, but he notices she can't resist taking some shots of the young rider who strikes an impressive pose on his handsome bay mare. They watch several more riders before Doog decides it's time to make sure everything is in place for the big night.

'I need to speak to Mrs Le Carre,' she says, but then she spots the next rider. 'That's the new bloke, Snow. I'll stay awhile.'

The five young steers are let into the yard where Snow sits on his horse waiting. Maroney looks at Doog. All her concentration is directed towards Snow.

'Please, let him at least cut the steer into the outer yard,' she murmurs.

The slight figure sits very still on a young colt named Solly. Maroney knows from the dinner-table talk that the snow-white colt is a good one. At least the blokes put him on a decent horse. Probably chosen to match his hair. What's he doing? Snow sits, neither man nor beast moving a muscle. The only movement comes from his eyes as they flick from the horse to the cattle and back again.

At last, Snow almost imperceptibly nods at the black steer. Man and horse spring into motion and in seconds the steer is separated and into the yard. He sees Doog snap several shots. There's a collective gasp from the crowd as horse and rider move in one sinuous body nudging the steer around the posts and through the gate. It's all over —in what? Seconds — it feels like seconds. The crowd is going wild.

'Bloody hell!' He yells. 'I know nothing about campdrafting but that looked good to me.'

But when he turns, Doog's not there and he sees her and her camera following Snow as he heads out of the ring with his saddle in his arms.

The Ball

DOOG wants to congratulate Snow but a small crowd has gathered. The young stockman strikes an awkward pose, while his hand is grabbed and his back is slapped. She can see he's uncomfortable being the centre of attention. What makes him so shy, she wonders? Jean Le Carre has risen with others in the grandstand clapping for Snow. Doog walks over and introduces herself. This is the first time they have met. How dare the woman exude so much elegance and charm in jeans and a checked shirt?

'Call me Jean.' Mrs Le Carre shakes her hand warmly.

The conversation starts with Snow's performance and then Doog explains the night's program. The station owner will need to welcome everyone and later announce the results of the campdraft. Doog gives her a brief background on the program for the night and then feels herself suddenly wilting. Her duties are over for this part of the day. As soon as is polite she takes her leave, blowing relief through her lips she heads towards her donga.

The water from the shower washes away the dust of the day. Despite her exhaustion, Doog's mood has been lifted by Snow's performance. She hopes she took some good shots of him. He's a nice young bloke, quiet and unassuming but she senses loss. He's like a photo taken in low light, too hard to pull into sharp focus. Out of the shower, drying her body with a towel, her mind turns to Maroney. She can't deny she's enjoying having him here and she knows he enjoys her company, but what's he hiding. There's a mystery. She knows there is. When she had asked him about performing tonight, he looked like a cornered brumby. She had asked him if he'd learned an instrument as a kid ... everyone did ... 'A recorder if nothing else,' she had said. She wasn't going to let him off the hook. 'It's just for a laugh, Maroney. Everyone makes a fool of themselves. What about the piano? The drums. The band wouldn't mind lending theirs ... or a guitar.' But every time he had shaken his head until she had spoken in frustration. 'Jesus, Snoopy, what sort of childhood did you have?' And he had turned away with half a smile, the most wistful half-smile she'd ever seen.

By the time Doog returns to the shearing shed, most people are standing around the barbeques or sitting on hay bales or picnic rugs, holding plates of food. All clean and spruced-up ready for the night, everyone looks relaxed and happy. The band starts playing and people drift into the shed. It fills with bodies, male and female, in a uniform of blue jeans and checked shirts. A few of the girls have mail-order rodeo outfits, bling-decorated hats, boots and flared skirts with low-cut necklines and tight bodices.

Inside the shed, the smell of hay is sweet after the sausage and onion smell of the barbeques. The place has been transformed with coloured lights and the kids' artwork — they were so proud of themselves. The tables look ready to collapse with the desserts and cakes Mrs C has loaded on them. Even Matt looks relaxed, beer in hand and a smile on his face. She pours herself a glass of bubbly and walks across to where Maroney is just finishing his steak burger.

'A quickie behind the shed, Snoopy?' She taps the pack of tobacco sticking out of her breast pocket. She loves it when he breaks into that broad smile of his.

'I'll give them half-an-hour and then I'll start the proceedings.' She looks up at the starry sky and drags the smoke into her lungs. 'I'll be glad when this part's over.'

'Where're the kids?' Maroney props himself against an old baling machine. Doog assures him they're in their element. 'Most of their little mates from Distance Ed are here. Kath Grey from Caloona Creek is letting them stay with her kids in their tent tonight. They'll be doing their bit on stage later on. Then Kath will put them to bed.' Doog doesn't envy her. Those kids are as crazy as cockatoos tonight. She stubs out her cigarette and drains her glass.

'Wish me luck,' she says.

'Break a leg,' Maroney calls as she walks away.

'Not appropriate for a campdraft, Snoopy.' She smiles but doesn't turn around.

Doog takes up the microphone and calls for attention. First, the routine but necessary chore of explaining the toilet and camping arrangements, the fire-safety rules, the location of first aid. She knows that nobody will be listening.

When she turns to introduce Jean Le Carre, Doog tries to hide her astonishment. The station-owner's get-up is breathtaking. A red cowgirl-style gown with a stand-up collar and long sleeves. The V-necked bodice plunges between her breasts and hugs her figure. The beaded, embroidered outfit sparkles as she glides across the stage in red high-heeled boots and an Akubra-style hat. Now, everyone is listening.

Doog sneaks a look at Maroney. His eyes and mouth are open. No wonder the media is banned. The only images of Jean Le Carre, on TV or in the papers, show her as the epitome of elegance and understated taste. The images are far from this vision of excess that has every male eye glued to her as she takes the microphone and flicks back her thick, honey-coloured fringe. Matt had said that the boss likes to *let her hair down* at the annual campdraft. And why not?

Jean Le Carre welcomes the visitors and thanks everyone at the station. Doog can't help nodding and smiling with admiration. No one is missed out. The woman's low sexy voice makes even this humdrum part of the speech interesting.

'Now let's see everyone dancing.' The station-owner calls over the microphone, and nods to the band.

When the band takes a break, she calls on various people to perform. After the girls and Mrs C have finished 'How Much is that Doggie in the Window?', it's Bruce's turn to sing, with Koop accompanying him on the guitar. They are at their clowning best and the crowd calls for more. Doog disappears before Bruce spots her. She is not singing tonight. Behind the shed she's enveloped in darkness and the feeling of peace the night sky always brings. The band and the voices seem far away. She'd like to stay here. Tonight, she doesn't belong inside the shed. She's not in the mood for merriment and she's finding it hard to fake. Her mind keeps returning to Lonsdale. She's glad she made the trip. Even without the records, she knows that's where she gave birth and she hugs the knowledge that she has come to the right region.

Back inside, Doog holds up her hands for quiet. She calls for Matt to announce the results, and Jean Le Carre to present the trophies. They go through the junior and the women's events and she can feel the crowd holding its breath as Matt breaks into an envelope with the results of the open. A fleeting look of surprise appears on his face.

'In third place,' he announces. 'Bruce McKay on his trusty steed, Galahad.'

Doog smiles as Bruce with a face like pickled pork, accepts the ribbon. That means ...

'In second place, we have Paul Gorski from Pardee, riding Tilda.' A loud whistle comes from a mate of Paul's, and she hears

Connor. 'Well done, my boy,' but Paul doesn't look any more pleased than Bruce as he accepts the ribbon.

Matt steps close to the microphone again. 'It seems at Bedarra, for the past few months, we've had a secret weapon in our midst that we didn't even know about. He's been hiding his light under the bonnet of a ute.'

All eyes turn to Snow, and a couple of people nudge the young stockman closer to the stage. Wary eyes look up from under his heavy brow. He looks ready to turn and run.

Matt's voice rises as he announces: 'Ladies and gentlemen, the winner of this year's open campdrafting event is Alexander, better known as Snow Kent, from Bedarra, on Solly.'

Doog almost feels sorry for Snow as he slinks onto the stage, but he can't hide his pleasure while he accepts the belt-buckle trophy.

'Not so fast, young man,' says Jean Le Carre in her husky voice, pinning Snow with her eyes as he tries to go. 'Now that we've managed to get you up on this stage, we're not letting you escape just yet I've been told you play the didgeridoo.'

Snow shakes his head as Doog pushes forward with the didge that Koop has ferreted out of Snow's room. The young stockman looks helplessly at the cheering crowd and back to her. She gives him a wink of encouragement.

Still shaking his head, he walks over to the front corner and crosses his legs before letting his body gracefully concertina onto the stage floor. There's a hush from the crowd as he holds the instrument out in front and lifts one end to his mouth. The sound that reverberates off the tin walls of the shed takes Doog by surprise.

The slow rhythmic drone becomes faster and faster then abruptly switches to the high-pitched sound of a kookaburra laugh and back to the drone again. She looks around. The people in the audience nod their heads, tap their feet and smile with obvious delight. When the sound changes to the thumping of an emu, one of the band members joins in with the drums and gradually the whole band follows with the audience clapping and stamping in time. The bashful young man has the whole crowd with him. When they stop, Doog crosses to the stage and whispers to Snow. He agrees to her request and she beckons to a young boy in the audience.

'Everyone, this is Jake,' she announces, as Jake leaps onto the stage.

The boy flings his white shirt to one side and moves in a slow dance. Spindly legs sprout from black footy shorts like the legs of a jabiru. Snow starts the low drone again and Jake moves gracefully around the stage. His stick-thin legs bend at the knees and his feet prance and stamp. Doog could swear his arms are made of rubber.

As if there's a telepathic line between himself and Snow, the boy gradually changes from twisting and turning, to hopping with arms held up in front. The didgeridoo copies with a hopping and clicking sound, stopping as the boy stops to look around like a watchful kangaroo. The pair incarnates one animal after another. The audience immediately recognises the emu, a howling dingo, a screeching cockatoo and a hissing snake. By the end of the performance, Snow is gasping for breath and Doog's convinced that after tonight much of his shyness will have disappeared.

The crowd claps Snow and Jake off the stage. Both of them look happy and proud, and Doog feels a flood of relief. Her job is over for the night. But before she retires to her donga, she walks around the campground. Most of the young ones are still in the shed dancing but many of the older ones sit around campfires drinking and yarning. Faces glow along with the fires. The warm night rings with festivity. Each time she pauses to say hello, Doog is offered a chair and a drink and more food.

"If I eat anymore, I'll burst.' She laughs as she accepts a glass of wine.

'Do you mind if I jot down your names.' I'm trying to remember who's who and where they come from but there are so many people here, I'm finding it hard.' Nobody appears to care and everyone is more than happy to talk about their families and where they're from.

'Young Harry Hooper did well today,' she says. 'He was only a whisker behind Bruce.'

'Yeah,' said a man pushing a mallee root onto the fire. 'Got a good horse. He'll be one to watch when he's got a bit more experience under his belt.'

'How old is he?' Doog asks.

'Twenty-three the man's wife says. 'Still remember the day he was born. I knew he'd be a good 'un.'

Doog crosses Harry Hooper off her list.

Rodeo

THE dawning sun shoots pale gold flares upwards as Doog jogs east towards the waterhole. The rhythm of her trainers on the hard track and from the shadows dancing from branches singing with cicadas usually make her mind drift, trance-like.

It always surprises her how running often brings the answer to a problem like an unbidden blessing. While she travels through the landscape consciousness becomes redundant. It's a process she has learned to trust.

But this morning the meditative state eludes her. Her mind hooks back to the campdraft, willing to bet that it would have infuriated Paul that Snow beat him. He'll be determined to be king of the heap today. The three-mile windmill is where she stops to do a few yoga stretches before turning around. Shit! She forgot to light the candle. She never forgets to light the candle.

Breakfast on rodeo day is a barbeque. Great trays of cooked steak, sausages and bacon are already on the table, with more sizzling on the hotplates. A line of women stands heaping fried tomatoes and mushrooms on to plates and waving at flies. She joins Maroney in the queue and they accept a spoonful of each.

'Don't ya want some meat, darl?' A thickset woman with tongs in her hand waves an enormous steak at Maroney. He smiles and shakes his head.

'That's not enough to keep a chook alive.' She looks at his plate and glares.

'I'll grab some eggs,' he assures her, and they walk over to where Connor is cooking eggs to everyone's preference.

'How d'you loike 'em?' It's plain to see the little Irishman is revelling in the job.

'Bleeding,' says Maroney, 'but could you turn them over?'

'Same for me,' Doog says.

'Bleedin' eggs, sunny-side down, coming up.' Connor strikes a professional pose with his egg slice.

'You like your eggs the same way as me,' says Maroney with a gawky grin. 'That makes us compatible.'

'Indubitably.' She raises her coffee cup to him and walks towards a hay bale, carrying her plate, feeling a warm flush of contentment.

Maroney follows with his plate and mug of coffee. 'What do you think my chances are of getting an interview out of Jean Le Carre?'

'Yesterday, my guess would have been between none and Buckley's but she was in a pretty good mood last night. You might get lucky.'

'If I could pull that off, I'd be golden boy with the editor. He might give me …'

'Might give you what?' Asks Doog when he doesn't go on.'

'Oh, um, more time up here, perhaps.'

Only the clinking of utensils disturbs their comfortable silence while they finish their breakfast and Doog knows it has been a long time since she has felt so at ease around anyone. She stands up, brushing the hay from her skirt.

'It's worth a try but I wouldn't get your hopes too high,' she says. 'Anyway, gotta go — things to do.' She walks towards the yard ignoring the urge to run back and tell him how much she likes being with him and tell him how she's dreading the day he says he has to leave.

The rodeo will start at ten o'clock with the junior events, followed by the ladies and the open. She wants to stay for the junior events and is thankful that Matt hasn't encouraged Jess or Cassie to participate. It's all a bit rough for her liking, but Jake and young Sam will take part. Jake was junior champion boy last year and although it will scare the hell out of her, she wants to cheer them on, take their photos. There will be dummy roping, bending and barrel races, steer wrestling and a list of other events where contestants can try to kill themselves. After that, she plans to escape to the waterhole with her book before its time to come back to take photographs of the final events. She mustn't miss the bull riding.

Snow sits alone up on the mini-grandstand watching the junior events. Maroney slides along the bench beside the spare-looking lad who keeps his gaze on the arena.

'That was quite a display you put on yesterday.' He leans forward with his elbows on his knees, smiling, trying to catch Snow's eye. The young man's expression remains wary.

'Where did you learn to ride like that?'

'Here and there,' comes the short reply.

'What? Did you grow up on a farm?'

Snow turns to face him. His prominent forehead descends into a frown and Maroney notices the nostrils of his broad nose flare slightly.

'Listen mate,' Snow says in his velvety voice. 'I appreciate you have a job to do, but leave me out of it, OK? I need to go … start warming up my horse.' He gets to his feet.

'Fair enough, mate. I've been baptised Snoopy around here, but I don't snoop where I'm not wanted. Good luck for the rodeo.' He watches Snow pick his way through the crowd and walk in the opposite direction from the horse paddock. This doesn't surprise him; it's too early to warm the horses for the open yet. He needs to drop it but an overwhelming curiosity and something about Snow's face is niggling. He feels a tap on his shoulder.

'Ten out of ten for discretion,' purrs the voice of Jean Le Carre. She puts out a small, exquisitely manicured hand. 'I am just going back to my marquee. Would you like to join me? Is it late enough to respectably have a gin and tonic, do you think?'

Walking towards the marquee, Maroney's in a whirl. What could she want with him? He tells himself not to be ridiculous and she's just being friendly. This could be his chance to interview her but he's not ready, damn it. A tribal rug lies in casual opulence on the marquee floor. At the back of marquee, he catches sight of a large Esky all but hidden by a screen. They settle into commodious canvas chairs and Jean Le Carre waves her hand as Willie emerges from behind the screen with a bottle of Bombay Sapphire dripping with condensation. She slices a lime and mixes drinks in crystal glasses on a small side table.

'Don't spare the gin,' Jean Le Carre commands with a smile, and waits until Willie has handed them drinks.

'Ten out of ten for ambience,' he says, looking around to see where the soft country music is coming from.

'Mr — may I call you Maroney?'

'Of course,' he says, nodding and holding up his glass.

They clink glasses and Jean Le Carre meets his eyes with a smile. 'You may think being one of the world's richest women is loads of fun,' she says. 'But mostly it's damned hard work and long hours. Things have a way of growing, and before you know it, you have more responsibilities than you ever asked for. This is one of the few places I can truly relax.'

'And I absolutely respect that, Mrs Le Carre.'

'Please call me Jean, Maroney. I read the piece you wrote about the snake-bite incident. You spun a good yarn, and you managed to put in information about what to do in that situation, without preaching. People shouldn't die of snake bite in this country. But ignorance, that's the killer. Well done.'

'Thank you,' he says. He takes another large sip of his drink. He feels the gin hit his bloodstream and tranquilise his nerves.

'I also liked the piece you did on the revegetation of the station. You … well, it could have been dry and scientific but you injected life and humanity into it. I happen to know the editor of the *Farmers' Monthly* and he liked it. A lot. I think you'll be hearing from him.'

By now Maroney is glowing and pleased to see that Willie has joined them, sitting opposite with a drink of her own. The hirelings are well treated.

'I have a favour to ask you,' she says.

Alertness returns and Maroney leans forward.

'I want you to stay on and do a series on the other environmental innovations that I've put in place on this station. I know for a fact that many of the other station owners think I'm as crazy as a cockatoo, a city farmer who plays around with fads and fashion.'

'And do you?' he asks, taking a gamble.

Jean Le Carre puts her drink on the small table in front of them. She brings her palms together and then points her fingers in his direction. 'You're a cheeky bugger but that is exactly the right question. However, when the whole world is crazy, it doesn't pay to be sane, I forget who said that.' Before he has time to reply she goes on, 'You have a right to be sceptical. I want you to keep working with Willie. She's my PA as well as my environmental manager, and she's well qualified. She will explain everything we're trying to do. If you're interested, she'll give you the scientific evidence for our methods and then it'll be up to you to make up your own mind.' Now, she leans towards him. 'I am evangelical about this Maroney. I want people to become aware of the innovations in land care. I think the future of this country depends on it.'

'What if I still think you're as crazy as a cockatoo?'

'You won't,' she says confidently. She reaches over and pats…no, caresses, Willie's hand.

Maroney can see she's enjoying watching for his reaction, but he's way ahead of her.

Emergency

BY the time Doog returns from the waterhole the sun is lower in the sky. If she can find a good position on the west side of the yard, she'll have the right light on the bull riders. She intends to shoot from low down, hoping to capture the way they explode from the chute. If the paper published one of her photos, she would be thrilled.

Doog passes the long paddock and spots Paul Gorski practising with his lariat. He catches her eye and with a smirk lifts his Akubra and bows deeply over the elegant neck of his horse. She feels her scowl deepen. *The Pardee Stud, now there's a name for an article in your paper, Maroney. Maybe I'm not being fair. I hardly know him. No, Matt's right. He's an arrogant prick.*

Her gaze falls on the large marquee. Maroney sits looking relaxed with a glass in his hand, deep in conversation with Willie. Even from this distance, she can feel the magnetism between them. She turns away aware that she's … let's face it, jealous. But why wouldn't he be attracted to this beautiful, intelligent, articulate, damn near perfect, let's not forget *young*, woman? He's a good-looking, *young* man. She walks to the ring and tries to concentrate on her task of worming through the crowd to a good vantage point for the photos.

Six finalists compete in the open. Four from surrounding stations, including Paul, plus Bruce and Snow from Bedarra. The bull riding, the first event, is to Doog's mind a potent metaphor of station life. Man in a herculean struggle, determined to dominate, muscles bulging and twisting in battle as the animal strains to dump the foe clinging parasite-like to its back. Aware of a smile hovering at the corners of her mouth, she knows she should feel traitorous for those thoughts as she snaps one picture after another.

Steer wrestling comes at last. In this final event, the rider dives from a galloping horse on to the neck of a steer, wrestling it to the ground. The steers used in the open event are fully grown, weighing up to half a tonne, with horns like enormous meat hooks. The rider grabs those horns and twists the steer's neck forcing the beast to the ground.

This is the deciding event. So far she thinks that Paul and Snow may have the edge, but all the contestants show brilliance in their horsemanship. Three visitors are up first. The first breaks the rope barrier and cops a ten-second penalty. The second wrestles the steer effortlessly, lifting his hat to the crowd as he walks away. The third misses the steer and receives a 'no time' from the timekeeper. Next comes Bruce. Doog can't fault him. He's as strong and as beefy as a steer himself. It's Snow she's worried about.

She cheers as Bruce leaves the yard with a bow and a wave of his hat. Her voice is lost in the noise of the crowd. She takes a rapid succession of shots of the crowd cheering and waving black hats in the air. She points the zoom lens towards the large marquee. It's empty.

The next steer erupts from its gate in an angry cloud of dust. The barrier is down and Snow bursts out, diving from his horse on to the steer's neck, grasping a horn in each hand. The animal is down and rolling on the ground before it knows what's hit it. Snow's not big but he sure is fast. She looks at the crowd; they're open-mouthed. He's finished before they've had time to rev up. As he walks out of the ring the clapping and cheering and whistling are deafening.

All eyes now turn to Paul, the final contestant. Behind the barrier, Doog can see man and horse frozen in concentrated fury. The official nods. The steer takes off as the barrier is pulled away. Horse and man leap into action as one. Her heart's racing. Snow's ride was smooth, but Paul looks slightly off balance and, at the speed he's going, she senses danger. He bends towards the steer just when the galloping horse bucks, throwing its legs into the air. The cloud of dust obscures everything except a tangled heap. All at once, the steer is up and tearing down the arena, leaving Paul lying on the ground. He's belly-down and not moving. Doog looks around to see where Matt is and then ducks between the wooden rails of the yard, racing towards the figure on the ground, yelling for someone to get the flying doctor kit from the homestead. Matt and Bruce sprint towards Paul from the grandstand.

Camera and lenses bounce up and down and she grabs them from around her neck as she runs. A hand reaches out to take them. Maroney is by her side. She reaches Paul and yells into the crowd for anyone with medical training. There's no response. She looks at Matt and Bruce.

'We'll manage.' says Matt. 'When we know what's going on I'll call the doc.'

In this situation, her Red Cross certificate doesn't spell confidence. The training kicks in as she drops beside Paul. His cheek rests on the gravel and she leans close to his turned face. His eyes are open and now he's not smirking.

'Don't move me,' he whispers.

'Do you think it's your back?'

'Back feels OK,' he says through gritted teeth. 'Leg hurts like a bastard.'

Relief almost overwhelms her and she closes her eyes for a moment. A man this young in a wheelchair is something she doesn't want to contemplate. His left leg is bent at a peculiar angle. She can deal with that. She passes her hands lightly over his body, feeling, checking, and she can see that his right arm is pinned underneath him.

'Paul, what about if I move your arm.'

'Don't touch it.'

'Why, Paul?'

'I'm holding … got his horn … not sure if my old fella's still hanging in there. Doog catches the hint of a twisted smile and smiles back. Sweat is running down her face and into her eyes. Matt's beside her with the first-aid kit.

'You guys, carry a marquee over here,' Matt barks. 'We need some shade.' She blesses his common sense. The shade is there in moments.

'Paul,' she says softly. 'We need to know what's going on. We're going to turn you over. We'll be as gentle as we can.' She looks up. 'I need six of you — two to support his broken leg as we turn him and two people on each side to put your arms under him and hold him every inch of the way while I roll him.'

There's not a sound from the watching crowd but Connor's face stands out. Stricken.

'Connor.' She flicks her head. Connor comes to her side. 'Talk to him,' she hisses in his ear. 'Tell him any blarney that comes to you.'

'Paul m'boy, d'y remember the time you came off your bike when you were nine and broke your arm. Yes, well … this is worse, I'll not deny it, but you are tough, me boy, and I am *so* proud of you.'

Jesus, Connor, Cinderella would be better than that, but Paul is smiling before a scream of agony erupts from his throat when they turn him. That's good. He can feel. But the next moment she sees blood pulsing from his leg to the ground. She puts her hand into the wound and Paul screams again as she pinches off the offending artery.

'Matt — call the doc now — femoral artery severed — emergency.'

'Bruce, belt. Yes Bruce — belt.' She points. Bruce looks flummoxed but hands her the belt holding on to his trousers with the other hand. 'Put it around his leg above where my hand is and pull as tight as you can. I need blankets — shock will set in. Koop, you can do a splint, can't you? No, don't raise his other leg for Christ sakes.'

Matt returns and she shoots him a questioning look.

'Doc should be here in less than an hour. We're lucky, he's just done a caesarean at the mission.'

'What about the bottom half of his leg?' A voice comes from the onlookers. 'It's not getting any blood supply.'

Doog hears a gasp and sees Connor standing chewing on his hand, his face drained of colour.

'He'll be OK. Got at least eight hours,' she says, knowing that is the absolute outside, optimistic best. 'I tell you what. It would really help if you could all go and get a beer in the shearing shed and leave us to this.'

Paul looks up with wide eyes.

'I won't lose my leg will I, Mrs Boss-Lady?'

'No, but I'm just about to cut your jeans off you, so as I warned you once before, you may yet lose your balls.' Connor lets out a choking sound, but she sees a smile flicker momentarily on Paul's white lips.

Blood

'I WOULD like you with me on the plane,' says the doctor as he kneels beside Doog in the dirt. 'We need to keep a close eye on that wound. I've sealed it for now but the slightest thing could open it up. You can make sure he doesn't move.'

In the plane, heading for Sandy Bay, the doctor radios ahead. 'Cath, it's an emergency, we need a blood ID as soon as we land. Can you get on to the mining company — see if their medivac jet is, by some miracle, available? If not, Royal Perth, and arrange the air ambulance, ASAP. Make sure you talk to the right person. We need emergency vascular surgery — femoral artery.'

Looking back over his shoulder the doctor asks Doog a list of questions. She can tell the doctor Paul's name, but no, she doesn't know his middle name. No, she doesn't know his next of kin. No, she doesn't know his date of birth. Paul seems to be slipping in and out of consciousness. She takes his hand.

'Paul, Paul, can you hear me? When's your birthday?'

'June … fourth,' He gives a twisted smile. 'Chinese horse … should have been able to outwit a bull.' Paul slides back into sleep and she looks at him again. June fourth. June fourth. He does have dark hair. But so does half the population. He doesn't look like … like anyone really. She thinks back to her school days … the boy who … he did have dark hair but did he look like Paul? She scarcely remembers. And lots of people have the same birthday — two of her friends, for a start.

She pushes away the thought. But memories of that date punch their way through, and she feels again the mewing bundle pulled from her and sees the tiny scalp of damp black hair disappearing through the door. Again she feels the drug take effect and the anger and frustration of her helplessness.

'Are you all right?' asks the doctor, looking back at her. Doog lifts her face from her hands and returns to the present.

'Do you think you'll be able to save his leg?' she says to divert his attention away from her.

Predictably, the doctor gives her an evasive answer. Something about doing their best and he's young and fit and has a good chance of a full recovery. They barely reach the emergency door of the hospital when someone has a needle in Paul's arm, drawing out blood. A team is running him down the corridor, she assumes to the operating theatre.

Left alone, she collapses onto a low garden wall outside the hospital and pulls out a cigarette she'd rolled on the plane under the censorial frown of the doctor. A frangipani reaches out like an exotic friend in the warm air. The nicotine hits her bloodstream. A hand touches her shoulder; she must have nodded off but the cigarette still burns between her fingers.

'Excuse me, are you a relative of the patient?' A tall nurse leans over her, concern on her pretty face. 'Paul Gorski? You brought him in tonight.'

Doog shakes her head. 'No … a neighbour. Why? Is he OK?'

'He's lost a lot of blood and he has an unusual blood type. Could take a while to track some down.'

'What blood type?' Doog tries to keep her voice steady.

'Type AB, it's … well, only three per cent of the population has it.' We'll give him serum, but it would be better if we could find someone with the same blood type. Do you know his next of kin?'

'No.' She's finding it hard to focus on what the young nurse is telling her. 'His parents were killed and he has no brothers or sis — shit!'

'Pardon, are you all right?'

She takes a deep breath. 'I have AB blood.'

'Are you sure?'

'Of course, I'm sure. I've been donating blood all my adult life.' She shouldn't be snapping at this Florence Nightingale but she can't help it.

'Well, that's wonderful. That is if you're happy to donate some now.'

Doog's head nods of its own accord. She feels numb, can't think. The nurse is still talking.

'We'll still have to make a positive ID, so if you'll come with me, we'll get started. If it's a match, we can send some down to Perth with him.' The nurse is smiling now. 'That'd be a big help.'

Doog sits in the chair with her arm on the table while the nurse swabs her and draws blood into a tiny phial.

'It won't take long to ID this. Stay there, I'll bring you a cup of tea. You're looking very pale, dear.'

Doog's head is spinning. The birthday, the blood, he's the right age. Can it be? She has to find out.

'Is Paul conscious? Can I talk to him?'

She'll have to wait, the nurse explains, Paul's being cleaned up and then they'll set his leg.

'He's still on a serum drip but if you are a match, when he's out of theatre they will have some of your blood ready for him. You may be able to talk to him in another couple of hours.' The nurse's forehead wrinkles with concern as she looks at Doog. 'After we take your blood, you should get some rest. There's a spare room in the nurse's quarters you can have for tonight. You can get something to eat at the canteen, or a pub meal just down on the main street. We need to get him to Perth for a vascular graft. He'll be in good hands. You don't need to worry.'

She's waited for twenty-five years, Doog tells herself, so she can wait a few more hours but right now it feels unbearable. She's ready to break wide open and she feels so alone.

After they've taken as much blood as they dare, she heads to the nurse's quarters and dumps her things. She doesn't want to stay in this tiny room. When she walks out the front entrance into the dark street, the small town is deserted. Her watch tells her it's eight o'clock but she's not remotely hungry. Fifty metres down the road is the pub, where she sits in a booth in the corner of the bar with a stranglehold on a glass of brandy and soda water. Dark wood fills the bar, wooden floor, wooden walls and furniture saturated in the smell of sweat, cigarettes and stale beer. She's thankful the few other people sitting hunched over drinks ignore her.

She knows now that whether it turns out to be true or not, she must tell Annie. She should have told her long ago, not waited for a crisis to completely upend her. It's tempting to have another glass but she hasn't eaten and the smell of the pub is turning her empty stomach. The jetty reaches out over dark water at the end of the main street. Not the place she'd usually go on her own at night. Right now she doesn't give a flying fig. A row of soft lights beckons her towards the end of the pier. Legs dangle over the edge. People fishing. When she was a little girl, her father took her fishing off the jetty in Fremantle. She'd always tangle her line and he'd help her. So gentle and patient; when did that stop? She's crying again. She's read about people who cry all the time. Maybe she's depressed. *Cut the melodrama.* She can't give in to self-pity but she really is terribly, terribly sad and very frightened right now. At the end of the jetty, she stands and feels the dark water drawing her down.

An hour later she returns to the nurses' quarters and the tall nurse rushes up to her. 'We've been searching for you everywhere,' she says.

'Why, what's wrong?'

'Nothing, nothing to worry about. The mining company has come good with the medivac jet. It's being fueled up now. We're just getting Paul ready for the transfer to the plane. The doctor asked if you'd go with him.'

'What, to Perth?'

'Yeah, it's a lot to ask, but Paul knows you, and of course, you're his blood supply. If he needs more, it could be hard to find.'

She closes her eyes in case the tears come again. She should be getting back to her job, the kids, but Paul needs her now. Son or not, it's the least she can do. She nods, returns to the room to pick up her bag and follows the nurse to the ambulance waiting at the emergency door. She should have eaten something. As if reading her thoughts, the nurse tells her that the paramedic on the plane will have something for her to eat and drink.

They take off and Doog looks around at the inside of the small jet. It reminds her of an intensive care unit she saw in Fremantle hospital when her nephew was ill, except that the four seats and the stretcher-bed where Paul lies are plush white leather. He's sedated and a drip hangs from a hook in the ceiling into his arm. His grey pallor has disguised his tan. Fear impales her.

'He's quite stable,' says the paramedic, whose olive skin is such a contrast to Paul's. She's not so sure.

'Do you know why he needs a graft?' she says. 'They told me they have sutured the artery and that blood's flowing to his leg.'

'It won't last. In Perth they can remove the damaged section and replace it with another piece of vein. The joins will be clean, and with what they can do with microsurgery, he can be back riding bulls next year.'

'Not if he's got any sense.' Doog tries to smile, then accepts the boxed sandwich and bottle of orange juice that he offers her.

Two hours later she is sitting in another hospital waiting room wondering why they're always so drab. Paul will return to this ward from the operating theatre. She should have rung the station. They all think she's stuck in Sandy Bay instead of a thousand kilometres south with her mind stuck in 1966. She approaches the nurses station just around the corner. Inarticulate with fatigue, she tries to explain who she is, that she has to make phone calls but isn't sure she has enough change. She tells the nurse she has to contact people on stations out from Sandy Bay.

The nurse directs her to a phone down the corridor and then says, 'Wait.' She opens a drawer and, with a wink, gives Doog a phonecard. But she's to keep quiet about it. All she has to do is swipe it and dial the numbers on the back followed by the station numbers.

It feels like an effort to walk down the corridor. She wants to lie down, right now on these bare boards and sleep. She lifts the receiver to dial Bedarra and changes her mind. She needs … she wants to ring her mother.

A sleepy voice answers. 'Doog, Doog, is that you? Do you know what time it is? Are you all right?'

She nods her head.

'Doog, are you there, love?'

Doog can't keep the quaver out of her voice. 'I'm here, Mum … I'm … I'm in Perth. There's been an accident on the station. I came down with someone.'

Her mother's voice rises. 'What's happened, Doog? Are you all right?'

'I'm fine, Mum. It was a young bloke from a neighbouring station — rodeo accident. I want to come home, Mum.'

'Where are you? Royal Perth? I'm on my way. I'll pick you up out the front in half-an-hour.'

'Mum!' But her mother has gone. Doog looks at her watch and sees how late it is. She'll phone the others in the morning. Back at the desk, she explains that her mother wants to take her home.

'Well, I'm glad to hear it,' says the nurse, as Doog returns the card. 'They took a lot of your blood in Sandy Bay. You should be resting. It's a wonder you can still stand.'

Home

BY the time Doog negotiates her way through the sprawl of the hospital, her mother is waiting in a five-minute zone. Doog thought she was too weary to raise a smile but she can't help herself. Some things never change. Even in the middle of the night, her mother looks immaculate. Lipstick carefully applied and not a dishevelled hair on her head.

'God, Mum, it's a wonder you didn't get picked up. It should take you an hour to drive from Freo.' Her otherwise law-abiding mother has always been a lead foot.

'Rubbish, not at this time in the morning. I was the only car on the road.' She pats the passenger seat. 'Get in, Doog. You look done in,' she adds, concern scoring her face.

Doog leans back against the headrest and sighs. 'Yeah, it's been a long day.' Being back with her mother unleashes a confusion of emotions. It's such a relief but she's on the verge of crying. She squeezes her eyelids together.

'What's wrong, Doog?'

'Nothing Mum, just tired. I gave blood. The nurse said I'd be tired.' She can hardly get the words out.

'Well, you can sleep in tomorrow. Sleep all day if you need to.'

'No, no, I have to … I have to see Paul, and I need to ring people.'

'Surely all that can wait.' It's dark but she can tell by her mother's voice that the wrinkles on her forehead are knitting together in a familiar pattern.

At eight o'clock the next morning, she's at the front desk of the hospital. The receptionist frowns and lifts the telephone.

'I'm sorry,' she says. 'Only next of kin can visit out of hours. You will have to come back at eleven o'clock.'

'But I just need a few minutes. Christ, I just saved his life and he's full of my blood. Isn't that next of kin enough for you?'

The face of the receptionist shuts like an elevator door. 'I'm not in charge of these decisions,' she snaps. 'Please come back at eleven o'clock.'

Doog wanders down to the street again. Connor, she remembers — she should have rung him last night. He'll be worried half to death. There's a phone box outside the hospital. She prays that it works.

'He's OK, Connor. His leg's broken and he'll have his wings clipped until the graft mends. He's a lucky boy but it looks like you'll have Pardee on your own for a while.' Suddenly she's blubbering again, this time into the phone. 'They won't let me see him.'

'Are you sure he's all right, Doogie? You're sounding upset.'

'I'm just tired, Connor. Is there someone else I should be phoning? Uncles, aunts? '

But Connor says, as far as he knows, Paul's on his own. He knew the Gorskis came out here after the war and they never mentioned anyone else, not even in their will. Everything passed on to Paul, the only son.

'Are you sure he's all right, Doog?' he says again.

The old man sounds so worried. She silently rebukes herself for being so selfish and tries to reassure him. 'Yes, he's fine, Connor. It's just been a rough couple of days. I'm a bit emotional. Can you phone Bedarra and let Matt and the rest know we're in Perth?'

At eleven o'clock she's back in the front foyer of the hospital but this time no one stops her when she makes her way to the nurses' station where she left Paul the night before. She's given his room number and marches down the corridor. And then she stops. What is she going to say? What will she ask him? Confusion, almost panic, make her want to turn and run back down the corridor.

She takes a deep breath and wills herself to calm down. OK, they have the same blood type. That might not mean a thing. She's not the only person in the world with AB blood. She'll just listen. Let him talk first.

She peeps around the door of the private ward and smiles.

'Mrs Boss-Lady,' he grins back. 'Come in, I need to thank you.'

'What for? Leaving your balls intact?'

'That too. No, seriously, Doog, the doctor says if it hadn't been for you, I would have bled to death in minutes. And how lucky am I that we have the same blood type?' He looks around. 'I can't believe I'm in Perth, I don't remember a thing.' The look in his eyes twists her heart. 'Thanks for coming down with me,' he says. 'I need a face from home right now even if she's hiding an elastrator in her pocket.'

'Paul, are there any relatives I should be contacting for you? I mean … I know your parents were killed in an accident, but aunts, uncles, grandparents?'

Paul's dark eyes seem to sadden. He's suddenly no longer the arrogant young cow cocky and she finds herself aching to hold him, son or not.

'No, there's no one. The Gorskis had both their families wiped out by the war and the Nazis, and you may as well know, now that we're blood buddies, that I was adopted.'

Doog holds her breath. 'Adopted, I didn't know that. Connor never said anything.'

'Yeah, well that's probably because I never told him.'

'I see,' she says slowly, although she doesn't see. From all accounts and from watching them together Connor is like a grandfather to him. They seem so close.

'Did you … did you ever try to find your real parents?'

'No, I didn't even know until after my … after the Gorskis died. I found my birth certificate. It had the Gorski's name on it but there was a sealed envelope with it. Inside was a piece of paper, barely legible but it seemed to be the same birth registered under a different name, stamped BFA.' He turns and gazes out the window. 'I found out that means Baby for Adoption. They should have told me.' There's an edge of bitterness in his voice now, and she hesitates but she has to ask.

'So, you know their names?' she says. 'Your real parents? Did you ever try to find them?'

'No, I couldn't read the names and they obviously didn't want me, so no point.'

Doog holds the edge of the chair. 'Did the Gorskis name you Paul?'

'Yes,' he murmurs, gazing out of the hospital window. 'The Gorskis called me Paul after her brother who died in a concentration camp. They told me that. I never asked about my middle name — Tom. It's not exactly a Polish name, especially shortened like that. Never was that curious until they died … now I don't know who I am.' He turns back to look at her. 'Christ Doog, don't look so horrified. I know you think I'm an arsehole, but that's not me, honestly. I want us to be friends. I hope you'll learn to like me, Doog.'

'I like you, Paul.' She swallows, trying to digest what this means. A worried frown scores his brow and she reaches out a shaking hand to touch his. 'So … so your adoptive parents — were they good to you?'

He turns and again gazes out of the window past the view of corrugated roofs. 'Yeah, yeah, they were — the best, but I was so shitty with them for getting themselves killed and for not telling me that I was adopted. I found the papers in a biscuit tin in their wardrobe. They should have told me.' His hands are twisting the bed sheets and she knows she needs to be careful, take things slowly. Nothing is certain. In those days adoptions were a lot more common than they are now.

'Perhaps they were scared of your reaction, scared of losing you,' she says quietly. 'They must have loved you a lot. I'm glad.'

A faraway look comes over Paul as he tells Doog about growing up on Pardee. On a horse from the moment he could walk.

'The old man let me start driving the ute on my twelfth birthday,' he says with a sad sort of smile.

Doog aches with envy when he tells her how Maria supervised his home-schooling even though she barely read English, how she made the best strudels in the district. And then, later, going away to boarding school. Hating it at first and then making friends and loving it. She clings to every word.

An orderly arrives with Paul's lunch tray and some medication. He'll need to sleep so she takes herself off for a cup of tea in the hospital canteen. The clatter of tin trays and crockery competes with the commotion in her brain. She can't get used to the fact that she may have found her son, after all these years.

The evidence is stacking up. She needs to tell him. And then thinks, no, she needs, she wants, to tell Annie first. She wolfs down some food and takes herself for a walk, over the road from the hospital down along the river. She has to decide how to tackle this. Should she risk telling Paul first? No, it has to be Annie. Christ, why hasn't she told her before now? How will she react? She thinks about the bitterness in Paul's voice when he said his biological parents didn't want him. The hurt and the anger have cut deep. If it turns out that he is her son, will he forgive her? He'll want to know about his father. Doog thinks about Alex and wonders what he's doing now. He was whisked off to Melbourne, she heard, although he shouldn't be hard to track down. She hasn't seen him since before she was spirited away in disgrace. There's not much to tell. They were both just stupid, naïve kids.

In the afternoon, she returns and listens while he talks. It sounds like he knows every plant, every animal and every rock on the station. While he describes the lake, Doog can feel the love for the place radiating from him.

The Gorskis had sent him to university. She wonders what sacrifices they made to do that. He says he didn't have a scholarship so paying the fees and accommodation in Perth would have been expensive. His life had been rich and full. It could have been so different.

Doog glances at the clock on the wall. The afternoon light is waning and her mother's expecting her home for dinner. She can't bring herself to rise from the chair by the bed, by the bedside of … who knows, maybe her son. Is it just the thick dark hair? No, she's almost sure she's found him. Just as swiftly she tells herself it could be wishful thinking. She'd stay all night if they let her, just to watch over him, wait as he drifted off to sleep. But how would she explain that to her mother?

'Paul, I'll come back tomorrow,' she promises, when his evening meal arrives. On her way out, she stops at the nurse's station and seeks assurance that he is completely out of danger. She's being irrational, she knows but she's terrified of losing him again.

The hospital is only a short walk to the station where the train leaves for Fremantle. She's only vaguely aware of the rush-hour crowds and the loudspeaker cutting through the hubbub. A train screeches to a standstill on the opposite side of the station. The steely glint of the rail lines draws her eyes all the way to the end of the platform and she needs to stop her mind from going down the dark tunnel of the past.

She tells herself that Paul seems to have had a good life. Paul … she's always thought of him as Tom but she doesn't mind Paul and it was nice of the Gorskis to keep Tom as a middle name if that's what they did. Surely that can't be another coincidence along with the birth date and the blood?

So, say he is her son. All these years wondering if he's been happy, if he's been treated well. You hear some horrible stories. Thank God for the Gorskis, they obviously adored him. But now they've gone and she only knows part of the story. She aches to know the rest.

First, she needs to tell Annie. It's not something that should be done on the phone but that can't be helped.

An angry voice breaks her thoughts. She looks down at a red-faced man in a wheelchair. She's blocking his path between the seats and the edge of the platform.

'Sorry,' she mumbles and steps back.

On the train she collapses into a seat and tries to imagine what it would feel like to be told, for the first time, at twenty-one, that you have a brother. Doog feels torn in two. Her mother … can she tell Claris she thinks she's found her baby? No, not yet. She needs to tell Annie first. Is she avoiding talking to her mother? This thing has been unspoken between them all these years. Round and round, her thoughts skitter without making connections until she feels the train scrape to a halt at the end of the line offering her the solid familiarity of Fremantle Station.

A stiff breeze sweeps her hair as she walks away from the station towards her mother's cottage in South Fremantle. She stops at a pub in Market Street for a bottle of white wine, smiling as she remembers how scandalised her parents had been when topless barmaids were employed in the 80s. It's good to be home.

The sun sets over the sea and bathes the foreshore in a mellow light. Old warehouses, restaurants and cafes hug the harbourfront. Smells of fish and chips come from Cicerello's replaced, as she keeps walking, by the salty smell of the boatyards where seaweed and barnacles careened from hulls lie scattered on the dry-dock. Seagulls whoop and screech overhead. She has missed the bustle of the port. She should have rung Frankie. There's an old ferryboat tied out the front of Cicerello's café. They would meet there and watch the boats on the harbour while they chased the seagulls off the table, drank cheap white wine and ate chips with salt and vinegar from paper packages. Slipping in and out of the past with an old school friend is one of life's greatest pleasures. Thinking about it makes her hungry — she hasn't eaten fish for months. God, she should have rung Frankie. Her old friend would be hurt if she found out she had been in Fremantle without looking her up but she just can't fit one more thing into her emotional timetable right now.

The light has turned from gold to violet by the time she crosses the road near the Fremantle Sailing Club and walks up the hill away from the harbour. Her mother still lives in what is now called a workers cottage. Her parents bought the place just after she was born, paying the bank, week by week. It was all they could afford but over the years real estate fashion has made this once dirt-poor, migrant-filled part of the city a *desirable* location. The cottage is weatherboard. From the outside it looks small but as you enter through the wooden front door, with its leadlight glass panel, there's a sense of space. The large rooms come off a central breezeway, broken elegantly by simple art-deco features. The ceilings are high and three-quarters of the way up the walls are picture rails from which hang the wishy-washy watercolours that her mother loves.

A delicious smell wafts down the breezeway when Doog opens the front door. Her mother is cooking fish. How did she know? Doog walks to the kitchen at the back of the house, plants a kiss on her mother's cheek and stuffs the bottle of wine in the crowded freezer. She turns back up the passageway to her bedroom.

'Just getting changed, Mum.'

'Dinner in ten minutes,' her mother calls back.

Her bedroom hasn't altered since she was a kid. The quilt is her mother's patchwork. The curtains, also made by her mother, are covered in pastel flowers. Even the sheets, she remembers, were made from raw linen, which Claris bleached and hemmed herself. She fingers the pictures stuck onto the back of the door. They were advertisements for diamond rings that she cut from Dad's old *Readers' Digests*. The photographs are of young women looking like princesses, sporting sparkling engagement rings, taken through a lens softened by Vaseline.

It feels strange being home, somehow vulnerable all over again. Last night she found her old photo album from the time before ... she looks so young and carefree. She'd forgotten about that girl — the girl blowing out thirteen candles on a cake, the girl in the mini-skirt posing on the front verandah before a school dance, the girl waving from the horse on the merry-go-round at the Perth Royal Show. In one photo the whole family is down at the beach. Her mother and father look happy, sitting on a picnic rug with a Thermos. But that was then.

Showered and changed into track pants and an old jumper that she'd left here with most of her winter clothes, she heads back to the kitchen. 'Have a wine with me, Mum.'

Her mother looks up from dressing a salad. Doog expects her to refuse. Then Claris straightens and says, 'Yes, I think I will.'

Doog pours the wine and sets the table. They sit down and eat in silence for a few minutes.

'I found Bedarra station on a map in the library,' her mother says after a while.

'One day we need to get you a computer so that you can look up maps or whatever else you want at home.'

'What's wrong with going to the library?'

'No, you're right Mum, there's nothing wrong with going to the library.'

'I didn't realise where it was.'

'What?'

'Bedarra station — I knew you'd gone north but I didn't know where.' Silence follows and Doog continues to eat, trying to decide what to say. 'Why did you go up that way?' Her mother's voice comes out in a whisper. When Doog doesn't answer she says. 'Was it to try and find him?'

Doog puts her knife and fork down, stares at her fish and nods.

'And did you … did you find him, Doog? Did you?'

Maroney

BACK at Bedarra, Maroney is missing Doog more than he thought possible. It's not just the nightly ritual by the tank stand of sharing a cigarette and the events of the day. Every part of him longs for this woman — emotionally, physically, and even intellectually. He's never felt such connection to another person. Now he stands by the tank stand every evening to gaze at the stars. He has never been one for romantic fancies but somehow being here bring him closer to her.

While Doog's away. Maroney again wonders whether he should track down the boys home when he goes back down south. Would he achieve anything by going back there? He can't imagine finding anyone he knows. Most of the boys would have been just as keen to leave the place as he was.

When he'd first left the boys home and made his way to Perth, he had been told Northbridge was the place to go. He had thought anything would be better than the home but those first few nights that he spent under a bush in a park he had been utterly lost and terrified. He had wandered around, hungry and cold, knocking on doors with signs *Rooms to Let*, promising to pay as soon as he got a job. Eventually he found a room in a boarding house where the widowed landlady agreed to wait until he got a job in exchange for chopping wood and looking after the vegies and chooks. Meanwhile she fed him, and even gave him some of her dead husband's clothes. Mrs Clemence, that was her name. She was the one that found the advertisement in the newspaper, a job selling *The Daily Mail* in the afternoons. It was a dream come true when he got that first job.

He could do anything. That's how he began in those years. He enrolled in the Perth Technical College just around the corner from the boarding house. The newspaper gave him a cadetship and soon he had enough subjects to get into university, again with the help of the paper. Meeting Rod and Maria was the next best thing that happened to him and, for a while, he made up his mind to push the past away and live in the present. And for a while he had succeeded.

Maroney keeps thinking back to Doog and the story she told him about having her baby taken, stolen. Yes, stolen is not too strong a word. He knows he should leave it alone. She doesn't want to share her story but curiosity is eating at him. He has heard about adoptions, especially in the 80s. Memories surface of stories about unwanted babies being lucky to be adopted into ideal families. Questions upon questions go around in his mind. How many women are out there with similar stories to Doog? How could this practice even be legal? Who was involved? Doog mentioned the church, what was their role in this? He needs to do some research just to satisfy himself and to get his mind off this merry-go-round. Doog doesn't need to know.

'Maria, I need a favour,' he says on the phone glancing down the breezeway to make sure no one is listening. He has a list of documents he wants her to find as well as a copy of the article in *The Women's Weekly*. 'I'm pretty sure it was mid-fifties,' he tells her. 'and if you come across any other stories related to adoption, I'll take anything. You can send them to my post box but if they're not too bulky could you try faxing them to the post office?' He reels off the number.

'Maroney, what's going on? I thought your supposed to be up their digging up stories about dry-land farming.'

'Yeah, well this is just an extra-curricular activity. Hush-hush please, especially with Toad.'

'Extra-curricular, Maroney? Your vocabulary is expanding. That wouldn't have anything to do with the school teacher, would it?'

'Gotta go, Madonna. I'm on the homestead phone. I'll tell you all about it one day.'

Paul

THE train from Fremantle stops and starts along the coast and then rattles eastwards through the suburbs until, finally, it pulls into Perth Central. Doog has had lots of time to think about the conversation from the night before. Her mother is more perceptive than she has given her credit for. When she was a little girl, she remembers being convinced that Claris had magic powers. The woman had an uncanny way of knowing what was going on before anyone told her. It's a relief now that her mother knows her suspicions about Paul. They'd shared the bottle of white wine and opened another one. Claris wanted to know all about Paul, what is he like, what does he look like, where he lives.

'When are you going to tell him, Doog? What about Annie?'

'I need a bit more time to think about that, Mum. Everything has happened so fast and I am so tired. I'll try to work it out tomorrow.'

Claris poured them both another wine and stared through the glass. 'I know its way past time to ask but tell me about what happened that night. Where did George take you?'

Doog tells her mother what she remembers. She wants to ask how they could have done that to her — but she won't — they were different days and she's worked out the answers now. She's done with blaming.

But when Claris asks about the hospital and the birth, Doog doesn't spare the details. Her mother had cried and hugged Doog, telling her how sorry she was, trying to explain how things were in those days.

'Yes, they were harsh times with some cruel attitudes,' said Doog. 'I have worked my way through it now and I am just holding on to the things I have to be thankful for.' She had leant over and put her hand over her mother's. 'That includes you, Mum.' She felt the rip in her heart start to mend.

At the hospital, she's pleased to find Paul propped up reading. His eyes are brighter and even his skin is a healthier colour, but he's not allowed to move until the graft heals.

'So bloody embarrassing,' he says. 'I have to piss in a bottle and worse, but I won't give you more information than your stomach can handle this time of a morning.'

'I thought you might be getting bored,' she says, 'so I brought you a present.'

Surprise shows on his young face and he opens the package.

'It's lovely, Doog.' He grins, and caresses the dark-grey object. 'But what is it?'

'It's a portable computer,' she explains. 'It's second-hand. They're making them these days for people who travel, or people who fall off horses.' He looks up and rewards her with a twisted smile.

Opening the lid and turning it on, Doog explains how he can do everything on it that he does on a big one, says she'll show him some of the programs he can use. That perhaps he'd like to do a bit of writing while he's laid low.

Paul glances up, a puzzled look on his face. 'How did you know I like to write?'

'No, I mean, I didn't know. *I* like to write things down – kept a diary ever since ... so maybe I assume everyone does. It'll take you a while to get used to it, but I hope you find it useful.' She looks up from the screen. Paul's looking out the window again.

'Don't you like it?'

When he turns back, he's wiping his cheek and he reaches for her hand.

'God, Doog, thanks, especially after me being such a prick. I don't know what to say. I'm, I'm ...'

'Paul, it's nothing. I got it cheap from Mum's neighbour. He services these things for a living and he put a couple of programs on for you.' She rises from the chair beside her bed and pours herself a glass of water, swallowing the tears that threaten. She sits down again, changing the subject. 'Tell me, what do you write about, Paul?'

'Oh, I've just been jotting down a bit about the station, some of the history and the native plants and animals. The old man was mad about all that. He taught me a lot.'

Once again, Doog feels the ache of having missed out on seeing her baby grow from infancy to manhood. She envies these people who had the intimacy of passing on knowledge to someone she's almost certain is her son, but she's grateful. She wants to know more about this couple from Europe who obviously loved him. That's for later. Now, she's delighted to find he has a thorough knowledge of the classics, as well as a love of poetry. She remembers seeing the shelves of books in the front room at Pardee.

'Did the Gorskis ... your parents, like to read?' she asks. Again, stabbed by loss, and envy of these people who knew him so well. Paul tells her that neither of them could read English very well, although the old man used to bring back the papers from Sandy Bay and pour over them. Paul wasn't sure if he was trying to learn to read English or pretending that he knew.

'When I went down to boarding school in Perth, I thought I'd hate reading. They handed out books with grotty green and maroon covers that kids had scrawled on over the years. But our English teacher, Mr Booth was great. I was hooked from the moment we started with *Moby-Dick*. When Mr Booth read, it wasn't just a story or another dumb poem.' Paul looks up with a helpless shrug. 'This probably sounds soft but he made us excited about good writing. We could … well, we could see the beauty in it. I think every single boy loved his class.'

'It doesn't sound soft at all, Paul. Sounds like you were lucky to have a good teacher.'

'Yes, he was good, Doog. When I first read poetry, it was just a jumble of words but he started us off with Paterson and Lawson. Suddenly I got it. I think most of the class did. He took us through all the great English and American poets as well as Homer and the *Iliad*.'

'I'm glad,' says Doog, patting his leg through the blankets. 'There are not too many things more important than reading.'

'You get plenty of time to read on a station,' he says. 'Especially when you're an only child.'

But he's not an only child and he needs to know that. Doog makes a decision to tell him. Lunch arrives and she leaves him to it and to rest. When she passes the nurses' station, she asks to have a word with Paul's doctor, but is told he won't be around until tomorrow.

'What about the nurse who'll be in charge of him this afternoon?' She asks and is introduced to a nurse who ushers her over to a seat.

'Look I have some news to give to Paul. I'm hoping he's well enough to hear it this afternoon.'

'Good or bad news?' asks the nurse.

'Good, I hope, but … well, I'm not sure how he'll take it and I really don't want to upset him. However, it is important, very important. I just wondered …'

'When you tell him,' interrupts the nurse, 'sit on the left side of his bed and press the button if you are worried about him becoming agitated. We'll come immediately. He mustn't move around.'

'That's what I thought,' whispers Doog. Telling Paul is suddenly real.

At three o'clock Doog walks back into Paul's room. *Thank goodness he has a private ward.* Paul sits, propped up with the computer on his lap.

'I'm not writing,' he says. 'I'm word processing. I found a tutorial attached to the program. It's fascinating, Doog. Thanks again.'

'Paul,' she says, lifting the chair around to the left of the bed. 'I need to talk to you about something.'

'Sounds serious, Doog,' he says, still smiling.

'It is, and I'm not sure … I'm not sure how you'll take it. Please, Paul,' She reaches for his hands and meets his eyes, feeling herself becoming tearful. 'Please, Paul. Remember your leg. Please stay calm.'

'OK, you're starting to scare me now. What are you on about?'

'No, no. I'm not trying to scare you but Paul, you have told me a lot about yourself. Now it's time for you to learn something about me.' She puts up her hands. 'No, don't speak, please listen. When I came north in March, I was searching for something, for some clue to the where abouts of something, someone … my baby stolen from me in 1966.' She hesitates, and looks into his confused eyes. 'I think I've found him, Paul,' she whispers.

He turns and stares through the window. For the longest time he doesn't speak.

'No, no, no, no.' His voice rises. 'Are you trying to tell me that you are the one who ditched me? And are you trying to tell me the Gorski's, Mum and Dad, *stole* me from you?'

Letter

WHEN Doog returns to the hospital the next day, she is not allowed to see Paul. He has barred visitors. She had half-expected this. Telling herself he needed time to process everything she has written him a letter and tucked it into an envelope, with a photo of Annie.

Dear Paul

I anticipated that you would be angry and not want to see me but I am hoping, that one day soon you can bring yourself to acknowledge me as your biological mother. In turn, I acknowledge that Tony and Anna Gorski were your real parents, who nurtured you lovingly until the day they died. I, in no way, blame them. Society and a cruel system entangled us all. When you were stolen from my arms, I was powerless to stop it. The Gorskis would have been told that the baby was unwanted. But I did want you, Paul, and I have wanted you every minute of the twenty-five years since. I would like to tell you the whole story one day. It is not a happy one.

Your biological father is Alex (Allesandro) Rossi. He may not even know of your existence. When I became pregnant, I was locked up and then banished up north. When I returned home, I heard Alex's parents had taken him to Melbourne. He shouldn't be hard to find and I will help in any way I can, if you want me to.

I have to go back to Bedarra. It is the end of term and my pupils need me there. I also have to tell Annie that she has a brother. (Yes, Paul. Please remember you have a sister who is innocent in all this.) I should have told her long before now.

Until we meet again, take care and please try to believe, from the day you were born, I never let go of the love I had for you.

Doog.

There is no short way for a woman to tell her daughter, a girl who has been an only child all her life, that she has an older brother. There is no short way for a woman to tell her daughter that her mother had another life, a secret life. And telling her on the phone is certainly not the way Doog would have chosen.

The phone box on South Street is the one where people made very important calls to other people far away. No one had a phone when Doog was a kid. She can't talk to her daughter with her mother listening, so now she's standing in that box with rain running down all sides, mirroring the tears running down her cheeks as she tries to tell Annie about Paul.

There is silence on the other end of the phone after Doog tells the story as gently as she can.

'Love, I knew this would be hard to explain on the phone. It's a lot to take in so I've posted you a letter that I hope will help. You should get it tomorrow.'

The silence persists. 'Annie?' she whimpers.

'Mum. You're right. It is a hell of a lot to take in, I need time to think about it. I'll get back to you.'

Col picks Doog up from the airport. His dusty smile lifts her. Col loves his trips to town. They arrive back just in time for dinner. Doog is exhausted but she needs to eat and the smell of Mrs C's Guinness casserole is heavenly. Her heart sinks when she finds Maroney has taken off for Sandy Bay.

'He'll be back tomorrow. Said he needed to pick up something from the post office,' said Col. 'Could've waited. Someone has to go in on Friday. They could've picked it up for him.'

The staff trawl for every detail of what happened down south. She tells them about Paul and the hospital but that is all. She's not about to get caught in the local gossip net. Tomorrow she needs to concentrate on school. The kids have had enough disruptions. As soon as she can, she says goodnight.

Turning away from the tank stand she walks in the moonlight towards the yard where all that's left of the campdraft is a bin full of empty beer cans and a tattered notice clinging to the wooden wall of the bar. She climbs into the grandstand. The familiar smell of horses in the warm night air soothes her. Sitting with her feet up on the wide wooden bench she hugs her knees, and hugs the knowledge of what has happened. Paul's face, filled with gratitude, when she gave him the portable computer, gives her such hope. He's angry now but with time … The moonlight picks out the posts and rails of the yard and she finds herself reliving the accident. Again, her insides turn to jelly to think how near he came to death.

The night is still and quiet, except for the soft lowing of cows in the distance. She looks around and sees a red eye glowing in the dark at the far end of the grandstand.

'Is someone there?' she calls out.

'It's only me, Doog.' She recognises Snow's soft voice and remembers he wasn't at dinner.

'Whatcha doing, kiddo? Besides smoking, which is bad for your health.' He sidles over and sits close.

'Contemplating.'

'Yeah?' she prompts but he doesn't answer.

'Jesus, Snow, you're a man of few words. What are you contemplating?'

'I won the campdraft *and* the rodeo.'

'And?'

'They reckon I ought to go in the finals, down south. And Matt's talkin' about sending me to the nationals in Tamworth over east. He reckons Mrs Le Carre would line me up with good horses and organise everything.' He pauses and clears his throat. 'I don't want to leave, Doog. I like it here.'

There's something she's not understanding. Yes, he's shy, but surely he'd be over the moon about his achievement, not sitting here as miserable as shit.

'But Snow, it's an honour that you've earned, and it's not as though you're going forever. You'll be back before you know it.'

'Don't need no honour, Doog, just want to stay here. I was starting to feel like I belong.'

Doog wishes that she could see his face. She reaches over and places her hand over his. 'Of course you belong, Snow,' she says.

'Dunno — never belonged anywhere else.'

They sit in silence for a while. Doog's not sure she has the right to ask but she feels his need to tell, and in this place the choice of people to trust is limited.

'Where did you grow up, Snow?' She asks at last.

He doesn't answer.

'You know, Snow, when you were up on the stage the other night receiving the trophy, and then playing the didgeridoo, I was so proud of you. I found myself wishing that you would turn out to be my son. I lost my son — a long time ago. But I knew it couldn't be you, although you're about the same age, because he was born with masses of dark hair.' She lights a cigarette and inhales deeply. 'No one here knows about that, by the way — not sure why I'm telling you now. Would appreciate it if you kept it to yourself.'

Snow nods slowly. 'I was born up north on Wongharra where my Dad was a stockman. He was Scottish but Mum was Aboriginal and when Dad died, they kicked Mum and me out. We ended up in a circus — a couple of freaks for their show.'

'Your Mum is Aboriginal?'

'Was, yeah, full blood. She's dead now.'

'How did she die, Snow?'

'Got bit by a snake. She was a city woman. Didn't know not to run. She died running to get help.'

Doog nods, remembering the night Snow had asked her how she knew what to do about snake bite.

'At the circus I'd started working with the horses,' he continues, 'and when she died, I went on to be a bareback-riding clown. The crowd loved my act but to the circus mob I was a boong. Couldn't even eat with them. When the circus came to Sandy Bay, I saw a job for a stockman who could sit on a horse so I applied and got the job. No one knows I'm an Abo. And that's the way I'd like it to stay.'

'Well, no one will hear it from me, Snow,' she tells him. 'I must say, with your blond hair I didn't pick it either.' But she can see his Aboriginality now, in the brow and the wide nose, and she remembers the negatives in the darkroom. 'Snow, I really don't think anyone here would care.'

'You don't know, Doog. This is not my mob. I don't even know who my mob is.'

'God Snow, you must feel caught between two worlds.'

'Yeah. Sometimes at night I creep down the creek and sit in the trees watching the mob down there singing and laughing and telling their stories. My heart goes down and sits with them, but my body has to stay here with the white mob … and they're OK,' he adds.

'So, I guess going to the campdraft finals could feel like being in the circus again.' He nods. 'Snow, you're a great rider. You wouldn't just be riding for yourself. You would be riding for the station. This is your chance to really belong. They believe in you enough to let you represent the station over east. They don't care whether you are black, white, or purple.'

Again, there is a long period of silence and again Doog sees the slight nod in the moonlight.

'Yeah, maybe you're right. Maybe I'll give it a go.'

The river of the Milky Way lights her way back to the Donga. She thinks about Snow not belonging. Is that how Paul felt when he discovered he was adopted? The Polish heritage suddenly swept away.

Lost

AFTER school the next day, Doog forgoes her cuppa with Mrs C. In her donga she changes into shorts and a singlet and pulls on her trainers. She needs to run after her time in the city, to hear the rhythmic thud of her footfalls on the baked earth and reconnect with the bush. It settles her mind. The sun slings low in the sky behind her so she's stomping on her own shadow. It's giving her the shits. Past the three-mile windmill, past the turnoff to the waterhole she veers left to get rid of the unwanted attachment. A large rocky outcrop rises like a mini mountain in front of her. It won't take long to do a loop around it and then head back. The sun sinking in the sky still radiates heat.

The solitude carries her. The outcrop has been encircled but there are two more out in front where there were none before and they both look the same. She turns around, backtracks but after running for another half hour she's aware that she's in the situation she warned the kids about. Everything looks the same. The setting sun points the direction but the path has vanished. Chances of finding it dim along with the light. A clump of spinifex trips her over and she comes up cursing, pulling spines from her hands. She startles a small mob of kangaroos and they thump away into the gloom. Fear and embarrassment compete. Not even her bum-bag or a water bottle. No one knows where she is and no matches to light a signal fire. Christ! It's going to be a long night if she can't find her way. Will anyone wonder where she is? Or will they all just assume she hasn't bothered to show up for dinner again. What a stuff-up.

The sun sinks. The deafening chorus of the birds precedes an eerie silence. *Bloody hell!* She has stumbled into an ants' nest. She feels them crawl all over her legs, up into her crotch. She's slapping and brushing like a madwoman, clawing and squeezing up under her shorts, the acrid smell of crushed ants escalating her disgust and dismay. What about snakes? Do snakes come out at night? She forces down a scream. She wants to cry but she's on her own. Tells herself to stop panicking. They'd hear her coming and get out of her way. Can snakes hear?

To her left, parallel threads of light on wire glitter and her hopes rise with the moon. She picks her way in the half-dark trying to avoid falling into spiny clumps or tripping over dead mulga shining white in the moonlight. By the time she reaches the fence line, her legs and arms are flayed. The fence is pointed more south than she knows she should be, but if she follows it, she must come to a track towards the homestead. Clouds darken the sky and she wills them to stay away from the moon.

All at once a figure looms over her. Small eyes glisten in the moonlight. Doog backs up in time to escape the knife-like claws at the end of scaly legs that rear up in alarm. The emu performs a shuddering pirouette and shoots like a spear with a tutu, its neck and head arrowed away from the fence. She lands on the earth, her heart thumping so hard it hurts. The shock of the encounter with the large bird in the dark dissolves the last of her defences. Bleakness takes hold. *What an idiot. She's lost. She's been bloody lost most of her life.*

The track, full of ruts and corrugations causes her to stumble and curse. Then there are lights. The car coming towards her, flashes headlights and Col and Koop are hanging out the windows whooping and cheering and waving their hats.

'Jeez, Doog, where ya been? Missed dinner. Mrs C was ready to have your guts for garters until we realised you was missing.'

Col moves over and she flops on to the front seat of the ute and closes her eyes. smiling away the mixture of relief and embarrassment and frustration with herself.

Koop uses the two-way to let the others know she's OK. 'They've all headed of in different directions looking for you,' he says. 'By the way, you look like you've been through the chaff machine, Doog.'

'Thanks, guys, got myself lost. Look, I'm shattered. Would you mind dropping me off at my donga and telling the others I'm sorry for causing so much trouble. I'll catch them tomorrow.'

Sure,' says Col. 'You go get a shower. I'll get Mrs C to send you down a plate of something.'

After her shower she flops on the bed but the donga feels like the inside of a kettle, and rivulets of sweat worm their way between her breasts. Bugger, she forgot to turn on the air-con before she went jogging. The night is unusually humid for this time of year, must be a storm brewing. She walks outside to give the air-con a chance to cool the place down.

'Can't sleep?' The familiar voice of Maroney comes from the darkness of the verandah of the old shearers' quarters.

'Nah, bit hot. Forgot the air-con.'

'I didn't want to disturb you. Sounds like you had quite an ordeal.' She smiles. Col and Koop would have given everyone a detailed description of her little adventure. 'Come and sit a bit, Doog — I promise no questions, but I sure as hell could use some company.'

'Before I went south you were joined at the hip with Willie. Isn't that enough for you?' she says, immediately cursing herself. *Talk about mouth before brain.*

He chuckles. 'I take heart from the fact that I detect a note of jealousy,' he says. 'And no, my association with Willie is strictly work.' He waits for her to step onto the verandah and flop into a chair. 'Doog, you must know that I …' He looks at her with a questioning frown. 'That I … enjoy … you must know by now that you're the one I want to be with, yet you've been avoiding me as if I had cholera.'

She's about to protest about the jealousy when what he's saying hits her. He's telling her something else now. She can hear it in his voice, telling her he wants to be with her. And all she can think of is that she's glad it's dark. Because the attraction is there, of course it is, but she feels like a fish being reeled in. He's interesting, articulate, educated. But he's younger than her. Is he playing with her? No, he's too sincere for that. She's been on her own for a long time now, telling herself she's fiercely guarding her independence but it has been lonely, and she can't deny the connection she feels to Maroney. He's looking at her now, waiting for her reaction.

'This is crazy,' she says at last.

'Why?' He stands up and moves behind her. He starts to massage her shoulders and neck. He's good, very good. 'You're uptight, Doog. I can see it and I can feel it in your shoulders. You've got a lot on. You're thinking now is not the time. But is there ever a right time, Doog? I'm not sure you can program what I feel for you.'

She feels herself letting go as his hands work away the knots in her shoulders and neck, and move down over her collarbones, stopping just short of her breasts before caressing their way back to her shoulders. Her eyes are closed and her head presses back into his body leaning behind her. Each time, part of her wills those hands to descend a little further, she wants them to keep going. She has to stop him but she doesn't want him to stop.

'I do have so much else to think about, I can't think about this right now,' she whispers. And she reaches up to restrain his hands.

He leans down and brushes his lips lightly over the nape of her neck before he sits and faces her, taking her hands in his. 'Something's happened. What is it? I could feel it this morning. Something's changed. Please, Doog, tell me.'

She can just see his eyes in the starlight, pleading. She stands and leans on rail of the verandah. This thing's been inside her for so long it's hard to let it out.

'I've found him … my son … I'm sure I've found him.' She doesn't want to cry but the relief of sharing with someone threatens to dissolve her. She stares at the stars through the branches of the fig tree and bites down on her lip. Maroney reaches out for her.

'Tell me,' he says quietly, as she sits down again.

She tells him about the flight to the hospital, about the matching blood, about Paul. She tells him about Fremantle and about her mother and about how angry Paul is about not being told he was adopted. She tells him how she had to tell Annie on the phone.

'And I know I have to give her time to take it all in but she was so quiet. She said she would ring me back. Not being able to talk about it face to face is killing me.'

Maroney is bursting with the research that Maria dug up for him but there is no way he can let Doog know what he's been up to. He has a fleeting thought that this would make a hell of a story, then immediately berates himself. Doog means more to him than any story. Perhaps one day, if everything gets resolved, she may agree to tell the world.

'I should have told her sooner. I hope she'll end up happy to have a half-brother but she's bound to be angry. Both of them — angry. I've made such a mess of things.'

'Messes can be cleaned up,' says Maroney quietly. 'It may be painful and it may take time.' He strokes her arm. 'Doog. Come, you are nearly falling off your chair.'

Diving In

FOR the first time since Paul's accident, the morning brings a feeling of peace. When Doog turns her head Maroney is awake, his blue eyes gazing at her, his face as serene as the morning. She rewinds last night.

He was comforting her and she didn't resist when he had carried her to his bed saying he wouldn't try to make love to her. He was saying she needed to sleep and he wanted her to sleep in his arms. His voice was soft and hypnotic and she wanted that too.

On the bed, he'd pulled her close and they lay like spoons. He smelled of soap as he had whispered goodnight and started to lower his head on to the pillow. But she'd reached up and grabbed the back of his neck. She'd pulled his lips to hers and, unexpectedly, all control threatened to fly through the glassless windows. Pent-up emotion erupted but Maroney kept caressing her with his hands and lips, all the time whispering, *Sleep now, Doog. You need to sleep.* She had lain back, sobbing, exhausted, saying she was sorry.

'Don't be sorry,' he whispered. And then she felt herself relax into his strength.

Before she'd fallen asleep, she remembered seeing the awning of stars through the open window. She'd felt sheltered.

She props herself up on one arm. Her sarong has come loose and her breasts are exposed but she makes no attempt to cover up and she sees his eyes soften. 'That was the best sleep I've had in ages,' she says.

Gratitude for the gentleness, the tenderness that he showed last night, rushes through her.

'Thank you for listening,' she says. 'I guess I needed to open up to someone. I'm glad it was you.'

'Over time, holding on to a secret can extract the very essence out of you,' he says, and again Doog glimpses that fleeting look. Far away and very sad.

'And thank you,' she continues, 'for stopping me.' She laughs. 'I think I almost raped you.'

'You were tired and emotional, Doog. I didn't want to take advantage of that, but ...'

'But?'

'But next time, go right ahead.'

She bends over and kisses him gently and before it can become more, she slides out of bed. He reaches out his hand to pull her back.

'It's a school day, Snoopy, some of us have work to do.' She tries to sound light-hearted. She'd like nothing better than to fall into his arms but she needs to stay focused.

'Doog, I'd love you to meet me down at the waterhole after school tomorrow.' he says.

'Uh-uh.' She shakes her head. 'Great idea, but no, I have a date with Matt and Miss Universe to learn about a hot new spreadsheet, whatever that is. On Friday, she needs to catch a plane. I'm pretty sure Matt's taking her to the airport, so that could work.'

Maroney says he'll understand if she can't make it. 'There will be other times, my love,' he whispers, and her heart does a cartwheel. She gazes out to the casuarinas and breathes deeply.

'OK,' she says slowly. 'If it works out you steal wine and I'll bring food. Can we go in your hire car? I've already got enough explaining to do. I need the ute on Sunday.'

Maroney sucks air through his teeth and makes a face as if trying to make a decision. 'I was going to surprise you,' he says. 'But I can't keep a secret, especially now. Doog, I've bought a car.' He pauses waiting for her reaction. She just looks at him.

'How?' she says.

'Rod had a mate check it out for me. Second-hand Land Cruiser. It arrives tomorrow. I'm going to return the hire car in the morning and pick up the new one from the freight yard. The boss was getting super techy about the cost of the hire-car and I think I'm becoming addicted to off-road driving.'

'You're full of surprises, Snoopy. Now I'm really peeved that I'm going to be stuck here.'

For the rest of that day, while Doog's busy in the classroom Maroney replays last night. The thing that really tears him apart is how the love and the loss of her child did not diminish over the years. It makes him wonder what happened to his own mother, who had lost two of her children. He can't shut it out any longer. He has to find out.

*****

The next two days fly. Willie has installed the farm program on the computer. Apparently, the spreadsheet, as Willie calls it, is just a glorified way of keeping facts and figures. It can be used to keep the accounts, as well as being adapted to monitor the results of farming experiments.

Doog wants to tell Willie that none of this fits her job description but she keeps quiet. When Jean or Willie visits the station, they can save it on a diskette and take a copy without needing to print it. Willie rattles on about computers replacing paper one day, saving trees. Doog finds her enthusiasm catching until Willie tells her to feel free to show it to Dan because he's working on an article on Jean's methods. Doog smiles to stop herself from snarling. *Mmm, Dan*! But she has to admit that Willie is disarming.

It's Thursday evening and she's feeling girlishly excited about her date with Maroney. After dinner, Matt beckons her over and points the way down the verandah, stepping out of earshot of the others.

'I need you to drive Willie to the airport tomorrow,' he says. 'Just do a half-day in the schoolroom. Take off at twelve and you can still be back by sundown.'

Doog just stares at him.

'You only do art on Friday arvo anyway, don't you?'

The art comment causes irritation to rise but she quashes it. 'I don't understand, Matt. I offered to take her. But no, you insisted on taking her so now, Matt, I've made other arrangements.'

'Doog, unarrange them. This is important. Don't argue, just do it, or … or you're fired.'

She breathes deeply. 'Yes boss, whatever you say, boss', she hisses with all the sarcasm she can muster and marches away with her teeth clenched.

'What was that all about,' asks Maroney as she stomps around to the back of the tank stand and starts to roll a cigarette.

'Fucking wanker!' She relates the conversation with Matt. 'No thought to what I might have planned, and it's no big deal because we *only do art* on Fridays. Fucking philistine!'

To her surprise and further irritation, he laughs.

'Are you going to let me in on the joke?' she says.

'I bet he came onto her.' Laughter bubbles from him.

'And? So?' She's getting impatient. Mat can take a brush-off. He's used to them and arrogant enough not to care. The scrapping of their excursion to the waterhole disappoints her but Maroney just laughs.

'She'd have given him the cold shoulder with a little surprise thrown in,' he says.

'What do you mean?'

'Willie wouldn't be interested in Matt. Besides anything else, she's gay and if I read Matt correctly that information would have been akin to her having a communicable disease.'

'Gay?' Doog is almost speechless. 'How do you know? She doesn't look gay.'

'And what do gay people look like? Doog, Doog — I can understand Matt stereotyping, he's lived in the bush all his life, led a very sheltered existence. But you were brought up in Freo. Where have you been? It was obvious.'

'Well, it wasn't obvious to me, Mr Sophisticated … Mr Cosmopolitan smartarse.' She stubs out her cigarette and starts striding towards the donga.

He catches up with her. 'Doog, Doog, what's wrong?'

She stops and grimaces. 'I'm tired and cranky … and disappointed,' she admits.

'Well, let's turn this around.'

'Meaning?'

'Instead of going to the waterhole, let me take you both to Sandy Bay, then you and I can stay and make a night of it.'

Doog takes a deep breath. This feels like jumping into a very deep billabong. She's not sure if there will be rocks below the surface but she finds herself saying, 'Yes.'

Mabel Springs

THAT night, surrounded by mosquito coils to deter bugs from dive-bombing into his lamp though the glassless windows Maroney punches out words on his typewriter. He makes himself a promise that next time he's in Perth he'll buy a portable computer like Maria's. At midnight he sets his travelling alarm clock for 5am. At that time, he'll go over what he's written with refreshed eyes.

The next morning, the bin fills with screwed-up paper as he makes changes. It has to be good. Good enough for the boss to give him a glowing reference. He skips breakfast to finish it, and then walks to the office in the homestead where Willie is working at the computer.

'First part of an article on the land-care innovations,' he explains. 'Would you mind taking a quick look before we take off. I'd like to post it from Sandy Bay today.'

She gives him a thumbs-up without taking her eyes off the screen.

After packing the car he returns to his room with a survey map. When Maroney had spoken the night before about wanting to explore the area, Matt had said he had a map he could borrow. It's just as he thought, Mabel Springs is not that far off the track to Sandy Bay. He tries to inscribe the area into in his memory by making a drawing of it. He tells himself to stop acting like a show-off kid as he tucks away the map and the drawing. *Pride goes before a fall*, he can hear Maria saying.

Next, he needs to write a letter to the boss. He inserts a clean sheet of paper into the typewriter. As he writes, the image of Maria and Rod intrudes. They're laughing at him in disbelief about what he's thinking of doing.

'Bugger off you two,' he says aloud. 'Get out of my headspace. 'I'm busy.'

'Talking to yourself now, Snoopy? That's a worry.' Doog has put her head through the window. 'If you want some lunch before we take off, you'd better come now. Mrs C is savage enough about the break in routine without you being late.'

He glances at his watch. Where did the morning go? He'll have to finish the letter in Sandy Bay. Into his backpack he pushes a few clothes and a towel, and then, enclosing his typewriter in its case, he follows Doog.

'What's with the bag and Esky in the back of your car?' she asks as they start off after lunch.

'Can I answer that when we get to The Bay?' Maroney rolls his eyeballs towards Willie in the back of the car.

'More secrets,' she murmurs, and gives him a quizzical look.

He keeps his eyes on the track. *Yes, more secrets* he thinks, pushing away fear.

He asks Doog to drop him off at the local coffee shop while she drives Willie to the airport.

'Make sure you look after that car,' he yells into the cloud of dust and flying gravel as she hits the accelerator.

He looks again at the ad seeking someone to take over the running of the local newspaper that has just come through the staff newsletter. He can't believe he's even considering it. *Any fool can have an idea*. Who said that? Does he have the courage to give it a go? He's being reckless. But he knows for sure he wants to stay here. To stay near Doog. She may not feel the same way but for the first time in a very long time he knows he's about to jump into an extremely deep pond and think about the consequences later. He sits and finishes the letter, glad he already knows what he needs to say, yet it's hard to concentrate, all the time praying he's not being a complete idiot. He walks to the postbox, closes his eyes and drops the letter and his article through the slot. After saluting his editor, he swivels on his heels and goosesteps across the road, imitating his favourite television character, Basil Fawlty. On to Dawson and Son, Stock and Station Agents. He will not look back.

A sign above a large shed tells him he has found the stock and station agents who seem to supply everything not sold at the chemist or supermarket. Maroney finds what he's looking for and again mentally tells Maria and Rod to stop laughing as he heads back to the general store, where he has arranged to meet Doog. The choice is surprisingly good if you're not too fussy about the fruit and vegetables. He fills a basket with cheeses, smoked salmon, dried tomatoes, some capers and crackers, and then he throws in paper plates. He contemplates plastic glasses and shudders and goes to the other side of the store where he finds real glasses in kitchenware. *Nothing's too good for M'Lady.* He's grinning and wondering if Doog likes smoked oysters when she arrives at his side.

'What *are* you up to, Maroney?'

'Anyone for a picnic?' He squirms, suddenly feeling like a witless git.

'A picnic? Where? In a motel?'

'No, no, Doog, listen. If the rest of the accommodation in this town is anything like when I first arrived, we don't want to go there. I have another plan. And … no laughing, Doog. I thought …' He stops and winces. 'I thought I would gear myself up for … camping. I said, no laughing.' But he's laughing himself. And then he tries to look serious while he explains how he has picked up a swag and a few other bits and pieces for camping and his idea of taking food and champagne on ice. And now he's almost too scared to look at her, afraid that she'll reject the idea that he has his heart set on. He clears his throat, feels his face go red then speaks — way too fast.

'Doog, I thought we could make a detour to Mabel Springs on the way back. Everyone says that place is amazing. Thought we could light a fire, have a picnic, sleep under the stars.'

'Camping? Sleeping out in the open? You told me you had an aversion to that sort of thing. Are you sure you're feeling OK?'

'I know, I know.' He can't help laughing himself. 'That's exactly what Rod and Maria would be asking.' He stops talking and meets her eyes. 'Please say you like the idea.'

She's hesitating. Perhaps he shouldn't have sprung this on her. Her own bag of worries is full right now. The other night they may have gone too far, too fast, but he senses that she wants this as much as he does. He's feeling like a schoolboy asking a girl to his first ball. Maria wouldn't believe his awkwardness. She'd give him such a hard time.

'I think it's a beautiful idea,' she says at last with a smile, 'I have to admit, the thought of a tryst in a Sandy Bay motel unit didn't really light my fire.' He lets go of the breath he has been holding.

They drive through the equanimity of the desert landscape. Nothing moves, except kites lazily looping overhead. Maroney and Doog enjoy the comfortable silence. The swag is rolled up in the back, together with the Esky filled with chilled champagne and food. Spare jerry cans of fuel and water are strapped on the roof rack. *You're getting to be quite the Boy Scout*, he'd said to himself, as he had made them secure.

'I don't usually go much for surprises,' said Doog after a while. 'But the promise of sleeping under the stars was more than I could resist.'

'And here was I hoping it was me you couldn't resist.'

She smiles but says nothing. He drives on, thinking how different he feels from the first time he came out on this track with Nev. The sun stains the earth a deeper red and rouses the kangaroos from their diurnal sleep. They veer off towards Mabel Springs, and have driven about fifty kilometres when the bare landscape changes. The bush becomes thicker and the journey more jarring. The track forks. He keeps driving until it forks again. Then with the memory of the map still fresh in his mind he turns down the smaller track to the left.

'Tell me you know where you're going, Maroney.'

He's enjoying showing off but she has a right to be suspicious of his display of confidence in this alien terrain.

He brings the vehicle to a standstill as the track ends in a small clearing.

'Just call me Livingstone,' he says with a grin and a shrug.

They leave the car and after scouting around the edge of the clearing, he finds a tiny boulder-strewn path. He points the way and follows Doog. They walk fifty metres, swiped by bushes that have almost grown over the path and all the time he's praying. He's going to look like the prince of fools if he's got this wrong. Ahead, he hears Doog gasp in surprise as the path opens out to reveal dark water. On three sides high red cliffs are reflected in the stillness, along with paperbark trees and sedges fringing the pool. The only sound comes from the soft cooing of spinifex pigeons and the rhythmic beat of the cicadas. Doog takes his hand and pulls it to her lips.

'This is perfection,' she whispers.

He lets out a sigh of relief and after a while he whispers in return: 'We need to set up camp before we lose the light.' Then, 'Why are we whispering?'

'Not sure. Somehow this place feels … sacred.'

They make two trips back to the car for all the gear. Doog carries the canvas bag. 'So, what *is* in here?' she asks.

'Sheets and pillows, of course.'

'Wow, I'm impressed, Snoopy. She laughs, he thinks, a little nervously. 'When you plan to seduce a girl, you really do it well.'

'Hey, I'll have you know, I don't make a habit of this.'

He's never spoken a truer word.

They set up the swag in the only flat space and light a small fire a metre away sending the smell of smoky eucalyptus into the air. When there's nothing left to do, Doog sits on a rock gazing at the still black pool. She's quiet and preoccupied.

'Do you think the champagne will have recovered from the journey by now? I could do with a little Dutch courage.'

The last thing he wants is for her to feel anxious. He takes her face between his hands.

'Doog, let's agree not to have any expectations. Let's just enjoy the moment in this Shangri-La, not spoil it by … you know … pressure on each other.'

She meets his eyes and her smile turns inwards as she lowers her gaze to the ground. Then she looks up again.

'OK, Snoopy,' she grins, 'but I still want that drink.'

By the time he has the bubbly poured into the glasses, she has spread their picnic out on the canvas top of the swag and is feeding dry sticks into the fire. He tells her what Nev had said about having a white man's fire, and as if on cue, a full moon rises over the cliffs in the eastern sky. They sit in quiet awe of the elemental beauty of the night.

After the second glass, when Maroney is beginning to feel mellow, with a beckoning toss of her head, Doog walks to the edge of the pool and starts to strip. She leaves her clothes on a rock and glides into the dark water. Thinking of ants, he pushes the remains of the picnic into the Esky and follows, shaking his head. Who else would think of ants at a time like this? *You're an idiot, Maroney!*

She has swum about halfway across the pool when he catches up.

'Watching you undress in the moonlight, in this place, it feels like we're the only people on earth.' He hears his own voice. It's husky with desire stronger than he's ever felt.

'It's magic,' she says, looking up at the stars.

They tread water face to face. He nibbles her lower lip and feels her nipples harden. She slides her face over his cheek, nuzzling his ear. His mind is butter but his body is primed and he pulls her forward, feeling himself rising against her. Eyes closed and head thrown back her legs start to entwine him before she pushes him gently and duck-dives away. And then she turns again to face him, smiling and beckoning towards the swag.

'There's another glass each left in the bottle,' she says holding it up as they stand dripping in the moonlight.

They lie down on the swag swathed in the tropical air. She smiles at the moon and Maroney smiles at her. His eyes travel over the smoothness of her body shining wet in the soft light, the rise of her breasts to the points of her brown nipples, the softness of her belly sloping down to the delta of darkness between her legs. He takes a mouthful of champagne and lowers the glass. The thrill of the bubbles against his tongue courses through his body. His lips against her belly, he looks up and sees her head thrown back and feels her legs part. Encouraged, he grasps her buttocks and lifts her to him. He hears her groan as he drinks her in.

Their voices couple, and echo around the gorge, as they explore one another again and again.

The night stays warm and they lie back on the swag in silent satisfaction beneath the soft glow of the stars.

After a while Doog traces her finger down the dip in the middle of his chest.

'You know a lot about me now, my love, but you're still a man of mystery,' she says. 'Yeah, I know you've told me about your job and your friends and your home in Freo, but who is Daniel Maroney?'

'Shh.' He buries his face in her hair. 'We can talk about that any time. Right now, enjoy the night, the magic.'

'C'mon, Snoopy. Spill the beans. Where are you from? Where is your family? You've never talked about that.'

He wants to tell her, just as she has trusted him with her story. She has given him that gift but he hasn't given her one in return. She has a right to ask, a right to know, but he feels apprehension intruding.

'I don't have a family,' he says at last.

'But you must have had one. Everyone has a family, even if they've lost track of it.'

He's not ready for this. Fearing he will crack wide open, he sits up and reaches into her bag and pulls out the tobacco pouch. He can feel her watching while he rolls two cigarettes and passes her one. He stares at the moon breaking up in the pool and lets out a sigh. He needs to open up to Doog but he's not sure he's ready to face it himself.

'I was nine and my ... I was nine the last time I saw my mother.' He drags on the cigarette. 'I remember her Irish accent, her thin arms and long fingers as she hugged us that last time. I remember the bones at the base of her neck but I can't ... I can't remember her face.' His words are choking him now and he's not sure he can go on. 'I can't remember her face,' he says again.

'Tell me.' She coaxes him gently pulling his hands towards her. 'Where were you?'

'I'm ... I'm not sure, England, Manchester, I think. At first, we were in some sort of place with a whole lot of other kids and the next thing we were on a ship. We spent weeks on that ship, sick most of the time. When we arrived ...' He can't go on. He needs to block out the screams. He lowers his head and puts his hands over his ears.

'And then I got sent to a boys home with a whole heap of others.'

She cradles his hands and nods.

'You were a child migrant. God, I'm so sorry. I've heard about them of course, but I guess things like that somehow don't feel real unless they affect you.'

He feels his mouth twist into a bitter smile. 'Oh, it was real, all right.'

'So, you never found out what happened to your mother?'

In the glow of the fire she looks so beautiful. He doesn't want to let this *thing* spoil tonight. He can't tell her why he couldn't face his mother, why he can't face himself. He shuts his eyes. He wants it to go away and he's shaking his head from side to side and she's trying once more to find him, telling him he must share this, calling him Daniel, and that only makes it worse and he can't stop his head from shaking, can't stop his body from rocking until at last, Doog pulls him gently back down onto the swag holding him tightly. That's the last thing he remembers.

The call of the birds wakes Maroney. He opens his eyes to the unsullied sky, smiling as he stretches in the memory of the night before. And then the torment of Doog's questions return. He watches while she sleeps, aware that, for the first time, in a very long time, he loves and needs another person. A jewelled gecko blinks at him from the rock beyond Doog's pillow. He takes it as a sign that he has found something precious. *Don't stuff this up, Maroney.* Without disturbing Doog he quietly climbs out of their makeshift bed, pulls on his clothes and wanders down the track.

When he emerges from the bushes with an armful of wood, Doog is sitting up in the swag stretching. She gives him a warm smile. Her outstretched arms and body reach for him. In that moment, in the glow of that smile he makes a decision. He will find out what happened to his mother.

They sit sipping tea and he tells her what he's decided.

'Doog, you and your story have made me see that I have to find out what happened to my mother. There's stuff I need to get my head around and I'll need to leave for a while. Doog, I haven't thought this through but I know, I don't want to lose you.'

Doog closes her eyes and nods. 'I feel the same,' she whispers.

They stand in silence, roll up the swag, pack the car and start the drive back to the station. She sits beside him staring out the window.

'Doog,' he tries. 'Doog I just need to —'

'I can see you're not ready to talk about it,' she says quietly. 'It's not my business.'

'No, no! Of course, it's your business … Doog.' He pleads softly. 'I just need time to sort some things out.'

'Yeah, you and me, both,' she murmurs, and continues to stare into the desert.

Pardee

THE next day Maroney's eyes follow the ute as Doog heads in the direction of Pardee. Perhaps he should have told her more. *She has a right to know after trusting me with her story.* But know what? His story is a jumbled mess in his mind. He spent so long trying to push it away it's going to take time to make sense of it even to himself. He will tell her everything as soon as he can. He walks down the track in the soft morning light knowing that for the first time since he was eight he has someone he can trust. There are some parallels with Doog's story and his research has confirmed something in his mind: for decades during the twentieth century children, both black and white, were commodities to be stolen, paid for, used as slave labour and worse. It really should be investigated.

When Maroney and his sister had arrived in Fremantle there were people everywhere. A man made a speech about how they were needed. Good strong, white boys and girls. Good British stock. *Work hard and you'll have a future in this country.* Afterwards, they were divided. Men in black herded the boys into a bus. Women in grey uniforms pushed the girls in another direction. The girls were sobbing and many of the boys were trying not to cry. His sister clung to him and screamed as a big woman tugged her. He has never forgotten those screams or the panic in her eyes or them dragging her away, and he hears his mother's voice over and over again. *Look after your wee sister, ——.* She didn't say, *Daniel.* That wasn't his name. Christ! Why can't he remember?

Doog's driving too fast over the bumpy track to Pardee. *You don't need this complication in your life right now, girl. You have more than enough already.* She slows down. But she can't control it, this thing that is happening– between her and Maroney. And right time or not, she doesn't want to control it. She's glad he's taking off for a while. It will give her time to think.

Connor meets her at the door. She surrenders to the cheeriness of the old Irishman while they have a cup of tea and discuss ways to make the homestead more manageable for Paul. Connor has already strengthened the rail on the steps to the verandah.

'Wouldn't want to see him go arse over tit and break the other leg,' he chuckles.

Connor has been sworn to secrecy. 'I'm not sure he would thank me for interfering,' she says. The old man doesn't understand but she makes him promise while she helps stack some of the chairs on the verandah and pushes the table over to one side so there's more room for Paul to maneouvre with crutches. The office is a mess but she decides to leave that alone. She won't intrude too much into Paul's life. She has a feeling he would resent it if he knew.

There are several rooms that have been kept tidy for guests. They just need vacuuming and dusting. Paul's bedroom, though, is quite a mess. It must have been the Gorskis' room. The furniture is all early Australian, dark and heavy. An old double bed sits high off the floor. Three hooked rugs in reds and blues with an ethnic pattern give relief from the dark jarrah floor.

She drags them out through the french window to the verandah and hangs them over the rail. She tells Connor they should roll them up in case Paul trips over them. Which room was

Paul's when he was a child, she wonders. There's no sign of old favourite toys or teenage posters. Just as well. If she had found a matchbox toy lurking under a bed, she would have been tempted to steal it. Sounds like he spent most of his time outdoors. She imagines the boy, Paul, happy tinkering with real cars in the shed or polishing saddles and bridles in the tack room.

The bed sheets need changing so she searches for the linen closet. The sheets and all the clothes strewn on the floor will make at least two loads of washing. After she has made the bed, she dusts the furniture with a damp cloth and on the bedside table, behind the radio and the lamp, an old biscuit tin confronts her. Is this the same one Paul spoke of? Does she have a right to open it?

She sits down on the bed, picks it up and puts it down again and fetches the vacuum cleaner. Connor has gone to muck out the stables. The vacuum cleaner is large and old and noisy, but its long tube extends to reach the high ceilings and suck up the dusty labyrinth of spider webs clinging to the A-frame trusses. The biscuit tin still beckons. Sitting on the bed again, she opens it before she can change her mind. A birth certificate is there, stamped with the date that is seared into her mind. It hurts to see the Gorskis named as the parents. She finds her maiden name, almost obliterated, inside a brown envelope, the paper Paul talked about, stamped BFA. This is the envelope that should have been sent to the department. Under the envelope is a tiny white hospital wristband inscribed with handwritten letters and numbers that are worn and barely legible. There's a surge of pain as the tiny band twists around her heart. A sob escapes her. There is something else in the box. A whisper-thin gold chain lies in the corner of the tin with the small amethyst pendant that her grandmother had given her. This, more than any piece of paper, tells her she has found her son.

The day he was born ... it's coming back to her. She had begged a nurse to make sure it went with the baby for luck. She had prayed that the nurse would be honest and not just keep it. How had she forgotten that? The drugs — she'd been groggy for days afterwards. She carefully puts everything back in the tin and replaces the lid. Holding the tin to her breast she sits on the bed with eyes closed, rocking back and forth. She hears Connor and opens her eyes with a start.

'Doog,' he says, frowning. 'Are you all right?'

She nods and tries to smile. Then she looks at her watch. Where had the day gone? She needs to get back to Bedarra.

Tonight Maroney won't be behind the tank stand. He has taken his swag and newly acquired camping gear to explore the surrounding stations and she's missing him already. He had joked, saying if he didn't watch out, he would turn into a rural reporter. Prattled on about being fascinated by the new methods. Stuff that Willie had told him. Old farming practices impacting on the land ... rebalancing the ecology ... reversing erosion ... salinity of the soil. He'd said something about Paul and Pardee ... innovations ... fit and healthy cattle. Stop the spread of exotic bloody weeds. Bring back the fucking native bee. She had to admit at that stage she was jealous of Willie and she had hardly listened. Now she regrets it and she wants so much to tell him what she found in the biscuit tin.

Where Emus Drink

MARONEY is away all week. Doog tries to banish him from her mind by immersing herself in the schoolroom. The children cross off the days on the school calendar and Doog knows the end of term is suddenly close and they need to complete the send-in work for Distance Ed before then. But the artless smile of Maroney, which she has grown so fond of, keeps intruding and she remembers the water trough that Willie had told him about.

After school, she packs her camera bag with various lenses and drives out to the shelterbelt until she catches sight of the windmill just off the track. The trough is two metres in front of her as she sits in the shade with her back against the cool of the concrete tank, her camera on her lap. The only sound is the rhythmic clank-clank of the windmill circling in the soft breeze. The best part of an hour passes. She relaxes into a yoga position and doesn't move. Birds begin to stir as the sun falls crowning the surrounding trees and bushes with a halo. The light is ideal.

She holds her breath as one emu after another emerges from the bush and starts to drink. Their salt-and-pepper feathers reflect the glow of the late afternoon. Some of them fold their legs, bending backwards at the knees and flopping like giant mops in front of the trough. They drink and drink until she thinks they must surely burst.

Bit by bit she raises her camera. The click-clack of the shutter is loud in the silent bush but the emus don't seem to notice and keep drinking. Kangaroos start to enter the clearing and stand as if patiently waiting their turn. Several come closer and take delicate sips from the overflow of the trough. Small heads poke from pouches on the bellies of some of the females. A large bungarra waddles from the bush and, oblivious to the emus, pulls its spotted body up the side of the trough, hanging on with urgent claws while it drinks deeply. She wishes she could share this moment With Maroney.

But she's glad she's alone, controlling the stillness, melding into the surrounds so the animals accept her. The children should see this. Then she thinks Jake, Sam and Molly probably have. The emus amble back into the bush, a few at a time. Only smaller kangaroos are left. Her stomach rumbles: it must be almost dinnertime. She's thinking of dragging herself away when a small amber clump shuffles towards her. At first, she's not sure what it is, and then the creamy spikes of the echidna, aglow in the setting sun, come into focus. The small animal with the comical gait stops by the overflow, stretches out its leathery neck and sips with its surprised face and pointed beak, while Doog snaps away, unable to believe her luck.

There is just time to shower and change before dinner. Again, she finds herself wishing Maroney were here. *Forget the bastard*, she chides herself but it's not the same without him.

'Connor rang and left a message for you,' Matt says as she walks up the steps to the verandah. 'He said to tell you he's picking Paul up from the airport on Saturday.'

She's surprised. She thought he'd be in hospital for at least another week.'

'Well, it looks like he's recovered,' says Matt. 'He's not our problem anymore.' Doog says nothing.

They raise their glasses and toast Snow. He's back from the state finals, having won almost everything there was to win. He has a whopping great buckle on his belt and a heap of ribbons to show them. Doog would swear he stands taller and she senses something else. The furtive look has gone and it's as if he has a delicious secret that he's keeping to himself.

Behind the tank stand that night, there's no Maroney. *Bugger you, Snoopy, I was quite happy here by myself before you came along. Now I have to admit I'm wishing you'd turn up to cadge a cigarette.*

Loose Ends

MARONEY has returned from the stations with the certainty that his life has changed, that he's changed. There is no going back. Questions go round and round in his mind. Unanswered What draws him to this country? Is it this woman? What need? What fear? Could it be that he is starting to face his fears, and is open to love for the first time?

Out here in the unforgiving space, there's nowhere to hide. Watching the folk on the smaller stations battle on, seeing their struggle against the odds farming in the desert country gives him no permission for regret. But now, he understands so clearly that he has to deal with the grief before he can move forward with Doog or anything else in his life. There is no going back. But first he must go back.

He should ring Maria. She had called earlier today.

'When are you coming home, Maroney? I hate to admit it but we actually miss you.' Her voice had reached down the phone line and squeezed his heart. He couldn't answer. He wanted her to hold him like she does her toddler. 'Maroney, you still there?' she yelled down the phone. He couldn't speak. He just gulped and nodded.

'Shit, we've been cut off,' he heard her say and the phone went dead.

Maroney knows that Doog feels for him. When he had started to open to her, telling her about leaving England, she had been gentle and understanding. Cared. But how can she help when he's not letting her? She had tried again when they met at the tank stand the night after they came back to Bedarra. She said she didn't think she could have a relationship with someone who shut himself away. It's history repeating itself, Gina had said the same thing. He said he needed more time. It sounded lame — he knows. She'd looked hurt and now she's shutting *him* out. Some nights at the tank stand, hardly a word passes between them. He mourns the light-hearted banter they had in the beginning, but he doesn't feel like frivolity. And he can sense she's obsessing about Annie and Paul and the whole damned catastrophe. He's powerless to help her.

During the day, Doog tells herself to switch off to everything except the kids and school. Even when school's finished, she tries not to think about Annie or Paul or Maroney. Or her mother. She must write to her mother. Claris will be wondering if she's made any progress with Paul.

When she was a little girl, she found a cracked golf ball and picked at it until she had peeled away the outer layer to see what was inside. The chaos of the compressed strands of rubber exploding out of the case filled her with a sense of powerlessness. There was no way of packing those strands back together into the body of the ball and, although she knew it was irrational, it had dismayed her.

'Life's not like that, Doog,' her friend Frankie had told her. 'You can't expect it to be all tidy with no loose ends.'

But she hated loose ends.

'I need to leave, Doog.' A pain stabs her chest and she's glad it's dark.

'When?' She's not surprised. It's what she's been expecting but it's too soon. It's like there's a chunk of him missing. She doesn't blame him, nothing's the same anymore but it's not what she wants.

'In the morning. I'll see if I can get on the afternoon plane.' 'I have to go back to Fremantle for a while.'

She nods. 'I wish … I just wish we'd had more time to talk.'

'I have to sort through some stuff, Doog,' he says gently, and places a soft kiss on her lips.

She can see the hurt in his eyes and wants to hold on to that kiss. 'Yeah, I know the feeling,' she whispers.

He frowns. 'Doog, I don't have the right to ask you to wait for me and I don't want to make promises I can't keep,' he says. But after … I *do* want to come back.' This time the kiss is long, almost desperate. She swallows hard as he walks away.

In the mirror in the donga, she catches sight of her belly. It's starting to sag. Fool, she says to the mirror. What did you expect? But Maroney's not that shallow, she knows that, so what is wrong with him? What is so damned wrong that he can't tell her?

She falls into bed but sleep only comes with the warble of magpies.

Dream Catcher

A FRAGMENT of a dream becomes stuck like an old LP on a turntable, revolving, repeating, frustrating, but when Maroney wakes feeling tense and still tired, it sidesteps memory. The Fremantle apartment looks different, everything is different, he's different. The shame still clings, he can feel it, only now he cares. He wants to do something about it. He can't connect, especially to Doog, with the past clawing at him. Who would have thought that he, of all people, would have come undone in the red desert country? It has picked apart his very existence. Insanely, at the same time, it has nurtured him and given him strength.

He takes his coffee out on to the balcony. The river persists past the apartment, homing to the ocean, towards England. Perhaps towards answers. He needs to go back to the organisation that helps link child migrants with their families. He's known about them for years … ever since he went looking for his sister. He was fourteen going on fifteen. That's when they put you on the street. 'Goodbye, we've trained you. Now go get a job.' They said his sister was dead. Part of him had been prepared to hear that but the other part felt like one of his dreams, the one where his guts are spread on the floor for all to see.

Leukemia killed her. The Department of Child Protection said she would have died whether she had stayed in England or not. They said that. But he doesn't believe it. Disease stalks unhappy people. They'd asked if he wanted more help. Did he want to try and find his mother? He remembers the idea filling him with dread. He'd stumbled out of the office unable to face anymore questions.

There was a river where he came from. He's sure of that. He has hazy images of boats. Gulls screaming and the smell of coal and rotting weed. He and his sister climbing on the railing. His mother calling them to get down. In his dreams his mother is always calling but he can't answer. He doesn't want to tell her. He's found his sister. But he's too late. He has failed.

Now he's back in the same department. A woman meets his scowl with an empathetic smile and tells him he must be prepared for the fact that his mother may be dead or infirm by now. He's craning his neck to see the contents of the file. She hands him his birth extract. How come they didn't do that last time? It's a jolt to see his real name after all the years. The woman's guessing how old his mother might be. Calculating that if he was born while his mother was in her early 20s, she could be in her early 60s.

'I can't see anything in the file to say your mother is dead. There's still a good chance.' He's already thought through all this a thousand times, but somehow it feels good to hear it put into words. He rises to go and then turns and shakes her hand.

'I'll let you know how I get on.'

She smiles and hands him a piece of paper. 'This is a good place to start,' she says. 'I will see if I can find anything more about your mother and if you need us, we're here for you.'

He glances down. It's the address of the registry office of births deaths and marriages in the United Kingdom. He was told about this place years ago but now he's ready to know. That night the dream returns. This time, he catches it. The cardboard suitcase in his hand bursts open and clothes spill out onto the deck. He's trying to gather them, but they keep spilling out and the wind picks them up. They fill with air and swoop on him like kites. He runs, trying to pull them back but Kitty is screaming for him.

He sits up in bed. They called her Kitty. Tears of relief run with the sweat on his face. For years, no matter how hard he'd tried, he couldn't remember her name. Oh, yes, they told him she'd been named Katherine, but he knew that wasn't right. All he remembered was how frightened she'd been on the boat. After lights-out she would sneak into the cabin he shared with three other boys. She'd curled up warm with his arms around her and he'd stroked her hair and called her Kitty-Cat while she fell asleep. No one cared what they did on the boat. They were left alone. He hadn't gone to visit the grave. Couldn't see the point, it wouldn't even have her real name on it. Now, with sudden certainty, he knows his mother would want him to make that visit. But when he thinks of telling his mother that Kitty is dead, courage evaporates.

He pushes himself off the bed, feeling as if he has been run over by a haul-pack. He has written down a plan of action. That way he knows he's more likely to force himself to carry it out. *Any fool can have an idea.* The first thing is to visit the grave, perhaps find a way to mark it with her right name. Second step: *What is the second step? Start the process to contact his mother? It shouldn't be hard. What if she's dead?* He splashes cold water on his face and sees dread in the mirror. That would be easier. He doesn't want to face her grief. *God, is he wishing his mother dead? What sort of a son wishes his mother dead? Why can't he remember her face?*

Before he has time to back out, he books a flight via Berlin that will land at Manchester Airport, eight kilometres from the city centre. And then he receives the news from the woman in the department that his mother died in 1974. For days he doesn't get out of bed until after dark. He walks along the river from Fremantle to Perth glad of the punishing cold. He returns, hugging the river until he reaches the apartment at dawn, burrowing back into bed, too exhausted to let grief keep him awake any longer.

The woman in the department said he had said he had another sister. He'd refused to believe it until he received the records. There had been three of them left in the home in Manchester. How come he didn't know that?

But through the fog of the years, he hears a baby crying. He remembers his mother, feeling her grief, but he still can't reach her face. Kitty was frightened and screaming for their mother. He remembers wanting to do the same but he had to be strong, to take care of her. They must have taken the baby to a nursery. His mother had turned away, shoulders shaking after she handed over the bundle. It must have been summer. He remembers her thin arms and the floral frock. He wills his memory to lift to her face but it's stuck on the bones at the base of her neck. They couldn't have been in the home very long. Kitty was about five and the next thing they were on the boat and all that mattered was that they were together and he was taking care of her just like his mother told him to.

He considers cancelling his flight but he can't. He owes that much to this unknown sister.

*****

As he walks through the crowded walkways to the baggage area of Manchester airport, the tangle of voices catch on the threads of memory. A porter pushes an old woman in a wheelchair.

'Coming through,' he calls out in a broad accent. 'Make way for m'lady, please folks.'

The accent, the people … it sounds ridiculous even to himself, but he suddenly feels a strong sense of belonging to this place. On the airport bus to the city, memories return of a trip around England with Maria and Rod in an old Kombi van. They drove past this metropolis, looking down from the motorway, shocked

231

at the coagulated mass of houses, on what must have been the outskirts of Manchester. All those years ago he'd been relieved when they'd decided not to stop. What would have been achieved? Trying to find his way back to something that didn't seem real. It was another world. Too far removed to worry about. Now, the English double-decker bus drones on through block after block of grey council flats. In his backpack is an address sent from the UK Registry Office.

The walls in the reception of the hotel he has booked are lined with English oak. The mixture of lavender and furniture polish remind Maroney of the old cottage where Maria and Rod live in Fremantle. As he walks up a small, dimly lit staircase, he smiles at the bric-a-brac and the furniture, darkly last century. The room is clean and comfortable but he stays only long enough to freshen up before going back downstairs in search of a beer and a snack. He feels like an interloper. White sash windows and a large gilt mirror are all that lift the saloon, a time warp of maroon wallpaper. He winces at the shelf running around the walls displaying a set of antique plates with gold borders.

The only other guests are an English couple, older. Their hands touch, their eyes and their smiles shutting out the rest of the world. He thinks of Doog. She'll be sleeping now, probably exhausted. It's almost the end of term and he's seen how much reporting she has to do. He can't imagine her not teaching. Enthusiasm for the job glows from her. He'd love to find a way to have her all to himself but he knows that wouldn't work. They both need their own lives. But surely, at times, those lives can merge.

He drinks his beer staring at the far wall, where a larger cracked gilt-edged-plate hangs alone. He turns away.

Outside, he hails a taxi to take him to the address he has been given. It's in an estate with red-bricked terraced houses compressed on both sides of meagre streets. All have identical doors at the top of sets of identical steps. The taxi pulls up outside one of them.

He pays the driver and asks him to wait five minutes. Before he has time to change his mind, he strides up the steps and raps the brass knocker. Someone opens the door and gazes up at him.

She's small, and has freckles, with sandy-coloured hair. Shock skewers him. Kitty. With her pointed chin and bright blue eyes. He feels the blood drain from his face and stumbles back down the stairs. A honk from the taxi demands his attention as he starts up the street. He dashes back and tells the driver not to wait. Around the corner is a pub where he orders a whiskey and water and sits with his hands wrapped around the glass while his stomach and mind begin to settle. The girl is Kitty's double. It has to be his niece, and he has to go back.

His heart thumps as he knocks on the door again. This time, a woman about thirty opens it. The little girl is behind her.

'That's him, Mam,' she whispers, with a squirm that is achingly familiar.

The woman frowns. 'What is it you want?' Her accent is thickly Manchester, and vaguely threatening.

'I'm Daniel … no, I mean I'm Patrick, Patrick Maroney. Your … your brother.'

A hand flies to her mouth. 'Where? Where …?'

'From Australia. I've been in Australia.' He's staring at the small girl and trying not to cry.

Maggie is her name. Well, it would be. She was Margaret on the records.

'I'm sorry; I should have given you warning. I wasn't going to come, and suddenly I knew I had to. They didn't give me a phone number.'

'No, we don't have a phone in the house. There's a phone box on the street.'

'Still, I suppose I could have written,' he says. 'Truth is, I wasn't sure you'd want to see me.' He's aware that he's sounding like a blubbering idiot but Maggie's eyes soften and her face quivers.

'And why, in God's name, did you think that?'

Her voice with its no-nonsense Manchester accent is harsh, but she opens her arms and pulls him into her softness. 'God love you, Paddy. Did you not know this would be like the second coming?'

He looks down at the girl and blinks back tears. They called her Kitty.

'Kitty, this is your uncle, turned up, all the way from Australia.'

He wipes his face and kneels down. 'Kitty, you had an Aunty we called Kitty and she looked just like you.' He bites his bottom lip. 'And I loved her very much.'

'Where is she now?'

He starts to tell his niece that Kitty is in heaven but instead he says, 'She died, Kitty. A long time ago.'

Maggie ushers them into the front room, sits him on a sofa covered in faded fabric printed with large cabbage roses. He runs his hand over the fabric. He has the same feeling of belonging that he felt in the airport. And again, he wonders if he's being fanciful. Maggie sets a cup of tea on a small doily-draped table in front of him. She brings out an old album the colour of cardboard with glace paper between the pages. The photos are mounted with ornate black photo corners and he feels as if he has stepped back in time.

'I've only a few of our Mam,' she says.

There's a studio picture of him lying stomach-down, naked on a blanket, holding his head up. He's smiling. Another looks like it has been taken with a Box Brownie. There's the four of them with baby Maggie propped up in the centre. The sepia picture of his mother, taken at the riverside eating an ice cream, smiling into the camera, crumples his face as memories return.

'How old were you when she died?' he croaks, trying not to break down again. His small niece stares at him with wide, unblinking eyes.

'I was about fourteen. I had just got myself a job as a housemaid at the pub around the corner. When she died they let me live in.'

Maggie leads him to the kitchen and he sits at the table. It's hard to listen while she tells him how, when their mother had learned that he and Kitty were no longer at the home, she had tried to find them.

'She took queer after a while when she couldn't find you. The neighbours told me that. She took me home and worked two jobs so she could keep a roof over our heads and pay the woman next door to look after me.' Maggie twists the hanky in her hand. 'She was always sick. Crying filled our house. I'm glad she didn't know that our Kitty was dead. She clung to the hope that you both had good lives somewhere in the colonies.' There's a pause while Maggie rises and starts to clear the table. 'It's funny,' she says, turning back to him, 'Mam always imagined you must have gone to Canada.'

A key clicks in the door. With a scream Kitty jumps up and dashes into the close. Maroney's head spins, ready to run after her, to protect her, the old feeling of terror erupting.

'It's all right — just my husband coming home. She loves her Da.'

'Stephen!' She rises to kiss a stocky man with a round beaming face. 'Stephen, you'll never guess …,' and she introduces Maroney.

Stephen takes off his cap and scratches his closely cropped head.

'Welcome to Munchester, mun,' he says with a broad smile, extending a hand. Maroney likes him immediately. 'Australia!' Stephen says. 'Well, I'll be. We were thinking about migrating there once, weren't we love?' He pronounces it *loov* and looks at

Maggie, and then back to Maroney. 'Well, well, you must have a tale or two to tell. I hope you'll be staying awhile.'

They offer to put him up but he explains about the luggage and the hotel. He had anticipated this offer, but now, more than ever, he needs space to take it all in.

'But you'll stay for your tea now and you'll come back, surely?' Maggie is setting the laminex table with knives and forks.

Over and over Maroney has imagined sitting around a table having a meal with … his mother … his family. He smiles and nods. 'Of course,' he says.

Maggie looks up with surprise on her face. She comes over to him with a teary smile and a hug. 'Christ almighty, Paddy, d'you know that's the first time you've smiled since you came through the door. I was beginning to think you didn't know how.'

The small gathering sits down at the table and Maroney feels warmth flood his desiccated heart. Stephen dishes out the stew while they ask him about Australia and he gives them a version.

'Can I ask a favour of you?' he says after a while. 'I've been called Daniel, and then just plain Maroney all this time in Australia. I don't think I could get used to Patrick right now. Do you mind?'

Maggie reaches across the table and puts her hand on top of his. 'Of course, we won't mind if that's what you want, but why? Why did you change your name Pa … Daniel?'

Silence closes in on the room. He needs to tell them this.

'I didn't change it. They did. They wanted us to forget who we were, and with most of us they succeeded. After I left the mission, when I went looking for Kitty, I found out my real name. I took back Maroney but I still had friends from the mission, and they knew me as Daniel.' He takes a breath and looks up at Maggie. She smiles with an encouraging nod and he goes on. 'Perhaps I would have felt entitled to hold on to my name if I had held on to Kitty's hand that day. I had let our Mam down and I didn't care anymore.'

'God love you, you were nine years old Patr ... Daniel.'

He smiles, wet eyes trying to blink back pain. 'I know that, but somehow ...'

'I'll hold your hand, Uncle Daniel.' says his niece, her elfin chin quivering with concern.

He wipes a hand across his eyes and puts out his other hand with a wet grin.

'Would you?' he whispers. 'I'd like that. I reckon that would fix me right up.'

The Sandy Bay Post

A MONTH later there's a call from Fremantle. Doog's heart leaps.

'I'd given up on you. Sent you a letter. No reply, Maroney.' She can't keep the accusation out of her voice.

'Yeah, sorry about that … had to go away for a while. A lot's happened Doog. I need to tell you.'

'I'm here. I'm listening.'

'I need to tell you everything, Doog.' he says. Is there a slurring to his words?

'Yes, Maroney, I'm listening,' she repeats. She asks him where he has been but he says he can't explain things right now.

'It's long story, Doog. There's no short version. Got some things to sort out in Fremantle. Can't say when I'll be back. But soon.'

'It's good to hear from you. I … I've missed you, Maroney.' But he's gone.

Doog puts the phone down and feels flat. Flat and very frustrated. Why did he bother to ring if he's not going to *say* anything? He hadn't asked about her or anyone else on the station. What is he saying? That it's all a mistake. That he needs to back out. *OK, stuff him. He's blown in, got what he wanted — a few articles for his paper — and now he'll blow back out again.* He has to come back to collect his car. He left it in Sandy Bay when he caught the plane. She curses. She was settled before he crashed her party.

The following Wednesday, Maroney arrives at the homestead just in time to join everyone for dinner. Doog is on the verandah when she sees his car pull up at the shearers' quarters. She watches as he takes his bag into his room and strides up through the casuarinas towards the homestead. She wants to run down to meet him, hold his broad shoulders, ruffle his sandy hair, have him all to herself. But all she can do is smile and wave from the verandah railing, and watch him walk up the steps to be greeted by the staff. Their eyes meet. His smile is warm. And worried. She hates the fact that she can't talk to him except for a polite hello. Others monopolise him and it's driving her insane.

After they've eaten, he triumphantly holds up a bundle of newspapers. One has a photo of Snow on a bucking colt The horse and man are airborne in a sunlit cloud of dust. A moment of doubt flits across Snow's face as the paper is passed around, but when he sees the photo, he gives Doog a nod and lets out a soft, *Wow!* As well as the campdraft in one paper, there is a double-page spread in another edition. It displays the story that Maroney has written on the new farming methods being trialled on the station. They all pore over photos that Doog took at the waterhole as well as several shots contrasting the rich valley of Tagasaste with the desert landscape.

'Thought you said you were just a dabbler,' says Matt. 'Time, I think, I had payment for the darkroom you're using.'

'On with you,' Doog says, and shrugs.

'No, I mean it. These are great.' Matt says, with a rare show of enthusiasm. 'I'd like to get a few blown up and framed for the homestead. I reckon Jean Le Carre would be interested in them as well.'

'Well, you might have to go through her agent.' Maroney smiles as he hands an envelope to Doog. 'Your first pay cheque, madame photographer.'

Now it's Doog's turn to say 'Wow!' She's already over the moon that her photos have been published. She hadn't expected to be paid. She wants to know more about how Maroney pulled this off. Their eyes meet. He looks at her and shrugs helplessly. Before she can ask him, Matt interrupts.

'What are your plans, Maroney? You've been here some time now. You must be thinking of moving on.'

Doog scowls, but Maroney turns to Matt. 'Yes, I know I've overstayed my welcome.'

'For Chrissakes Matt,' Doog snaps. 'He's been in the old shearers' quarters, which are hardly fit for a dog, and he's contributed in more ways than one.'

'No, Doog, Matt's right, I can't stay here forever. I'm putting some plans in place. Never meant to stay this long.'

Doog feels as if she has been punched. So, Maroney is planning to move on after all. She feels her hopes being thrashed around like a thread in the breeze, one minute buoyed by the publishing of the photos, the next minute crashing in a gully.

Maroney looks around. 'You guys will never know how much being out here has changed my life.'

'We won't know if you don't tell us,' says Koop.

'Yeah, well perhaps another time. Right now, I'm bushed. Gotta hit the sack.' And he rises to go.

Yeah, Maroney, Doog thinks. *We won't know if you don't tell us.* She stays to help clear the table and then follows him. He's not at the tank stand and she tells herself not to care. She keeps on towards the donga.

'Join me?' Maroney's voice comes from the dark of the verandah of the shearers' quarters. Clouds hide the moon and stars.

Doog slumps into a chair. 'It's good to have you back, Snoopy,' she says, 'but now you're talking about leaving us.'

'Well, not entirely.' He lights a candle and leans towards her. Takes both her hands in his. 'Doog, before anything else I need to apologise.' He closes his eyes and rocks slightly. When he opens them, his eyes search hers. 'I shouldn't have phoned the other night. I was a mess. I'd been drinking with Rod,' he says. 'I didn't know how … where, to start. I knew I wasn't making sense, but I couldn't help it. I just wanted to hear your voice.'

'You said you wanted to talk to me.' Doog is aware that her voice sounds as brittle as she feels. And then she sees that he's smiling as he pours them both a drink. He tells her yes, he does want to talk to her. He has so much to tell her but first he wants to propose some toasts.

'Here's to Ms Doogie Wilson, the northwest's most celebrated photographer,' he says as he clinks her glass. 'And here's to the new editor of *The Sandy Bay Post*.'

It takes a while for the words to sink in. 'What, you? How?'

Doog learns it's something he has been working on it for a while. *The Post* is part of the same group as his paper, he tells her. His friend, Maria, noticed the ad and mentioned it because he was up this way.

'I don't think she dreamt, for one minute, I might consider it. Matter of fact neither did I, but once the idea became implanted in my mind it took hold.' He grimaces. 'Maybe I should have told you what I was planning, but it seemed too unreal, too impossible. Part of me didn't think I'd go through with it.' He stops and laughs. 'It's a very small concern, The *Sandy Bay Post*. Probably the highlight of the year will be the show results, but I'm hoping to build it up.' He pauses, looks at her intently. 'What do you think, Doog?'

Doog's mind can't keep up. She really *is* tired and she's not sure she understands. Maroney had never struck her as reckless but that's what this feels like. Can he possibly be happy if he dumps his city life and starts anew up here?

'God, Snoopy. I'm not sure what to think.'

'Well, I've done it now,' he says. 'And I was hoping you might help me.'

'Me? Help with a newspaper? How?' she says.

'Your photographs, for a start. And I know it's a dream … but I thought that during school holidays you and I could go walkabout to find stories. Document this country. Who knows, maybe one day we'll have enough material to make a best-selling coffee-table book. We'll be rich and famous and live happily ever after,' he says, and grins.

'Yeah,' she says. 'Right.'

Maroney reaches for her hands and meets her eyes. He's telling her he doesn't care what they do as long as they do it together. Says he's not trying to rush her into anything and she is not responsible. That he made this crazy career move all on his own. His life had to change and this just might work.

'And my life has changed, Doog. Not just because meeting you is the best thing that's happened to me and not just because of the reconnection to my family. There's something more, something intangible about the desert. It's as though it holds a hidden well that sustains me.'

He stops and she looks at him but she can't find the words.

'You think I've lost the plot, don't you?'

'No,' she says slowly. 'But you sure *are* full of surprises.' They sit together in silence, both smiling. 'And I *am* glad you're staying.'

'I'd be tied up with the paper, Doog, and you'll have your job here, but there will be plenty of opportunities to get together, on the weekends, whenever you're not working. And I'm sure I'll find any excuse to visit out this way. Who knows? For now, let's just wing it.' He stops and draws breath. 'Now,' he continues, 'is anyone going to ask how my trip to Manchester went?'

'Came over for that express purpose, Snoopy, but I haven't been able to get a word in.'

Maroney's story takes Doog from outrage to sadness. She's heard about the child migrants, of course she has. Even visited Fairbridge Farm and read of the misery there, including one tale of a child suicide. All that had seemed in the distant past, nothing to do with life today. Yet here is Daniel Maroney, on the surface a confident man who's made a successful life for himself, damaged and haunted by what amounts to kidnapping, child abuse, slavery and yes, murder is not too strong a word, all happening in the so-called civilised world. Little kids, arriving without their parents, after weeks at sea, lost and frightened. She pictures them standing on the wharf with their little cardboard suitcases and brims with anger and pity. She had felt Maroney's pain and panic as he told of his sister wrenched from his arms. The guilt that has torn him apart through the years was thick in his voice and the misery of the memory shrouded him.

'Since I've been here, I've started to face what I've tried to forget,' he had said last night. He told her that before arriving at Bedarra he hadn't confronted his past but up here, meeting her, it seemed impossible to avoid. He paused and then tenderness had filled his eyes. 'While I was in Manchester, I realised how much I cherished you. I know that's an old-fashioned word but somehow it describes how I feel about you. I decided that if we have any chance of moving forward, I needed to tell you about my past, Doog.' He'd closed his eyes, one hand dragging down over his mouth. 'I'm not sure what telling you will achieve but my sister, Maggie in Manchester and all the new-age wisdom says I should share it with someone.'

He'd talked in a monotone voice as if he'd rehearsed what he needed to tell her. Doog tried to encourage him, taking his hands in hers. Secrets are better not kept. They are too corrosive. She knows.

'Somehow I could never write it down like you did. But it comes to me in nightmares and even in the daytime it sometimes possesses me when I'm least expecting it.' He'd sat staring into the dark and his silent tears glistened in the candlelight.

'Tell me,' she had whispered.

'There was one priest … Brother Timothy. He was old. Scary. Eyes everywhere. Bullied all of us. He liked to … he touched us. Mainly the smaller boys. Me, he tried once but I reacted pretty violently and after that he would lock me in a dark shed.' He shuddered. 'Told me to stay there and think about what I'd done. I never knew what I'd done. Sometimes it was hours. Dark. Before he came back. He'd … he'd …' Maroney paused. Doog could see him struggling. She'd stroked the back of his hands and he continued. 'He would make me strip naked while he beat me. The weird thing was, he would cry while he did it.'

She'd leant forward and grabbed his arm. 'Did he …?'

He shook his head. 'No, he never tried again,' he said, and then a look of pure misery transformed Maroney's face. 'But I would hear him go to Jimmy's bed in the middle of the night and afterwards … Jimmy … he was only six. He would cry and cry. I should have done something, told someone. I was too frightened.'

'Of course, you were. You were a child,' she said and urged him to continue.' She didn't want to hear but Maroney needed to tell her.

'It was such a long way down.' He rocked as he described waking early one morning and looking down from the second-floor dormitory. 'Jimmy lay on the pavement in his little shorts and singlet like a rag doll. His legs stuck out at a funny angle and his face was a like a mask, a white, frightened mask looking up at me. His eyes and mouth were empty holes.'

Doog felt her insides go cold but she'd continued to stroke his hands and asked him what had happened.

'That was the worst bit — nothing happened. Jimmy's body disappeared. It was as if he had never existed.'

If she were in Fremantle Doog would be phoning Frankie. They would go down to the boat harbour and talk over several glasses of wine.

A relationship is not what I expected right now, she writes to her friend, *but we seem to be on an irreversible course. I'm hoping it's not just because we're both lonely and need someone to share our problems. Honestly, Frankie, you should have heard him tell the story the other night. Pain in his every word.*

Doog chews the end of the pen and thinks about what Maroney had told her. Could years of suffering be vanquished by a visit to Manchester? The brief reunion with what's left of his family? She doubts it.

It's all very well to say that we have grown to love each other. I'm pragmatic enough to know that love won't last at our age if it's swamped by too many difficulties. We've both grown used to being on our own. Not having to answer to anyone.

She finishes the letter.

Take a risk, I hear you saying. And any other time I would. You know I would. I probably will if he hangs around. But I'm not sure I can help him through his problems and right now I have my own mess to sort out. It's just all a bit overwhelming — tell you all about it at Cicerello's at Christmas, girlfriend — can't wait, love Doog.

Mother Duck

DOOG tries several times to ring Paul. Connor always answers the phone and Paul is always off working in the paddocks. Once she rings in the evening. Again, Connor answers the phone. He's sounding sheepish.

'Doog,' he says, putting on a surprised voice. 'Lovely to hear from you.'

'I was hoping to have a word with Paul, Connor.'

'Och, I'll need to get him to ring you back, Doog. One of the horses is having a foal.'

Paul doesn't call back.

Maroney is heading off to Sandy Bay to line up accommodation and get his head around the newspaper he has just taken over. He's going via Pardee to ostensibly continue his research in farming practices.

'I'll see if I can get him to talk about you, Doog. I'll let him know my unbiased opinion of you and I'll give you a ring when I check out Sandy Bay.'

'Maroney,' Doog says, fixing her eyes on his. 'Why me, why now?'

He takes her hands in his. 'I've actually asked myself that question. I've enjoyed a simple life but I haven't been celibate. And much to Maria's chagrin, no relationship has lasted past the first or second date.' He presses his forehead to hers. 'Doog, I'm not sure what I want or where this will lead. I'm used to living on my own, but that's not the same as being lonely. There's nothing lonelier than being with someone you don't connect to. I'm sure this is different, my love.' He holds her face between his hands.

'Doog let's just agree to go on being friends and, I hope, lovers — if things evolve, that's fine. Let's just enjoy life without any expectations.'

With closed eyes, Doog smiles and nods gratefully.

'Unless …'

'Unless what?' she opens her eyes.

'You want a big wedding with a white dress and six bridesmaids.'

She pulls a face. 'Bugger off, Snoopy,' she's smiling now. 'I have things to do.'

A letter arrives form Annie. She hopes Doog doesn't mind but she'd shared the story with the college councillor. She needs time to talk to her mother and connect to her brother. The councillor has helped in getting her studies deferred until next semester. Meanwhile, if she can produce a decent documentary, she'll get a credit so she's had the idea of visiting Bedarra before they meet in Fremantle at Christmas.

The next afternoon, Matt corners her as she finishes teaching. He invites her to join him on the verandah for a cuppa, says he has just made a fresh brew. She tries to hide her surprise. Matt doesn't sit around drinking tea with people for no reason. He hands her a cup.

'What's up, Matt?'

It turns out, nothing's up. But Matt's worried because the end of term is approaching. Tells her she has made a huge difference to the kid's lives and he's saying he doesn't want things to change, that they need some stability. He says he wouldn't blame her if she wanted to take off but he's hoping she'll stay.

'At least until the end of the year would be good, Doog. The kids … they like you.'

He says she's the best thing that's happened to them for a while and Doog feels a warm glow of pleasure at Matt's awkward words of praise.

'The feeling's mutual,' she says. 'And I probably should have decided by now but the truth is I've had a few problems of my own and I really haven't had time to think about it.'

Matt nods slowly. 'Yeah, I figured that.'

Doog thinks of Paul. Even if he won't talk to her, could she leave? And of course, there's Maroney. Although he's adamant that she's not responsible for his career move, he'd surely be devastated if she left now. *He'd better be.*

Snow reappears at breakfast the next morning.

'Be nice if you'd let us know if you're not turning up for dinner,' grumbles Mrs C.

Snow keeps his head down, keeps eating. 'Yeah, sorry about that.'

'An explanation wouldn't go astray,' says Bruce.

Doog glares at him, but he deliberately avoids her eye.

'I'm sure Snow had a reason for skipping dinner. He's already apologised, and he has just as much right as anyone else to a bit of privacy around here.' She didn't mean her voice to harness so much emotion.

'Jesus, Doog, keep ya hair on. We was just stirring you up, son. Didn't expect no woman to leap up and defend you. What is she? Ya mother or something?' says Koop.

'Nah, Mum's dead,' says Snow into his teacup.

Doog just shakes her head. 'You're an insensitive mob of bastards. Lucky Matt's asked me to stay on until the end of the year. Might just give me time to knock a bit of refinement into you.'

This time she catches the hint of a smile in Bruce's eyes and she realises the decision's been made.

'That's wonderful, lovey,' says Mrs C putting a big sweaty arm around her shoulder.

That evening after dinner, Maroney phones from Sandy Bay, his voice full of excitement.

'You have to see this, Doog,' he says. '*The Post* — I didn't realise how old it is. It's been up and running since the First World War. There's an old printing press here that's out of the ark. I think it's nineteenth century. It's not in use of course, but technically it's a historical gem. The process for printing photographs is almost like etching. It could have all sorts of possibilities. Maybe get some art students, from Freo or somewhere to come up. I'm sure it could be used for printmaking in some way.'

'Have you found somewhere to live, Maroney?'

'Sort of,' His voice is sheepish.

'Yeah?'

'Well, *The Post* is in this building that houses the old printing press. It's huge, I don't need that sort of space working from a computer and sending the copy to Geraldton to be printed, but the rent is peanuts. It's got everything I need: lav, running water. I can set up a shower and a kitchen with basic equipment. Curtain off a nice little boudoir to seduce sheilas in.'

'Ha, ha. And council by-laws? Have you thought about that? Not sure you're allowed to just camp in commercial premises.'

'Yep, I did think about that, Doog, and I reckon that any sensible councillor around here is going to want to keep on the good side of the local editor.'

'Ye gods, Snoopy! The power of it all — it's already corrupting you.'

'Yes, wonderful, isn't it? You and I, we could become the next media barons.'

Doog laughs. 'Leave me out of that, Snoopy.'

Maroney goes on to tell her that by renting his apartment in Fremantle and living cheaply in the office premises, he thinks he can afford to buy an off-road van.

'It could be our little home-away-from-home for collecting stories and photographing the outback.'

'Can't wait to hear what your Freo friends think of that idea.'

'Yeah, might have to keep that a secret. Anyway, we have plenty of time to work all that out.'

'Did you see Paul. How did you find him?'

'Yes, I called in. He was calm, almost too calm, but I told him your story from my perspective. He's a pretty cool character when he wants to be, but I'm sure I put a dent in the spinifex ring he's grown around himself.'

After Maroney had had the awkward conversation about Doog, he changed the subject to innovations in farming and Paul became quite animated. He showed Maroney his success in bringing back native grasses and reclaiming the eroded river banks. Maroney ended up staying the night, pleased with the rapport he managed to build up with Paul, telling him he'd like to return and do a follow-up investigation.

Doog makes her way back to the donga via the tank stand. She spies the red glow of the end of a cigarette and guesses who has tracked her.

'This is *my* sanctuary, Snow. Can't you find your own?'

She's rewarded with a rare smile.

'Actually, I think I have. That's what I came to tell you, Doog.'

She waits, sensing this shy young man is about to open up. She doesn't want to spoil it.

'When I went down south, Doog, they said my name over the loudspeaker — not Snow — Alexander Kent. I thought no one would know me down that way. Anyway, this old bloke comes up and almost squeezes the breath out of me.'

Doog feels her mouth hang open.

'He was hugging me and calling me, Murranjarra. I was thinking poor old coot, he's lost the plot, but he turns out to be me uncle, me mother's brother. He knew me when I was a little tacker. He recognised me.'

Doog couldn't be more pleased, but she feels protective towards Snow. She's full of questions. It seems he has been reunited with a whole clan. His mother had left after she married Snow's Scottish father. This is his grandmother's family.

'So, what now, Snow, you think you can join them? You might find it all a bit different from what you're used to.'

'Yeah, I know, but I gotta give it a go, Doog. I figure it's worth it for family.'

Doog puts a hand on his arm. 'You got that right, kiddo, but maybe you don't need to cut your ties with the station. If anyone can handle a foot in each camp, I reckon you can. Do yourself a favour, talk to Matt. At least give it a chance, Snow.'

Doog walks back to the donga, lighter than she's felt in the past week. It was good to hear from Maroney. And another thought has struck her. Jean Le Carre would be interested in what Paul wants to achieve on Pardee. They must be on the same wavelength. At the risk of being called a mother duck, she'll enlist Maroney's help in bringing them together.

Connective Tissue

MARONEY has returned to collect his things before moving into Sandy Bay. 'Tell me about Paul,' Doog stares into space knowing she hates the thought of Maroney leaving. 'I hope he's not putting too much stress on that injury. The connective tissue in the graft needs time to bond.' She lets out a sigh. It's not so much the connective tissue of the graft she's worried about as her own desperate need to connect and bond with her son.

Maroney assures Doog that Paul is doing well. 'I gave him copies of some of the stuff I dug up about adoptions. He's pretty quiet but he seems to have lost his anger.'

'Research about adoptions? What have you been up to, Maroney?'

Maroney tells her what he's been learning. 'Jeez, Doog, I knew it was bad but it's much worse. It's hard to believe what went on right up until very recent times. There were all sorts of people and organisations involved in what amounts to a baby-selling industry. And for the most part it's been covered up.'

Doog's mouth twists in a wry smile. 'You're not telling me anything I don't know. I've been digging stuff out of the library and keeping a record of it all. It's the way I've coped over the years. Some women have found the courage to write about it and I still remember how much it meant to find out I was not the only one.'

'Are you not tempted to tell your story, to help others like they helped you?

'It may surprise you to learn that, yes, I am tempted. When … if I sort things out with Annie and Paul, I may give you that material along with the interview I know you're hoping for but I'm not sure I could use my real name. I think it would kill my mother.'

The idea scares the hell out of Doog but she thinks of the Anais Nin quote that she keeps in her scaredy-cat drawer: *Life shrinks or expands according to one's courage.*

'You got a phone call, Doog – It's Paul Gorski,' Matt's brows raise with curiosity.

'Doog.' Paul's voice has lost all trace of arrogance. 'Doog,' he repeats I'd like to talk to you.'

She's trying not to cry. 'I'd like that too, Paul, very much.'

He tells her he's had a letter from Annie, that he hopes he can meet her too. 'I want to hear your story, Doog. And I need to apologise for being such an arsehole.'

'No, you don't, Paul. With that sort of revelation coming out of the blue, you were bound to be upset — more than upset, totally shocked.'

On Saturday afternoon Doog drives over to Pardee. She finds it hard to drag her eyes from Paul's face as they sit on the verandah with a cup of tea. She decides that he looks a bit like photos of her father in his younger days. Eyes dark enough to shut out the rest of the world. They both sense there is no hurry to dive straight into the deep stuff. He's telling her about the great rock on the station.

'It's our own Uluru,' he says, and she feels his love of this country as he describes how he takes the tourists on a hike up the rock to see the sunset.

'On some occasions', he says, 'a special moon rises shortly before the sun sinks on the opposite side.'

'I'd love to see that,' she says. 'When's the next full moon?'.

'About two weeks away. Hopefully I'll be off crutches by then and I'll take you up there.'

'Two weeks could be a bit premature, Paul. The broken leg will be fine, the connective tissue in your artery needs time to mesh with the graft. Some wounds heal slowly.'

He wants to know how she knows all this medical stuff. She tells him about keeping up her Red Cross qualifications and gives him the pep talk about how everyone should do that, especially out here. What she doesn't say is that she'd also learned a hell of a lot by hounding the doctors and nurses at Royal Perth.

'Anyway,' he says. 'I've got a better place to show you, Doog. It's a place I don't let many people go. Connor's seen it, and of course my parents, but that's all.'

'I'm honoured,' she says.

'Well, it's a fair swap for a couple of pints of blood and I thought it would be a good place for us to sit and have a decent talk.' He leans over and puts a hand on her shoulder. His touch sends the longing through her body, but now there's more than an empty picture frame, and the memory of a tiny vernix-coated body. Her hand goes up to cover his.

'You'll have to drive,' Paul adds.

Connor helps them load some ice and a bottle of champagne into an Esky. Doog drives while Paul guides her on the track past the lake with birds swimming, some standing on stick legs among the reeds. Cockatoos and galahs clown in the branches of the ghost gums that grow on the shore, their white branches mirrored in the still water. On the left side the earth erupts sharply and soon a cliff towers over them.

'That's where we're going.' Paul points up to the top of the cliff.

'You're not climbing up there,' she says with ferocity.

'OK, don't get your knickers in a twist — we're driving — I'll show you the way.'

The way through the bushes doesn't warrant the name of track. She would never have found it on her own. By the time they reach the top, her hands strangle the steering wheel until the ground flattens out and she releases the low-range gear, exhaling loudly with relief. They are high above the lake.

'Come on,' he calls. He climbs out and hops over to one side of the car with more agility than he should have on crutches. They walk along the side of the flattened ridge and sit in the shade of a single ghost gum twisted and bent by wind looking east down over the lake. A creek meanders, dotted with billabongs and fringed with more ghost gums. Paul tells her the names of the different plants and formations. He knows them all. They cross to the western side of the narrow plateau and the vastness of the space they are surrounded by fills Doog with awe. Dropping his crutches Paul sits on the edge of the cliff with his legs dangling over.

'Doog, I should be the host, but would you mind grabbing the bottle and the glasses from the Esky.'

When she returns, he has a rapturous look on his face The high-pitched twittering of the grass wrens darting from clump-to-clump of saltbush is the only sound in this endless space that moment by moment becomes redder and richer in the late afternoon light.

'I miss this place so much when I'm away,' he murmurs.

Doog uncorks the bottle and fills the glasses. 'Here's to you having returned safely,' she says, clinking his glass.

He has something in his hand, her grandmother's amethyst pendant that she saw in the biscuit tin.

'I thought to get this ball rolling, you might like to start with telling me about this,' he says with smile that's gives her hope.

He had been silent while she told her story all the while staring out across the empty space, sometimes shaking his head, occasionally turning with a shocked look in his eyes.

'Shit, Doog! I don't know what to say.'

'There's no need to say anything, Paul. It happened but now it's history. I'd like to think we can move on from here — all of us.'

He nodded. 'Yes, I'd like to meet my half-sister. And I have a grandmother. Still can't get used to that idea. It's good that Annie's coming to Bedarra.'

'Paul, I hope you don't mind me asking, where are the Gorskis buried?'

'They're out by the rock. I got permission to bury them on the station. And I went to Sandy Bay to ask the local Aboriginal people to give me their blessing. I invited them to the burial ceremony. This is their country but they don't come here anymore. They sat me down and performed a ritual on me instead — smoke everywhere — by the end I was crying my eyes out, and it wasn't just the smoke.'

'Would you mind if I visited their graves, leave some flowers? I'd like to tell them how grateful I am that fate delivered my baby to a very special couple.'

She gazes up through the tangle of branches of the ghost gum that reaches over them, at the torn pieces of blue sky shining through. Sunlight sparkles on leaves, dissolving the holes. Connecting.

The End

Acknowledgements

I am grateful for the opportunity to have been a volunteer for V.I.S.E. (Volunteers for Isolated Children's Education). My work on some unique properties with amazing children and their families has helped colour the pages of this book.

A big thank you to Susan Midalia, Shelley Kenigsberg and Jane Messer who helped steer me through the many drafts of my manuscript, encouraging me to *kill my darlings* along the way.

Thank you to my family who have always encouraged me. They unwittingly lured me away from the visual arts into the more portable art of writing by being scattered to the far corners of the world. Thanks to my sons, John and Rob. You have both have taught me so much through your innate affinity for animals and your passion for the environment. And an extra thanks to John for introducing me to my first camp draft on the station where he worked, and where he wowed everyone with his playing of the didgeridoo.

Thank you to my precious three sisters for keeping me half sane.

And thank you to Mark Butler for your brilliant editing skills and to Ian Hooper of Leschenault Press for publishing my work.

About the Author

Christine Eyres, a writer and artist living in Fremantle, Western Australia, was born in Scotland, and raised in the southwest WA town of Albany.

She qualified as a teacher and completed a B.A. of Fine Art and a Graduate Diploma of English at Curtin University. After raising a family on an alpaca farm, Christine spent time in Queensland where she completed a Graduate Diplcma of Research Methods at James Cook University while living on a boat and working in her studio in Cairns.

Besides exhibiting art, Christine conducted workshops and curated exhibitions for community art groups in Far-North Queensland as well as being an active member of Tropical Writers in Cairns.

Christine worked as a volunteer with V.I.S.E. (Volunteers for Isolated Children's' Education), an experience that has informed the background of No Use Crying Now.

No Use Crying Now is her second novel. Her first, The White Apron, an historical fiction of a working-class family's struggle in Scotland during the Industrial Revolution was released in 2018.

A member of the Fellowship of Australian Writers, Western Australia and the Australian Society of Authors, Christine regularly contributes articles to magazines, including most recently, a series that featured in Southerly. She also publishes a blog that you can follow on her website at

http://www.christine-eyres.com.au

9 781922 670281